I0760664

praise for chill out, josey

How I love Susan May Warren's Russian stories. This one is no exception. I highly recommend it.

— Melanie Dickerson, *New York Times* bestselling romance author

Don't read this book in public. All of the snickering and snorting will draw attention to yourself, and you won't be able to hold it back. Lest you think you will get only humor from this book, let me set you straight now. Josey gains insight into her inner life and motivations, and as a reader you will do some soul-examining along with her. The spiritual message is wonderful.

— Michelle, Goodreads

This novel was delightful! Honestly refreshing, humorous, engaging and filled with some wonderful spiritual truths.

— Kindle Customer, Amazon

Susan May Warren has done it again. She's brought Josie back for another tour of duty in Russia! The whole book was a delight—one I'll be sure to read over and over!

— J. Ohlmann, Amazon

chill out, josey

The Josey Series || Book Two

susan may warren

Chill Out, Josey
The Josey Series, Book 2

(Originally published 2007 by Steeple Hill)
Ebook ISBN: 978-1-962036-11-5
Print ISBN: 978-1-962036-12-2 (hc.)
Print ISBN: 978-1-962036-10-8 (pb.)

For more information about Susan May Warren, please access the author's website at the following address: www.susanmaywarren.com.

Published in the United States of America.

Cover design by Courtney Walsh

happily ever after

. . .

There is only one happiness in life,
to love and be loved.
~George Sand

Mr. and Mrs. Erland Berglund
request the honor of your presence
at the marriage of their daughter
Josey Lyn
to
Chase Anderson
On Saturday the 5th of August
Two thousand and six
At 2:00
Gull Lake Community Church
34 Chester Street, Gull Lake, MN

A Reception will follow
At Berglund Acres
2210 Berglund Road, Gull Lake

not quite happily ever after

. . .

I DON'T EXPECT TO LIVE HAPPILY EVER AFTER ALL THE TIME. Really, I don't. In fact, I'm not even sure what that looks like. There's nothing wrong, either, with having high—or even reasonable expectations for life. Like not having my sister/matron of honor go into labor during my wedding ceremony. Or needing to take over as labor and delivery coach after said sister's husband keels over in the hallway. Like expecting my new husband/dream man who chased me to Russia and back to refrain from playing football in his rented tuxedo while waiting for the baby to appear. Or having a dream-come-true honeymoon in the beautiful Canadian Rockies. (Okay, that did happen).

Most of all, a gal would expect that her mother would be on her side, and try not to sabotage her fledgling attempts to be the perfect wife.

Maybe she's not wholly to blame for the Chicken Kiev fiasco, but my mother is known for her diabolical plots. She knew what she was doing.

Let me back up to the Sunday after we arrive home from our honeymoon. Chase and I have known each other all our lives, ever since the first day of kindergarten when he decided to show his affection with a snide remark about my lunchbox (which earned him a thunk over the head). However, despite that obvious display of love, and living next door to him my entire life, it took my going to Moscow to see that Chase, with his tousled golden brown hair, his swagger and laughter, and my hometown of Gull Lake, Minnesota, are everything I ever wanted. And, although Chase is adventure and sweetness wrapped up in a delicious package of hard muscles and twinkling blue eyes, the best thing about Chase is that he loves me.

I couldn't wait for us to move into my tiny apartment above the local convenience store—the one with the view of Gull Lake and the free-of-charge seagull crying in the background. It's a cheap little love nest and I even cleaned out half a closet and two drawers. Not that Chase needed much room. His earthly possessions consisted of two duffel bags, one which held his wadded dirty clothes, the other his high school letterman jacket, his arrowhead collection, an army hat he once wore hunting, and a camp stove. I have a sad feeling he used that stove more than once in his childhood, camping out to avoid going home. We moved the lot in before we left on our honeymoon. So I spend an hour unpacking on Sunday.

I love Sundays. Normally, I fill the morning with church, then spend the afternoon with a good book, some iced tea, and finish with a pedicure while watching the Sunday Night Movie. I know it's not high entertainment, but it's my life, okay?

Emphasis on MY.

So, our first Sunday back, I unpack our bags. The sun is still high and hot above the bay and the smell of late summer thickens the air. Chase has gone out for groceries, and I grab the newest Grisham for some couch time.

Chase returns. My hunter-gatherer, bringing home the kill.

He kisses me, goes to the kitchen, fills the fridge, and joins me on the sofa. The foot rub is nice.

But, you know, it tickles just a bit too, so I pull away and smile at him.

He smiles back. Picks up the remote.

I have to interject here that the first commitment Chase made to our marriage, even before the I Do, was a satellite TV order in our names.

Yeah, okay, I liked seeing the bill addressed to "Chase and Josey Anderson." But to be honest, I am not thrilled with watching the National Geographic Channel every waking hour. The life cycle of the praying mantis just doesn't do it for me.

I close my book. Get up.

There are only two rooms in this apartment. I go to the bedroom.

Uh oh . . . Chase appears at the door, a kooky smile on his face.

I get up, act innocent, and brush past him. "I'm going out for a walk."

A half hour later, I'm back, and he's on the sofa. Oh yippee, there's a riveting show about the mating habits of the Siberian Tiger.

I check my watch.

"I'll give you a thousand dollars for use of the remote."

He glances at me, smiles. "I have a better offer."

Okay, I was sorta kidding, and he better be also, because the movie starts in ten minutes. I don't smile. "Can I watch TV?" I ask, cutting through the innuendo.

His beautiful smile vanishes and I feel like a heel. So much for wanting to be the perfect wife. But hello, we're talking the Sunday Night Movie here.

He hands me the remote. Gets up.

And I realize something. *He's not leaving.*

Which I know I should have been up to speed on when the pastor said "Man and Wife," but, well . . . .He's. Not. Leaving.

He's here. Making noise in my kitchen. Bringing out a bowl of chips and cheese, and bumping me as I put on my nail polish.

Crunch.

Crumbs spill, onto his jeans, the sofa, my toes.

Crunch.

I pump up the volume, focusing on the heroine kicking . . .

Crunch. "Want some?"

Did he forget I'm on a diet? I take a chip, hating myself for my weakness.

Crunch.

I stare at him, at his rumpled hair, his dirty T-shirt, his ripped jeans, and . . . is that a smell coming from his bare feet? And the truth hits me like a bulldozer.

He's staying.

Like . . . For-ev-er. This is a picture of my Sunday nights from here to eternity.

There are nasty, non-newlywed words forming as an image of us fills my brain. I'm a chip-eating, three-hundred-pound couch potato who can't even reach her toes. My brain is filled with useless facts about pygmies in Borneo, and I'm reduced to bargaining marital favors for the remote. Sorta makes a girl wanna get up and run. And not for exercise.

But Chase didn't marry me for my propensity to throw in the towel. Just two years ago at this time, he showed up at my sister's wedding toting a buff and tough fiancée, a woman who made me feel like a cave girl in a poppy-colored dress. And did I take that sitting down?

Nyet! I ran off to Moscow. Where I taught English for a year, learned how to surf the Moscow metro, manhandled Russian into workable communication, dated a guy who worked for the

American Embassy (yes, say it, em . . . ba . . . see. Has a nice ring, doesn't it?), and even led an old lady to the door of salvation.

I can fix this.

I can be the wife he needs, the wife who helps him eat healthy, who creates a home of refuge and happiness, a home Chase never had.

Proverbs 18:22 says, "Whoso findeth a wife findeth a good thing, and obtaineth favour of the LORD." I want to be that good thing for Chase. And no, I don't aspire to be June Cleaver, but a morph, perhaps of June and Lara Croft . . . a woman of wisdom, courage, and incredible curves. A woman who takes his breath away. In fact, I'm even thinking that God might have some input on that. Lately, and especially since my stint in Moscow, God and I have been on regular chatting terms. I do most of the chatting. But occasionally He chats back. Sometimes He does it through the Bible. Other times, He uses people.

Take, for example, the conversation I had with my mother on Monday on the telephone, in between proofing the police beat, transcribing the city commissioner's report, and choosing the recipes for this week's *Gull Lake Gazette.*

Mom: Are you coming to Jasmine's baby shower on Saturday? You know, it's a couple's shower, so bring Chase.

Me: Chase has football practice. (Translation: Chase would rather have his molars ripped out by a bobcat than go to a baby shower.) Can I bring something? (I'm really good at the conversational bait and switch.)

Mom: No. Jas and I have it covered.

Of course. Because, while neither of them will say it, they don't think I'm capable of cooking even the most modest of grilled cheese sandwiches.

Okay, I admit it—yes, I once tried to make a grilled cheese sandwich in a toaster. But good grief, I was ten, and who knew the cheese part would come unglued from the bread and meld into the grates of the toaster? We needed a new toaster anyway.

Haven't they ever heard of forgive and forget?

Me: Are you sure I can't bring something? (At the very least, the sub shop has that party platter.)

Mom: How are you and Chase settling in?

(Where do you think I got the bait and switch from?)

Mom: Have you used the cookbook I gave you?

The Joy of Cooking. It's about the size of *War and Peace*, with such essentials as how to can pumpkin and de-vein shrimp. Yeah, I'll use that information every day. Still, it was considerate of her to think of my weaknesses . . . or maybe I should read that as a challenge? I mean, how would my mother feel if I gave her a dictionary for Christmas? Yeah, I can spot a dare when I see one.

And, I did pick up a *Martha Stewart* magazine on my honeymoon . . .

Me: I'm trying something new tonight.

Mom: What?

I reach for the magazine, paging through it. And this is when my day takes a nose dive . . .

Chicken Kiev. Of course Martha's helper is posing with a delicious looking meal, and it's like a lightning bolt to the brain.

Me: Chicken Kiev.

Was that a chuckle coming from my mother's end of the telephone? I'm going to say it was a . . . burp. It better have been a burp.

I arrive home on Monday night, after work, to find Chase already home from in-teacher training at school. Which is only slightly weird, because I thought he had football practice.

He's parked . . . guess where? And I'm only momentarily snagged by the bathing habits of the hippopotamus. Pay attention, Chase.

I'm headed off to the kitchen with my fixin's for Chicken Kiev.

How hard can this be?

"Really, GI, I don't need gourmet." Chase says this as we watch Clark, our fire chief, emerge with the offending pot. Smoke continues to filter out of the apartment, and it's brought the locals out for some summertime entertainment. Unfortunately, his use of my nickname, as in G.I. Joe, only slightly dulls the pain.

Please, just shoot me. Now.

Who knew that grease had a combustion point? And a thank-you-oh-so-much goes to the dime store for the automatic smoke detectors that dialed the fire department. I think I could have figured out how to put out the fire.

Maybe.

I have tears running down my face and it doesn't help at all that while Chase's arms are around me, he can barely hold in his laughter.

Yeah, hardy har har, chip-boy. We're both going to starve to death.

I should have learned something from the grilled cheese sandwich episode.

I push away from him, walk down to the park, and sit on a bench.

The sun is turning to liquid on the horizon, and the gulls wander the beach. Every morning during tourist season, the park department comes out with rakes and spends the morning, ah, grooming the beach.

It's a while before Chase joins me. He's probably consorting with the local hose draggers while they chortle at his fate. Methinks that a bunch of guys who call training a night of viewing *Third Watch* while eating buffalo wings and downing Heinies should mind what they say.

Chase sits down beside me. "You're the greatest," he says.

Oh, I'm feeling like the greatest. That's me, Great Josey, the Chicken Kiev Killer.

Thankfully, because I'm the newspaper editor, this story *won't* be making even the police beat.

He puts his arm around me. Unfortunately, Chase knows just how to yank me out of self-pity, right into gratefulness. He's tender and kind and grinning as he pulls me onto his lap. "Besides, I don't even like Chicken Kiev."

Now he tells me.

He runs his hands through my hair and pulls me to him. So I can't cook. Maybe there are other things I can do. But it's starting to dawn on me that this wife thing might be a bit more unwieldy than I thought. I mean, I wanted to take his breath away . . . not suffocate him.

Hours later, I'm lying in bed watching the ceiling, Chase beside me. The apartment smells of grease and smoke, and my stomach still roils from the tacos we had down at Jakey's Tacos and Burgers.

But I'm not thinking about tacos. I'm thinking of the time when Chase was ten, and one night under the Milky Way sky, he snuck over to my house, climbed up our gutter, and we sat together on my roof (while Jasmine eavesdropped in the bedroom). He said nothing for the first half hour (and I in my jeans and jammies nearly froze my backside). Then he started crying.

That rattled me. But, because we were ten and I had no idea at the time that I loved him, I put my arm around him. We sat there until Jasmine fell asleep and the lights went out at his house.

I never asked, but three days later, I saw his mother in the grocery store, took in her dark glasses (hello, who needs shades in the dairy department?) and I didn't have to guess further.

Chase and I spent years of cold evenings on the roof until, of course, he got a motorcycle.

Then we'd go for long, windy drives.

I don't want Chase to start tuning up his Kawasaki, maybe taking a spin alone.

Lord, help me be the wife Chase needs. Help me be the Proverbs 31 wife, one that brings him good, not harm, all his days. Help me love him the way he needs to be loved.

I say all this because I know that God listens. At least He did when I was in Moscow. And, I know God put Chase and me together. And, I do want to learn to love Chase like God wants me to.

In fact, I'd like to know that kind of love too. To live Happily Ever After.

And have a two-story Cape Cod on one acre of Gull Lake

And maybe a GMC Denali. Black. With the multi-media package.

And a boy and a girl and a dog named Boo.

Okay, not all at once!

I roll over and nudge into Chase's embrace. He makes a warm and happy noise and puts his arm around me, pulls me tight.

Maybe God is trying to tell me that, in a seedling way, I already have all that . . .

First thing I do tomorrow on the way home is buy a fire extinguisher.

liposuction

. . .

Gull Lake is a great place to live and raise a family. Population five thousand, including the summer residents, it's located about three hours north of Minneapolis, smack in the middle of Minnesota. We have one stoplight, two grocery stores, two hardware stores, a smoked fish shack, a library, a hairdresser, two cafés, and one coffee shop—the Java Cup. And, we're surrounded on all sides by resorts. Including Berglund Acres, where I grew up.

As I drive through town, I'm seeing the groomed streets, bungalows, and Victorians lining the sidewalks, their hanging plants on the porches overflowing with impatiens. Children's bicycles, skateboards, and water guns lay strewn in yards; a few have trampolines.

I want skateboards in my front yard.

This maternal thing has only recently kicked in, I have to add. I never saw myself as a mother. Up until a year ago, I dreamed of being an investigative reporter, a sort of Lara Croft and Lois Lane morph who uncovers conspiracies and shuts down things like slave trade and nuclear smuggling. And while I like kids . . . usually clean ones, without snot running out of their noses . . . having one permanently attached to my hip seemed like an unnecessary, and frankly, cumbersome, accessory.

Until I met Amelia. The raisin turned most-beautiful-baby-I've-ever-seen. I held her the entire time during Jasmine's couple's shower. (Okay, what's with my brother-in-law Milton and his enthusiasm for the game of "dress your husband up like he's pregnant"? I so didn't need to see Milton wearing a couple of grapefruit and a pillow. Then again, when Chase walked in, glowing with sweat, in his muscle shirt, athletic shorts, and tousled hair and gave Milton a one-eyebrow-up glance, I again had the opportunity to thank God for his intervention in my life.) Sweet Amelia cooed and gurgled in my arms, completely capturing my heart.

I want one.

But first, I want a place to put one. Hence the appointment with Carla from Gull Lake Realty.

Won't Chase be surprised?

I even did the legwork and found the perfect house.

> Charming 3 BR, 1 Ba Cape-Cod-style house on half acre corner lot. Dining room, den, large kitchen, view of Gull Lake. Large garage outbuilding. Call Carla at Gull Lake Realty. 555-2438

I drove by it twice. It's yellow, with a red door (love that!), a dormer window, and petunias on the porch. It has a fence, and a dog—a golden retriever—met me at the gate. (I wonder if he comes with the house?) Most of all, it's next door to the mayor and his wife (handy, especially if I need to subtly hint that we need to make more bike paths in the city, or post a full-time lifeguard at the beach), and across the street from a church. Not mine, but still, atmosphere counts. A church looming over our front yard will remind my daughter that Someone might be watching so no, she shouldn't take out her brother for flattening her sandcastle.

I meet Carla, who is still perky and cute, even six years after high school graduation. I remember her as a cheerleader, one who got pregnant her senior year, and dropped out of school to marry Bo Williams.

Not sure where Bo is now, but their daughter is in first grade and attended our vacation Bible school last summer.

I'm wanting this to work out for Carla because I entertain lingering missionary aspirations, and she looks like ready prey.

She smiles, and around her eyes I see fatigue, even though she looks prim and tidy in a linen suit.

"Hey Carla," I say, and we do small talk while she unlocks the door.

The owners aren't home, which allows me to critique their decorating choices without recrimination.

The walls are peach, the furniture a light-blue velour, and is that a couple of stuffed mallards above the kitchen door? In the kitchen, the owner has stenciled some sort of poppy—and for personal reasons, I have an aversion to poppies.

The upstairs is better—lavender walls, green shag carpet, but I'm guessing that under all that fur is hardwood floors. And, like the ad said, a view of Gull Lake from the master bedroom.

The floors squeak, and there is an air of age in the house, but for a starter home, I'm loving it. I see Chase Junior in the tiny bedroom with the alcove, playing with his Hot Wheels. And little Jenny we'll put in the other bedroom—the pink one. And Chase can build her a dollhouse in the garage-workshop. We'll modify the kitchen, of course—get a decent six-burner stainless steel range and grill top, and I'm there when Chase gets home, working on an article from my kitchen computer while I wait for the dough to rise. He comes in, puts down his briefcase (have to get him one of those), and nuzzles me behind my ear. "Jose, what would I do without you?"

"I don't know, Chase—"

"When do you think you'll have your loan approved?" Carla asks, her eyes bright.

Rats. Just when things were going to turn fun. "I just have to get Chase's okay."

But I know he'll agree. Even Chase knows we can't survive in the apartment longer than eight hours together. Every Saturday for the last two weeks we've managed to alternate our time, like a couple of tag team wrestlers. The fact is, it's starting to affect his mood.

He's suddenly turned sullen and mopey and aside from the occasional smile, he looks like he'd rather have his fingernails gnawed off by gutter rats than be married to me. No, I'm not overreacting. The seven night mini-series on the vast loneliness of the Serengeti that Chase glued himself to should be enough to know something's not right.

But Chase will be happy in a home. Our home. The one I make for us.

I'm driving back to work, seeing the smile on his face . . . and the ensuing celebration . . . when my heart stops dead in the middle of my throat.

Really. I know you think that's a cliché, but there it is, a big ball of shock. I'm having trouble breathing. I might have to give myself the Heimlich maneuver.

Or maybe I could get out of the car and stumble over to *Chase and the blonde he's walking down the street with.*

It's a good thing he doesn't have his arm around her, because I'm telling you right now, he'd lose that appendage for sure.

I'm at the stoplight, and they don't see me. Chase is smiling —smiling—something he hasn't done with *his new bride* for two weeks (okay, like I said, it happens occasionally . . . okay, often.

For goodness' sake, we're still newlyweds). I wonder if I could plead insanity if I ran them over?

Not only that, but it's only three o'clock in the afternoon. Doesn't he have school?

I can hardly believe he's walking with a man-stealer in broad daylight. Hello, this is a small town. Does he think that no one will see him as he walks into the Java Cup with her?

My Java Cup, located in the same building as *my* newspaper. They'd better not be ordering white chocolate lattes.

I slowly drive by. Chase is in there, at a table, sipping a coffee.

I hope it's laced with arsenic.

He has to know that in about thirteen-point-two seconds any number of my loyal lifelong friends will spot him and he'll be dog meat by supper.

Wanna bet he comes home with a lamebrain excuse? Some sort of cover-up?

But I'm onto him.

I stop the car, but instead of going inside, I sit there. Watch them as Chase listens with that cute, smug smile of his, then stands up and shakes her hand.

I feel sick. In fact, I might just be ill right here on the sidewalk outside the Blue Moose Café. Which will do wonders for their business, I'll bet.

I watch him leave. He opens the door for her, of course, then walks her to her car. If he gets in with her, I swear, I'll follow and run them off the road like the Dukes of Hazzard. Chase would do well to remember that I did jail time, and I'm not afraid to go back. (Okay, it was only for an hour, and it was for skinny-dipping in Gull Lake. And, Chase bailed me out, and shoot, if you didn't know all that, it would have made that statement more powerful.)

Besides, I really am thinking the insanity plea might hold.

After all, most of the people in this town think I'm just a bit off—especially after moving to Russia for a year. It wouldn't take much. Just a few key witnesses. H, for one, who knows the identity of the person who stole the mascot of the Bakersfield Bulldogs and let him loose after a bacon-greased cat at our senior homecoming game.

Chase doesn't get in with the blonde, preserving his existence just a few moments longer, but waves as she drives away.

Waves.

When is the last time he waved to me?

Okay! This morning. But still. A man should only wave to one woman in his life.

He walks back inside Java Cup and I'm left to contemplate my next action.

1. Follow the seductress and find out where she lives. Then again, if I'm caught, this could work against me in the way of premeditated murder charges.
2. Confront the two-timing weasel while the impression is still fresh. However, not all the words I want to say have fully formed, and this may leave me at a disadvantage.
3. Go home, draw a bubble bath, and plot my revenge.

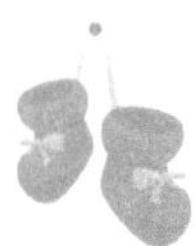

I have two soul friends in Gull Lake. The first, of course, is Jasmine, my little sister. Yes, she married the guy I brought home from college (and foolishly thought I would marry at the time. Thank God He doesn't give us what we ask for!), but Jas and I shared a bedroom until the day she left on her honeymoon, and frankly, once your sister has seen you in a thong, there's nothing much left to hide.

My other best friend is H. Just H, nothing more, although at one time she might have been named after a flower. But she doesn't like to talk about that, and she's not a flower type, with her multiple piercings, her multi-colored hair, and her belief that punk rock music is the language of the soul.

Jasmine is the one I turn to when I want to, say, pick out a nice dress for dinner with Chase, or complain about our mother's propensity to solve our problems with lasagna and pot roast. She's the nice one.

H is the one I turn to when murder is on my mind.

She, of anyone, would know how to hire an assassin.

I'm on the telephone with her when Chase walks in. I hear him dump his keys on the kitchen table and my blood heats, even though I'm up to my chin in hot soapy bubbles.

"I gotta go, H," I say into my cell phone.

"Remember, solar plexus, instep, nose, and groin. I got that from *Miss Congeniality* and have actually used it with some success."

I don't comment. Because, although I once threatened Chase that if I got angry enough I might be able to take him, certainly that wouldn't be while naked. And, frankly, now that I'm calm . . . *er* . . . I want to plot my revenge. Slowly.

Painfully.

Please, Lord, let him be innocent.

I'd hate to think that our marriage only lasted three weeks.

"Josey, are you here?"

No, it's just me, Gullible Girl, turning into a prune in the tub. I don't answer, and instead turn on the water. It's getting a tad cold. I also add more rose bubble bath. Maybe I can just hide inside the foam.

"GI?" He knocks on the door. I turn off the water and draw the curtain.

Not fair, calling me by my favorite Chase nickname.

"I know you're in there. What's the matter?"

I hear guilt in his voice, and it slides under the door and contaminates my bath. I actually have a stomach spasm. "Nothing," I say, sweetly lying.

Because, really, who wants to have a big fight in the raw? Besides, that girl he was with looked thinner than me, and if I get a glimpse of my wet, stringy-haired, bulgy self in the mirror as I'm accusing him of cheating . . . well, you get the picture.

No, I need bravado. I need chutzpah.

I need to lose ten pounds.

Why, oh, why do my digressions always take me to the scale?

I wince, because I hear Chase knock again, and then, to my horror, come in. I thought I locked that door!

Then again, this is Chase, and he knows how to unlock stuff. Like my heart.

I picture him sitting on the toilet (cover down), wearing his dress pants, his dress shirt—slightly un-tucked, his hair rumpled, those blue eyes staring at the bath curtain—

Stop it!

"Go away, I'm soaking here."

He pauses, and through the tiniest of cracks, I see him sigh then run his hands through his hair. Yeah, buddy, you'd better be feeling guilt.

"I have something to tell you."

Here it comes. The Big Cover-up. I freeze—which isn't hard to do because the bath water has cooled and some of the bubbles have deflated. I can see through them to skin, and well, right now I'd do anything for a towel. And some chocolate. And maybe a 9mm Glock—oh, okay, I wouldn't know how to use it anyway.

"I've been keeping something from you. And it's time I told you."

Oh wow, that really hurt. Like a shot right to the center of my chest. I actually can't breathe for a long moment. I'm trying to suck in air when he continues.

"Today I met with a representative from WorldMar, a non-profit agency out of Minneapolis."

And? This has what to do with your lying, cheating heart? Except, the smallest seed of hope takes root.

"How would you like to go back to Russia?"

"Russia?" Oh, that sounded like a squeak, but frankly, well, I'm stunned. Russia? Maybe I have foam in my ears.

"Yeah. I mean, you loved it last time."

Loved? That's an interesting synonym for *endured*. Tolerated. Suffered in. "I did?" I can't help it. I peek around the curtain. Chase is sitting there, blue eyes searching mine. I'm thinking, suddenly, there's room for two in this tub.

See, I'm so easily sidetracked. Russia. Blonde. Cheating!

"Why?"

Chase suddenly doesn't meet my gaze. "Well, I ah . . . I got a job in Russia."

I need to take this sentence apart, slowly. He. Got a *job*. In . . . *Russia*. I'm so very confused, because, you know . . . *he has a job.*

Which then prompts me to ask: "Forgive my confusion, but I thought you already had a job?" (I think I'm being very calm here, don't you?)

He winces, like my words sting. But I'm not the one who is rearranging our life like an episode of *Extreme Makeover: Home Edition*.

"I got fired two months ago."

Fired?

Oh. Hence the weirdness in our relationship. Note to self: next time he goes silent and mopes around the house I'll know it's because *he's been lying to me.*

But let's, just for a moment, go back to the *fired* part. "Fired? How?"

He winces again.

Stop that. I'm naked and wet. Do you think I'm going to karate chop you or something?

"Actually, it was more like pink slipped."

So not fired. Laid off. That's not so bad. But still . . . *.lying!* "Why did you keep this from me?" I reach out and put my hand on his leg, leaving a nice wet mark. But he looks up and smiles at me.

"I'm so sorry. I just didn't want to wreck our married life so soon after the wedding."

Translation: He wanted to be my perfect husband. At least, that's how I'm choosing to translate it. And, it doesn't help that I'm a sucker for his smile. Bang, suddenly he morphs from lying cheater to remorseful running back who needs a hug . . . at *least* a hug. "C'mere."

He leans down and I give him a wet, soapy embrace. He pulls back and kisses me, running his hands through my hair. "I love you, Jose."

Me too, Chase. I lift my face for another one of those kisses when I see something in his eyes . . . something that looks like relief. And just like that, I realize that he thinks I've said yes.

Wait—back up to the *Russia* part!

Russia, that place two thousand miles over the *ocean*, and so far that when I talk to Jasmine on the telephone we can hear our own words echo back, like the twilight zone. Russia, with the garbled language that makes me feel like I'm spitting, rusty elevators the size of phone booths, all-leather, size-two fashions, and dog-fur coats. Russia, empire of fish and fatback and red caviar and beets, the place where laws were made to be broken.

The place where I went beyond myself and found the Josey

who God was still creating, and a relationship with the Almighty that gave me strength and hope.

Russia, the place where my true love chased me . . . caught me, gave me a little gold ring, and reminded me that I can never truly leave home.

Russia, the land that gets under a person's skin, like liposuction, and changes her forever.

"Josey?"

His voice is muffled, because I'm under the rose-scented water, trying to drown myself.

kgb tricks

. . .

"HE WANTS YOU TO DO WHAT?"

Thank you, H. See, that is exactly the reaction I hoped for when I tiptoed out of our quiet and tomb-cold flat, despite the sweltering August evening, and drove down to the Hungry Wolf to solicit my best friend's advice.

I nod solemnly, eyes big, matching her disbelief. "I know, can you believe it?"

"So the blonde was a recruiter?"

I shrug. "If that's what you want to call her." *Homewrecker* would have been my label. "I can't believe he'd even consider this after I'd found him our dream home. Doesn't he care about Chase Junior and Jenny?"

H's eyebrow ring tweaks up. "Is there something you're not telling me?"

It takes me longer than a second to catch on, and I feel the instant rush of heat to my face. "No, no, I'm not—"

"What house?" she asks, dropping her cigarette to the parking lot and pounding it out with her black chunky-heeled boots. We're standing in the back entrance alcove of the Wolf, the side that faces the lake. Overhead, the moon is hazy, as if mimicking my thoughts, and it turns the lake dark and murky. The beat inside the Wolf is loud and country-western. I lean against Chase's truck and fold my arms.

"The Cape Cod across from the community church. The one with the red door."

"Oh." She makes a face.

"What?"

She hitches a shoulder, stares out into the surf. "I've just never seen you barefoot and pregnant, cooking up dinner for the hubby. That house is a Jasmine house. Not a G.I. Josey house." She turns to me and shakes her head. "I always saw you in some big city, chasing down a story. Or overseas. Didn't you want to be a foreign correspondent or something?"

Lara Croft, to be exact. I've always appreciated H for her ability to sort through the rubble and find the nugget of truth. Like when she told me that if I didn't go to Russia, I might regret it forever. And, probably, she's right. But well, that was then and this is now.

"I'm married now. It's time to settle down."

She looks at me as if I've turned green. Or maybe dyed my hair purple, like hers. (I sorta miss the orange.) "Who are you, June Cleaver?" She reaches out and, before I can stop her, whacks me on my forehead.

"Ouch!" I step back before she can bean me again. "What was that for?"

"I'm just trying to shake your brain loose from whatever insanity has taken it hostage." She shakes her head again, and I can sense a "For Pete's Sake" looming.

"My brain's not hostage," I say. But all at once, I'm remembering the old Josey, the one who wore leather and attended the embassy ball and sang karaoke at the Grey Pony in Moscow. I think the song was "Stand by Your Man," if I can remember correctly. Oh, shoot.

"H. Focus!" I say, my tone more for myself than for her. "I

said he wants us to move to Moscow. Not Minneapolis. I *did* the G.I. Josey thing." And, I might add, I was expecting just a bit more understanding here.

H hoists herself up on the hood of Chase's truck, crosses her legs beneath her, and pulls out another cigarette. At least I *think* it's a cigarette. It smells really sweet, and I try not to inhale.

"You can't tell me you're surprised. You knew this was coming. Chase is a traveler. He always was. You spent enough hours on the back of his motorcycle touring the countryside with him to know that."

Oh, is that what we were doing? I thought I was just hanging on, glad to have a reason to wrap my arms around him.

"I thought when we got married he'd want to stick around, build a life with me. We were going to buy a house, I'd learn how to make a pot roast, and Chase would earn tenure at the high school . . . " Even to my ears, those words seem . . . so Jasmine. H is right . . . I'm planning Jasmine's version of Happily Ever After. Maybe it was seeing her holding baby Amelia, but in a flash of insight, I realize I don't exactly know what Happily Ever After for Chase and me might be. I make a face and H nods.

"Think about it. Chase has spent his entire life trying to escape Gull Lake. I think the only reason he ever returned was for you, and you ditched town—to a former communist country, no less. Chase married the girl who can keep up with him, who isn't afraid of chasing his dreams with him. What did you expect—that marriage would kill the adventurer inside him?"

I close my eyes, let the night breeze calm my razed nerves. The last two days have been quietly agonizing, and intellectually demanding, with me dodging Chase every time he brings up the subject. Poor Chase jumps every time I enter the apartment (and it doesn't help that, now that the jig is up, he's lounging about in his cutoff sweatpants and muscle shirt, which is like a cluster bomb to my resolve). Our conversations resemble those of an old married couple with their hearing aids cutting out.

Him: So, Jose, about what I said—
Me: Yeah, I'd like tacos tonight also.

Or,

Him: We really need to talk about—
Me: Discovery channel has a special on Mt. Everest tonight.

So far I'm winning. But victory has never felt so bitter.

Hence the last-ditch grab for sanity outside the Hungry Wolf. Remind me not to do this again.

"Did you think about Chase at all when you married him?" H asks.

Oh, hardy har har. Of course I did.

I think.

Really.

But the longer H stares at me, the more I realize the truth.

I thought about what Chase could give me—strong arms, sweet laughter. Someone to face life with. But really, did I think about the *real* Chase, or just the Chase I wanted him to be? Did I consider for a moment what I could give him?

No, not that.

I love Chase for himself. Which includes the adventurous hunter-gatherer inside him. But I think I expected Chase to be my knight, and for him to surrender himself in the process.

But what about me? What am I surrendering?

Chase Junior. My Denali. A dog named Boo. My dreams.

But are they really my dreams? Or simply the dreams I think I'm *supposed* to have?

"I can't go to Russia, H."

She slides off the car, gives me a hug. "Now that you got the gold ring, what are you going to do about it?"

H returns inside and I stand there, the car keys jangling in my hand. I blow out a breath and stare at the hazy covering of stars, trying to remember if they really are brighter over Moscow.

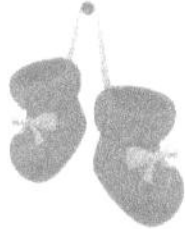

My parents run a small resort/bakery/convenience store located on Gull Lake. It's been in the Berglund family for two generations, and Jasmine and Milton are poised to take over the business when my parents decide to sell out and move to Florida. Roughly when they hit their late nineties.

Don't want to hand over the reins too soon.

Meanwhile, Jasmine and Milton live over the restaurant in a cozy (read: cluttered and painfully small) one-bedroom apartment. Of course the place continually smells of baked goodies—*kringle*, Danishes, brioche, and Jas's other concoctions. While I inherited some rare and remote wandering gene, like Bilbo Baggins, my sister got the full array of Berglund, including the baker's thumb.

I tell myself that this is a good thing. Just think of the damage I'd do to my waistline if I could actually create this stuff at home? I'm thinking this as I cut myself a healthy piece of almond *kringle* and slide it onto a paper napkin. Jasmine is sitting on the sofa, nursing baby Amelia, a blanket over her shoulder. Outside, it's a gorgeous Labor Day, with the sky a periwinkle blue, nary a cloud to shadow the traditional Berglund picnic that Milton and my father are setting up on the grounds.

"So, how are you and Chase?" Jas asks with a soft smile. "Any baby ideas?"

My eyes widen as I wipe the flakes from my mouth before I choke. "What? No. Absolutely not." And it's kinda freaky that my two best friends have broached this topic in the course of one week.

My sister quirks an eyebrow.

Oh, that's right. Jasmine and Milton were "trying" within a month of their nuptials. But the way things are going between Chase and me, well, it would have to be a miraculous conception of divine proportions for me to be pregnant. After living for nearly twenty-four years without . . . *it* . . . one would think a week wouldn't faze me.

A *week*.

I take another bite of *kringle*. "We aren't ready for children. We need to figure out . . . some things."

Like if we want to live in the same country. I drove by The House twice this week, by the way. The For Sale sign is still up. Mocking me. And once I even saw a tricycle out front on the sidewalk. Chase Junior's tricycle.

Still, after my talk with H, I'm ready to admit that while my dream fits Jasmine, I've never been the stay-in-one-place type of gal. But isn't that what a couple does when they get married?

I'm so confused.

"Like what?" Jasmine asks as she burps baby Amelia. I watch that little downy head tuck into Jasmine's neck and another wave of longing surges over me. What is wrong with me? Chase and I can't even agree on a television channel. We certainly aren't ready to figure out how to raise a child together.

I blow out a breath. "Chase lost his job at the school." Saying it obliterates my appetite. The one and only good byproduct of this entire fiasco. I wrap up the *kringle*, toss it in the trash.

Jas says nothing, but I see concern on her face. I hate the

fact I'm that transparent. Apparently I need to be more like Chase, the Secret-Keeper.

"More than that, he wants us to move to . . . " The word stumbles for a moment in my throat, but when it emerges, I feel an odd exhilaration. " . . . Moscow."

Jasmine stops in mid-burp. "What?"

I nod, staring out the window. Below, in the yard, I see Milton and Chase standing with my father. Milton already has a Berglund paunch and is wearing an apron and barbeque mitts. My father has on his lawn-mowing overalls, complete with the grass stains and grease. And next to them, wearing his baseball hat backwards and in a pair of jeans, a white Gull Lake Gulls T-shirt and bare feet, my hero. Is this the sign of things to come? How long before Chase has his own apron, his own shiny barbeque mitts?

"You can't go to Moscow, Josey," Jasmine says, cutting through my silence.

I turn to her, a strange feeling in my gut. I hate it when people tell me what I can't do.

"Why not?"

"Because your life is here. In Gull Lake."

Funny, I thought my life was with Chase.

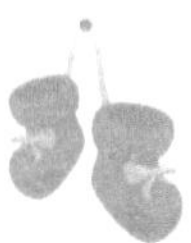

Occasionally during Jasmine's pregnancy, I dreamed that I, too, was pregnant. Maybe it was watching her expand from her petite size six to roughly the size of an award-winning pumpkin, but I found myself, more than once in the middle of Gull Lake, standing in my underwear, my stomach so large I resembled an oompa loompa. And sadly, the pervading thought wasn't, how did I get this way? But . . . what would my mother think?

I suppose the theme of the dream, then, wasn't the pregnancy so much as the fear that my mother would find out. And that bad things might happen. It's just that every major change in my life has been met with a full-out block from my mother, who missed her calling as a linebacker for the Vikings. She still has her diabolical ways, however, like reaching past me to hand the first helping of pot roast to Chase, or Milton. Or conveniently forgetting me when the leftovers of the cinnamon buns are being passed out.

So maybe it wasn't pregnancy that made me large in my dream.

Whatever the case, the dream again finds me, slinking into my subconscious and transporting me. Only this time, instead of being surrounded by the *Gull Lake Gazette* offices, the local Blue Moose café, and the sound of seagulls, I'm barefoot and fat in the middle of Red Square with Lenin's mausoleum looking shiny and black to the right, and the colorful church of St. Basils at the far end. Pigeons coo, their heads bobbing, as they scatter at my feet. As I stand there, registering my surroundings, my hands over my ballooned stomach, panic swills through me. And it's not because I'm pregnant. Or even that my mother might find out. But this panic is new, and choking.

In my dream, I know Chase is not there. I'm in this by myself.

I awaken wet and sweaty, my shirt sticking to me like cellophane. My Tasmanian Devil shirt has been in my possession since college, when I first discovered that I wasn't required to wear Gramma Netta's frilly polyester nightgowns. Taz and I made it through my four years of late-night papers and occasional lonely Saturday nights, then Taz hung with me during my stint in Moscow—my bedrock reminder of the true

Josey Berglund during my ugly forays into leather. When Chase asked me to marry him, I paged briefly through a Victoria's Secret catalog (which I had to hide from nearly everyone I knew), only to decide that not only would a black silk teddy on me look like I'm trying too hard, but like I'd spent a small fortune on something that might stay on my body for less than, say, five minutes.

And my Norwegian practicality kicked in and asked the obvious . . . why bother? In the end, I couldn't justify the expense. Not if I wanted my two-story Cape Cod, the Denali, or braces for my two adorable children.

Which, if Chase gets his way, won't be happening anyway. I should have purchased their entire summer line.

I blink to adjust my eyes and relief nearly takes out my breath at the form of Chase's body breathing next to me. I put a hand on his shoulder, just to affirm the truth. Despite my less-than-enthusiastic response to his grand plans, he's still here.

He's spent the day in Minneapolis, talking with the folks at WorldMar, going through a final interview. The fact that he went there without us agreeing on our final destination tells me 1. He's optimistic. 2. He's desperate. 3. He might go without me?

No. Not that. He did return home, after all. Which means that I'm still in his life, and it's time we had the Russia discussion. At least with real words instead of disbelieving harrumphs.

I was in the tub (of course) when he got home. I heard him thumping around the kitchen, doing his typical acts of vandalism. I hid in the tub until pruned-over, then, clad in my Taz armor, I tiptoed out to the kitchen. While he sat with his feet up on the sofa watching *Survivorman* (a show that he should probably be paying apt attention to for when I leave him with only a nail clipper in the middle of Siberia), I poured myself a bowl of Lucky Charms and crept back into the bedroom.

Exhausted, I fell asleep with his side of the bed cold and flat.

Cold and flat. Is this going to be my life? Chase and I agreed to this "till death do us part" clause, which means one of us is going to win this battle over Moscow. But what hits will we take to our marriage?

Is this my Happily Ever After?

I slip out of bed. Outside, the lake is awake also and tumbling onto the shore. I pad to the window, wrap my arms around myself, a sickness inside that feels like something has crawled in my gut to die. Maybe my dreams.

What if loving Chase isn't about living my dreams, but rather believing in his? Except, *Russia?* When I'd gone to Russia a year ago, I had great dreams of changing the world. Of having orphanages named after me, biographies written. Maybe a parade. No, not really, but I did hope to change my corner of the world. Instead, I discovered that God planned to change me, and if someone else got saved, well, that was a byproduct. I discovered that maybe God could use a girl like me, even if I didn't have it all together. That, in fact, He liked me, with my bagel and popcorn addiction, my occasional over-trying. I'd even go so far as to admit that living in Russia made me a better Josey. But now that I've healed . . . well, I'm not sure I'm ready to sound like a kindergartner (or worse), live in a high-rise, and subsist on pig fat and potatoes and caviar. Call me strange, but I hate caviar. Little red fish eggs exploding in your mouth? Nearly as bad as eating a snail.

I can't go to Russia. I'm supposed to be starting my Happily Ever After.

This isn't fair, Lord. I rub my arms, smelling the scent of a storm on the horizon. Hence, probably, why the waves seem to be trying to escape onto land. A welcome breeze drifts into the open window, lifts my hair off my neck. I cut it while in Russia, but its grown this past year, past my shoulders. For the first time in my life, I like it.

Lord, this wasn't in the plan. I thought we had this settled.

Chase stirs and I turn, wondering if he senses that I'm not there beside him. In the darkness, with the moon silvering his outline, he takes my breath away. I've been waiting for my Chase-Me to finally catch me since I was fighting him for room in his sandbox. And he's loved me since the day I skinned myself raw trying to beat him in a wagon race down Bloomquist Mountain.

Once, as we sat on the shores of Gull Lake, feeding the water stones, I asked him why he loved me. He told me that it was because I loved him back. At the time, I wanted a list. Either of the following would have sufficed:

1. For my brains
2. For my great curves.

But as I pondered it, I realized his answer would outlive my brains, the curves. He loves me because I love him.

The only outstanding question is, of course, what if I stop loving him? Since that will never happen, I suppose I don't need an answer. I agreed to love him for richer or poorer, in sickness and in health, for better or worse.

I'm starting to realize that surrendering my Sunday night viewing preferences to him aren't exactly the extent of "worse."

Russia.

Here are my options as I see them:

1. Inform Chase that he's temporarily insane, open the want ads, and convince him that a job making blizzards at Dairy Queen is the perfect place to study American culture. (Which isn't so far from the truth.)

2. Call my mother and beg her to take Chase on as a lawn boy/dishwasher/maintenance man at Berglund Acres. But I suddenly have a visual of Dad and his coveralls . . . okay, enough said.
3. Set down ground rules and agree to a short but productive, and very temporary relocation, with the firm agreement that we return to Gull Lake after a year to reassess (including the option to buy the Cape Cod from Carla).

But what if My Dream House is sold by the time we return? What if Chase loves Russia and wants to stay forever?

What if something happens to my family and I'm stuck three thousand miles across the ocean? What if Chase decides he's made a mistake and leaves me for a shapely Russian redhead?

Where do I go for *kringle?*

Probably I need some ice cream, or, at the very least, a bag of popcorn, to mull these options over.

I turn and tiptoe back into the kitchen. Open the refrigerator. My feet are cold against the kitchen linoleum. Bathed in the bright light of the refrigerator, I see a bag. From a bagel shop in Minneapolis. A lumpy bag.

He didn't, did he? I open it, and inside are a dozen bagels.

Oh, Chase.

Me smells a diabolical plot. I was in Russia. I can spot KGB.

Only . . . it's working. I close my eyes, and the fridge. *Lord, not again.*

For we are God's workmanship, created in Christ Jesus to do good works, which God prepared in advance for us to do.

Oh not fair, bringing to mind the verse that sent me to Russia in the first place. Only, I can feel it, the tingling that starts in my spine and spreads throughout my body and should send me running away, screaming. The forewarning that says God's up to something.

And I'll never be the same.

Tears are welling in my eyes as I head back to the bedroom. The sky is turning the pallor of a Moscow pigeon on the horizon as I slip into bed next to Chase. I wrap my arm around his waist. He stirs and I lean up, whisper into his ear. "It's only for a year, right?"

He grunts, rolls over onto his back. I slide into his arms.

"Promise you won't leave me for a sexy redhead, alone and pregnant in Red Square?"

I hear a muffled grunt of confusion. But as he tightens his embrace around me, I know he's figured things out.

I love him.

And we're going to Russia.

#144

. . .

"YOU'RE DOING WHAT?"

Now, the first couple of times I heard that, from H, then Jas, respectively, that response gave me strength, courage. The wherewithal to uphold my righteous indignation and stand against the urge to smooch Chase's sun-kissed face, with the smattering of blond whiskers and Matthew McConaughey smile. I held out for what felt like an eternity.

But that same tone, that same question from my mother has me wanting to slink under the table where we were, until a few moments ago, enjoying a perfectly innocent pot roast, mashed potatoes, gravy, homemade rolls, a jello salad, and fresh green beans.

Now I'm not sure I'll be able to finish my beans.

Mom turns to my father, as if Chase has spoken Taiwanese, and says, "Did he say they were moving to Russia?"

Now, see, this is where I interject and point out to Chase that I was the one who said that breaking the news to my parents over Sunday dinner might not be the best idea. Not only would dessert be in jeopardy, but we have at least three more Sundays before we have to leave, and it's the one decent meal we get a week. My suggestion was to wait until Myrtle called and told my mother I was quitting, and then to dodge Mom until the day before our flight. And even then I wasn't sure if I'd deliver the news in person.

Because in person, Mom can take me down with The Look.

My mother should register The Look as a concealed weapon, because when she draws, people get hurt. Like the time in third grade during our Christmas choral performance when I was yanking on Stephanie Lindquist's ponytail.

I am pretty sure I still bear the scars of my mother's fifth-row scorcher.

I avert my gaze to my mashed potatoes before she can zing me.

"Did he say Russia?" my mother persists.

"I'll be working with the sustainable living and small enterprise departments to help them create capital opportunities for our partner clients," Chase says, cutting his pot roast.

Oh, well, when put like that—

"Huh?" Mom says. Yeah, me too, Mom. I spent an hour on the website yesterday and I still don't understand what they do.

WorldMar International is committed to building long-term relationships with the goal toward developing sustainable communities, cultivating healthy opportunities for economic growth and promoting international relationships. A non-profit organization, WorldMar works with people and industries around the world to create and increase economic opportunities, sustain and protect natural resources, and benefit the environment. Using innovative approaches, WorldMar utilizes local resources to develop leaders in the community, assist small business enterprises, and meet their unique needs.

"I think it's sorta like teaching someone to fish," I say to my mother.

Chase raises one of those sexy blond eyebrows at me.

Yes, we've reverted back to newlyweds and there are times I have a hard time focusing.

"That old saying—give a guy a fish, feed him for a day, teach him how to fish, feed him for a lifetime," I explain.

Chase is grinning at me, as if he can read my mind. Or maybe it's because I get it, the whole Russia thing, the adventurous spirit inside him, the desire to do something different with his life. The Chase Spark. Bottom line—I'm such a good wife.

"But what about your job, Chase?" my mother asks.

From across the table, I see Jas making trails through her potatoes. She glances at me, hurt on her face. Well, she started it with that whole, *you can't go to Russia* bit. She was privy to the times I climbed out of my bedroom window after being grounded. She knows better than to tell me what I can and cannot do.

"I got pink-slipped," Chase says, reaching for the rolls. Apparently he hasn't noticed that he's the only one still eating. Well, except for Milton, but then again, a tornado could whip through the living room and Milton would dive to save the *kringle*. The man has priorities.

"I heard they were making cuts at the school," Dad says, and ladles more gravy onto his potatoes. One down, two to go.

"But Russia! Can't you find a job in Minneapolis?" Mom asks, the die-hard that she is.

Chase cuts his pot roast. "I don't want a job in Minneapolis. When I went to visit Josey last year in Moscow, the city spoke to me. I want to learn more about the people, help them, if I can."

I remember that time as The Week of Confusion. He might have heard the city speak; I heard the shattering of my heart, believing that Chase and I would never be together. I heard no speaking city, no future in the wind. Apparently I'm not a very good listener.

"That's well and good, Chase, but what about Josey? What about her job at the newspaper?'

I look up and flash Mom a smile. Hurrah for Mom, who has managed to say the right thing, after all. *What about Josey?*

I sigh, reach for Chase's hand, and very Proverbs 31-like, say, "I think a year in Russia will be good for us. Besides, it's a golden opportunity for Chase."

Chase squeezes my hand back. My mother stares at me, and then, as if both bewildered and resigned, she shakes her head. "Anyone want more salad?"

After dinner, Jasmine and I sit on the front porch, watching Chase clobber Milton in croquet. The sun is low, and from the kitchen, I hear the sounds of my mother doing the dishes. She likes to handle the after-Sunday dinner clean-up alone, probably to mull over our conversations and prepare for her Sunday evening follow-up phone calls.

"Are you sure this is what you want to do?" Jasmine is holding Amelia, who has fallen asleep on her lap, her mouth open and making occasional baby sounds that have my heart turning to mush.

"I don't know, Jas," I say honestly, picking at the paint on the porch. "I think it'll be fun. Last time I went to Russia, I learned a lot."

"You came back a skeleton."

I hardly think that a size ten is a skeleton, but who am I to argue? "I learned another language and nourished my independent side. Who knows what will happen this time?"

She looks unconvinced as she runs a finger down Amelia's cheek. The baby gives an involuntary smile.

"Besides, I want Chase to be happy. And I think this is what loving someone is all about."

Jasmine glances at Milton, and a soft look comes over her

face. "I guess so." She reaches out and touches my hand. "Just promise me that you'll come back in one piece."

Yes, I nod. One very skinny piece.

The night shoos the day into the horizon as Chase and I bid my parents and Jas goodnight and stroll along the lake. Chase holds my hand. "I hope your bistro is still there," he says softly.

I grin. My bistro, the Venetsia, across from the Moscow McDonalds, the place where Chase found me and proposed.

Overhead, a sliver moon carves out the sky. A star falls. Chase is warm and strong next to me and, suddenly, anticipation swooshes through me like fire.

I can do this. Chase needs me. I know Russia better than Chase. I can help him survive, help him navigate the subway system, barter for bread in the market. I can be his true helpmate, the one who stands beside him in a foreign world.

We're going to have the perfect life.

WorldMar International
Office of Personnel
2241 Hennepin Ave, Ste. 233
Minneapolis, MN 55401

Dear Chase Anderson,

Congratulations on becoming a member of WorldMar, where we put ideas to work today for a productive tomorrow. We are pleased to have you as a member of our Russia staff and look forward to working with you. Enclosed is your membership packet. Please fill out the forms and return them to our office by September 15. If you have any questions, please contact the personnel office at 763-473-2060. Welcome to WorldMar!

Sincerely,

Richard Olafson

Director of Personnel

Enclosures

Checklist of forms:

1. Medical information and release form
2. Life insurance policy number and name of representative
3. Permanent Address form
4. Emergency Contacts
5. Immunization forms
6. Doctor's exam and release
7. HIV Test results

Gull Lake has a clinic in town that gives HIV tests every third Friday of the month. It's not with a little relief that I discover that this is two Fridays too late for our purposes. It's been two weeks since The Big Decision, and WorldMar has us on a fast track to departure. Evidently the guy in Chase's position resigned (or bailed, as blonde and still-alive-but-barely Stephanie Mills defined it), and they need Chase to take over immediately.

I'm happy for him. For us. For the twinkle of adventure that I see in Chase's eye, and the way it makes me tingle down to my toes.

And our trip to a clinic specializing in HIV testing in

Minneapolis is the first step on our grand adventure. Although something is wrong with my stomach. As in, it's acting like a walleye trying to get off the hook.

Not that I have a problem with HIV tests—well, I mean, because you know, I *waited*, and I didn't ever think I'd need one. But it seems so suddenly vulnerable. As Chase and I park in a ramp, cross the street, and descend into the bowels of some nearly abandoned building complete with the smell of musty carpet emanating from the painted cinderblock walls, I suddenly get a hint of how it might feel to wonder if you have a ticking bomb inside you.

Really, I know that in all likelihood, the test will come back negative, but what about that woman in Florida who got it from her dentist? I'm just saying that it feels creepy to walk into a small, poorly identified office with a dimly lit waiting room and know that everyone else here feels the same sort of panic. Probably my gimpy stomach is due to Mom's lasagna (although usually I can eat cold lasagna for breakfast and have little or no aftereffects). Or maybe it was getting up at 6 a.m. for our three-hour trek to Minneapolis. Nevertheless, I'm realizing that for everyone else in the room, this could be the worst day of their lives, and I'm feeling their pain.

With Chase at my elbow, I approach the counter, expecting to sign in. Instead, the woman behind the desk, late forties, long grayish hair tied into a ponytail, gives me a number. #144. That's me. No name, just a number. I take my new identity and sit in one of the molded vinyl chairs in the waiting room. The other clients run their gazes over us and I wonder what they think. I wonder if they wonder what I think. I wonder if they think I'm wondering about what they're wondering. All of the wondering makes me cross my arms over my chest and duck my head.

"Are you okay?" Chase asks softly. I look up and give him a death-ray silencer. Of course I'm okay. Now what are they going to think, that I'm not okay? That I'm going to keel over, right here, in the middle of the waiting room?

"Of course," I hiss, and Chase widens his eyes.

I glance at him and suddenly I realize that maybe I *do* have something to worry about. Not me . . . him. Although Chase and I . . . uh, abstained before marriage, he was engaged to a shapely blonde before he wizened up, and well, although we haven't discussed it, I suddenly have a sick, nauseous feeling on top of my already churning stomach.

That ad is running through my head. The one that says that when you, *ahem*, with someone, you also . . . *you know* . . . with everyone they've ever *you knowed* with. Which is suddenly so very, very gross I'm holding my gut and sorta doubling over.

"Are you okay?" Chase says louder.

Of course I am, I nearly snap, but a wave of fresh concern rushes over me, taking the edge off my words. "I'm fine." But I'm not, really, thinking of the scenarios. What if he is HIV positive? What would that mean for us? No Chase Junior? No Jenny? What if I'm infected? What if I'm not, but he is?

What if Chase dies?

I sit back, beads of sweat across my forehead. Across from me, a toddler takes toys from a milk crate. The little girl has her hair in amber pigtails that stick out like Pippi Longstocking. She's plopping the toys in the lap of her mother/sister/caregiver who lazily drops them back into the milk crate. It's a game. The woman has pretty bright red hair, but she's thin and wears exhaustion on her face that ages her a decade or two. She's wearing overalls, and unless she collects her body fat around her hips, she's expecting.

I suddenly have a horrible thought. What if Chase dies and leaves me with Chase Junior and Jenny, alone? Can I be a single mom? I don't want to be a single mom. I don't even know if I can be a non-single mom. I'm not ready to face momhood by myself. I turn to Chase, who is watching me with concern on his face.

"I can't do it," I say under my breath.

He frowns as the room starts to swim. I feel lightheaded and grip the edge of my chair. My number falls off my lap to the ground.

"Josey?"

His voice comes from far away, as if through a tunnel, and as I turn and look at him, I'm seeing spots, leopard spots, now giant black holes piercing through my brain and—

"Josey?!"

I'm under a blanket, I know that, but the smells aren't my bedroom and as I open my eyes, I see bright lights and hear unfamiliar voices. "Where––"

"G.I." Chase suddenly appears over me, his hair mussed, fear in his eyes. "You passed out."

"What?" I look around and realize I'm in a doctor's office, judging by the blood pressure unit on the wall, the rolling chair, the eye chart, the row of antiseptic supplies—cotton balls, tongue depressors, really long Q-tips.

"Where am I?"

Chase takes my hand. "In an exam room." He runs his hands over my hair, pushes it back. I see that he has a Band-Aid and a piece of cotton in the crook of his arm.

"The HIV test," I say, it all coming back to me. I am feeling weak, even woozy. "Did you get your results?"

Chase smiles. "No, we don't get them for two weeks. But I was tested when I went to Peru a few years ago. I'm fine."

"But what about Buffy?"

Chase quirks one of those cute blonde eyebrows. "Buffy?"

Oh shoot, now not only have I forgotten his former fiancé's name, but he knows that I named her myself. Which means he now knows I was jealous. Can't a girl keep any of her secrets? "What's-her-name—the girl before me."

He chuckles. "Buffy, huh? Well, we never . . . ah . . . " I see him turning a little red, and can't help but grab him by the collar and pull him down for a kiss. He's slightly shocked, but my future is again intact and all is well with the world.

I hear a knock at the door, and it opens, the voices in the hall now less muffled. A thin blond doctor enters. He looks younger than me. "Number 144?" he asks.

"That's me." I sit up and prop myself for a moment while my head clears of spots. "The lasagna this morning didn't agree with me, that's for sure."

"I'm Doctor Pike. I'd like to just check a few vitals before we draw blood." He takes out his stethoscope and presses it to my upper chest, listening.

"I had a physical last week. I'm fine."

"I'm sure you are." He moves the stethoscope to my back, listens again. Then takes my pulse.

"Well?" I ask, in my told-you-so voice. "It was just low blood sugar."

He quirks an eyebrow. "Do you have a doctor you regularly see we could forward these tests to should they show any abnormalities?"

"I promise, they'll be negative."

He says nothing and it bothers me.

"Listen, I'm telling you, I'm fine."

"Send them to Dr. Everson, Gull Lake Clinic," Chase says quietly.

I look at him, feeling a sense of betrayal. But more than that, I'm wondering, does he think the HIV test will be positive? As if reading my thoughts he turns to me. "You really scared me. Let's just let them run a few extra tests. Just to make sure."

I sorta like this Dr. Chase I married. I shrug. "Okay. But I'm fine, I promise."

"We're not going if you're sick, Jose."

"I'm not sick. I'm just . . . well, I panicked. I wondered if . . . if . . . " Suddenly I can't look at him, or even the doctor. "Being here just spooked me, that's all. I don't want to lose you," I whisper.

The doctor leaves as Chase puts his arms around me and pulls me tight. He smells of cotton and his minty-fresh soap, and he feels so warm and solid I sink into him. "Don't worry, #144. You won't lose me."

Josey's Packing for Russia list:

- sheepskin slippers
- wool socks
- leather boots
- 5-lb bag popcorn
- all five seasons of *Alias* on DVD
- the first two seasons of *Lost* on DVD
- books 12-24
- pictures of Jasmine, Mom, Dad, and Amelia
- medicines – Ibuprofen, Acetaminophen, 5-lb bag chocolate chips
- toiletries
- Taz T-shirt
- leather skirt (for potential embassy event)
- leather pants (for second potential embassy event)

- a year's supply of Tampax
- power converter (for new hairdryer)
- computer
- Gap jeans (size ten and new size eight, just in case)
- capris, black dress pants
- white blouse
- underwear & socks (new)
- University of MN sweatshirt
- my collection of tees
- my mules
- hiking boots
- Birkenstock sandals
- slingback sandals
- black pumps
- black ankle boots
- black high boots
- passport

Chase's packing list:

- passport

I'm a little worried about our weight limit. According to KLM and Northwest, I can only take fifty-five pounds in each bag, with two bags apiece. I dragged out all the luggage in our collective possession—Chase's army duffel bag and two bright orange-poppy-colored suitcases passed down from my grandma Netta.

Chase's idea over the past two weeks of helping me pack has been to rustle up the grimy gear he brought into this marriage and dump it into the corner of the room. While I can appreciate his attention to minimalism, I've decided that the guy needs more than one change of clothes and a toothbrush. However, for every pair of pants I pack for Chase, I have to surrender a pair of capris, or perhaps . . . one of my shoe choices.

Yes, I'm a Proverbs 31 wife, but I don't remember any verses about shoe sacrifice.

I've done the brave thing and whittled down my shoe selection to the essentials, which has left enough room for two sizes of Gap jeans in three styles, my Old Navy tee collection, three sweaters, my leather pants (that I purchased last time I was in Russia for the hopping New Year's Eve ball at the *em-ba-see*, yes, I said *ball*), and plenty of essentials like bath oil (because I tell myself that the rusty water that comes out of the taps is really an expensive mineral bath at a French Spa), chocolate chips, and my collection of *Martha* magazines to date (we're going to forgive her for that little jail thing because she knows how to make soap from scratch).

Most importantly, not only have I packed like a pro, not forgetting even the tiniest detail, but I also packed for Chase, including the very, very few things I despise (like the suit coat he got from Buffy which looks great on him but reminds me of the *other* woman every time he wears it), his fifteen-pound, 528-page Cultural Anthropology textbook (I had to remove my two hardback Nora Roberts anthologies, which were roughly the same length), and of course his Scary Pants.

Chase alleges that Scary Pants appeared one day in his duffel bag, much like a gift left by the tooth fairy. And, instead of being suspect of the origin of the pants, Chase, like all men, simply looked at the windfall and didn't ask any questions. I think he should have put someone to the screws because the pants look like something that should be in the bottom of a dumpster, plugging holes. Blue polyester with a white pinstripe along the outer edge, in a former life they were stirrup pants—you can imagine the shape. Scary Pants take a perfectly good looking pair of appendages and turn them into Scrawny Chicken Legs.

Personally, I'm not attracted to a man with scrawny chicken legs. But, being the Wife of Noble Character, I packed them anyway. And took out my wedge-heel espadrilles.

But I'm determined that we're going to have the best year of our lives. Chase is about to see that I'm the best thing that ever happened to him.

And I'm not just window dressing, either. I'm not only going to look good, (aiming for that size eight this time around) but I still have that missionary spirit, I can speak Russian, and I know how to get around Moscow. I can see God's wisdom in putting me with Chase and sending us to Russia. Not that I'm being presumptuous or anything, but now I understand that verse, where the husband rises up (from what, I'm not sure) and says, "Many women do noble things, but you surpass them all."

Surpass them all.

And, as I've been praying about this, I've come to believe that God has something cooking for me. (And on that note, I'm hoping He also provides someone who knows *how* to cook. Because last time I subsisted on raw carrots, Nutella, and a puffy chocolate-filled cereal called *padushki*, which means "little pillows," and certainly filled my mouth with comfort and joy.) I just have this feeling inside that there's something special waiting for me across the ocean.

Hence why I've spent the past two weeks cramming socks and movies and Tampax into Zip-loc bags and find myself the Thursday before we depart surrounded by plastic bundles.

Jas is in the kitchen cleaning the fridge in hopes we'll get our deposit back on the apartment. I'm hoping she doesn't inquire about what that green stuff in the vegetable bin used to be. Meanwhile, Chase and my father are loading the boxes of our wedding gifts—the china, pictures, pottery, appliances, and everything else I've only enjoyed for less than two months into Dad's truck for shuttle to the Berglund basement.

Chase is the town hero. Not that I mind—I mean, I already

knew this, but because of the feature article about him in the *Gull Lake Gazette*, he's become something of a celebrity. (Yes, I wrote the article, but I didn't think it would bring casseroles to my door. Come to think of it, that worked out well for both of us.)

Oddly enough, no one wrote headlines about *me* when I went to Russia. To *serve God.*

But it's not about me. It's about *serving* my husband.

Okay, I admit I feel a little like a Sherpa. You know, the baggage carriers for the explorers who climb Mt. Everest? Has anyone ever acknowledged the Sherpas? I mean, they climb the mountain *too*, and without the billion-dollar sleeping bags and the titanium-steeled crampons. Just their moccasins and an old blanket. (I know this because of our recent commitment to Discovery Channel.) I just think that someone needs to say a word for the Sherpas.

I suppose if I were the kind of person who felt sorry for herself, I might say, What About Josey? Did anyone notice that I had to quit my job, give up my chair and my great view? And instead of a well-attended good-bye barbeque tomorrow night, Mom is off to her quilter's club at the community center, and Dad has an elder meeting.

Good thing I'm not that kind of person.

Chase and I are staying with my parents, then Milton is driving us to the airport on Saturday. No flags, no parties.

"Josey, do you want me to throw these bagels away?" Jasmine appears with the last of the crushed bag.

Sorta feels like *some* people don't care.

"No," I say as I stand up and swipe the bag out of her hand. She shrugs, and as I look at my life's belongings squished into plastic like forensic evidence around me on our tiny bedroom floor, suddenly I feel nothing but dread.

Please, God, tell me that we're doing the right thing.

Tears well in my eyes and I blink them away, grabbing a bag

of socks. I don't know what is wrong with me. I change moods faster than the housewives change partners on Wisteria Lane.

"Josey, are you okay?" Apparently Jasmine hasn't left, and from the way I'm clutching my bagels, well, no, maybe I'm not okay. The first step is admitting it, right?

"I think I'm going crazy." I wipe my eyes. "One second I'm thrilled about Russia, the next, I'm . . . .I guess I'm just tired."

Jas comes over, wraps me in a hug. She says nothing, because she's still hoping I'll throw myself between Chase and this insanity. The truth is, if I simply said no, it would all go away.

But do I want it to?

Jas pulls away, and is about to say something when we hear, "Hello?"

Kathy Simpson, my landlord, comes into the room. "Oh, still packing. Okay. Well, my new tenant is here and she wants a look-see."

So much for second thoughts.

I climb to my feet and follow Jas into the family room where Kathy stands with . . . H? She's looking very punk today in an orange and black tank and a full-length skirt that looks homemade from a pair of army surplus pants. She has enough chains draping the skirt to supply the Gull Lake police force for an entire year. I do like her orange toenails that peek out from beneath, however. Apparently this is a no-shoes day.

"I thought you were playing at a gig in Brainerd this weekend." H's new hard-rock/punk band, the Sugar Monkeys, is gaining popularity all over the state, although I have yet to make out even one lyric.

"I'm the new tenant," H says, beaming at me. "Rex and I are moving in."

"Rex, your drummer? I thought he lived at home." In fact, to my knowledge, he still drives his mother to the library every Thursday for senior discussion hour. They debate hot topics like alternative energy sources and the war on terror. I wonder sometimes if perhaps someone should listen in, maybe take notes, send them to Washington. "Why does he want to––"

H smiles at me.

Oh. Shoot, I'm out of the loop again. "When did this happen?"

"After that gig in Detroit Lakes. The rest of the band went home and––"

I hold up my hand. Really, that's enough information. I try and smile. I know I shouldn't be surprised, but I am sad all the same because of my mother's voice is in my head, something about free milk and buying the cow. "Wow," I manage. "That's . . . that's . . . "

H is shrugging, ignoring my stuttering. She's walking through the apartment. "Is the table staying?"

The table Uncle Bert gave us? "No."

"How about the comforter?" She's ducked her head into the bedroom. "I like blue."

I'm starting to feel grumpy again. Or maybe just grumpier.

"And you don't need the television, do you?"

No, but . . .

"And I really like that driftwood coat rack––"

"I'm not dying, H. I'm coming back in a year!" Okay, so that came out a wee more passionately than I intended, but for Pete's sake, I'm not the Salvation Army store.

H stares at me, as if baffled by my response. Jas frowns, leans against the wall.

"You both act as if I'm never coming back. Chase and I are going for *one* year. One." I hold up my finger, as if they might need help counting. "I'm coming back for all this stuff."

Jas smiles, nods, gets it. H, however, is still staring at me. "Are you serious? What happens when a year is up? Do you seriously think Chase is going to return home and you'll buy your dream house, have two point three children, and live happily ever after?"

Uh, *yes.*

But her words have sucker punched me. What if . . . what if she's right? (And H is so often right, it's painful.) I sink down on my former sofa, sighing. "I thought it might be something he just needs to get out of his system."

Silence fills the room, like we're waiting for the results of a loved one's triple-bypass surgery. Kathy turns toward the window, admiring the view of the lake. Jas begins to sweep the kitchen floor. H continues to stare at me.

Finally, she utters the Minnesotan epitaph for all arguments. "Whatever."

I'm about to "Whatever" her back when Chase and my father thunder up the stairs. Chase is sweating, his red muscle shirt just a little soiled, his hair sticking out in spikes under his baseball cap. He leans against the doorjamb.

"Time for the furniture."

I look around, at the television—it's my parents' RCA from the eighties, with the push buttons and the remote control attached to the television with a cord. And the orange sofa, a hand-me-down from my aunt Myrtle, still in excellent condition due to the plastic wrap she kept on it for the first twenty or so years. The driftwood coat rack I got as a wedding present from who knows who. So, maybe I'm not going to use it . . . in the near future.

I look at Chase, at the way his blue eyes twinkle with excitement. I've never seen him so happy (well, with the exception of our honeymoon), and frankly, I don't want the dismal old Chase back. Ever. I like the sense of adventure that imbibes our marriage.

I like it when Chase is happy.

But what about Josey? I feel a wail inside, but I clamp down on the feeling that my insides are being shredded and paste on a smile. “Naw. H is moving in. We’ll let her use it.”

Chase shrugs. Shrugs! Like the sofa where we watched the Sunday night movie for the first month of our marriage means *nothing* to him.

I’m a little miffed as my father treads past Chase into the room. He plops down on our former sofa. “I picked up the mail for you.”

He hands me the stack. I sort through it and find a piece from the clinic in Minneapolis. Addressed to Chase. I hand him his envelope and look for mine. When I find it, it is considerably thinner and, while Chase is reading his results with all the interest of a hibernating bear, I am tearing mine open.

> *Your test results have been forwarded to the doctor’s office on file in your account. Please refer to your local doctor/clinic for further information.*

I feel another faint coming on as I sink onto the sofa by my father.

Picking a doctor in our small town isn’t easy. Every doctor in the Gull Lake clinic is either 1. Related to me. 2. Goes to my church. 3. Is in the quilter’s club with my mother, or 4. Attended high school with me. Sorta makes a gal want to find a nice anonymous clinic in Minneapolis. Especially when she has those once-a-year exams. What exactly do you say to your gynecologist when you meet her in the chips section at the Red Rooster? Especially when she knows how much you weigh.

Anyway, thankfully, Chase named the only doctor in town I would consider seeing. Maggie Everson is older than time, probably delivered every baby in Gull Lake, and has known me since I bit her back in '82. And I feel about seven again as she knocks on the door and walks into the exam room. I remember two things about Dr. Everson. She has bony hands. And she carries lollipops in her lab coat.

I'm hoping I get lucky with a lollipop today. Because my stomach is churning again, I'm shivering uncontrollably, and I'm wishing Chase had come with me. But I had visions of standing on that scale, the nurse tapping it higher and higher, and well, there are simply some humiliations a girl should endure alone. Besides, I have a gut feeling there is a mix-up.

I can't be HIV positive, can I?

"What's wrong with me?" I blurt out before Dr. Everson even gets a chance to sit down. I'm sitting on the exam table, my feet dangling. They didn't weigh me or ask me to put on a gown, and now that omission suddenly seems ominous. I can nearly hear the soundtrack of doom.

Dr. Everson takes out her thin bifocals, sets them on her nose, and opens my file. "You been feeling okay, Josey?"

"Fine. Tired maybe."

"Moody?"

"No," I snap. "I just have a lot to do."

She looks up at me.

"Sorry."

"Stomach bothering you?" She glances at the way my arm is curled around my waist. I'm still shivering.

"A little. What's going on? Am I going to die, or not?"

Dr. Everson closes the folder. Sets it on the desk. She stands and takes out her stethoscope. "No," she says cryptically. She leans me back onto the table, presses on my abdomen. "Mm hmm," she says.

"What? Do I have a tumor? Diabetes? What's the matter

with me?" Now I really wish I'd agreed to let Chase come with me. After all, he knows what I look like and hence can probably deal with the scale's verdict.

Dr. Everson sits down, folds her arms over her chest. She is a typical Norwegian, tall and slender and strong. She wears her white hair fluffy around her face like a grandma, and as she smiles, I see delight in her eyes.

"What?" I sit up.

"Well, you're not dying, not yet. But some think they will from this ailment. Certainly will change your life."

I am HIV positive. I feel the blood drain from my face. "But how?"

"The old fashioned way, I guess." She's smiling brightly now, apparently enjoying this game she's playing.

I just stare at her, uncomprehending.

"Have you missed anything lately?"

Huh?

"Josey." She leans over, puts her hand on my knee, softens her smile. "You're not dying. You're pregnant."

the bumpkin

• • •

I'M PREGNANT. EXPECTING. WITH CHILD. COOKING A BUN IN THE oven.

Okay, maybe that's going too far.

But, I'm going to have a baby! I get into Chase's truck, sucking the grape lollipop I scored (hey, I'm still a patient!) and lodged in my cheek, and simply sit in the cab, absorbing Dr. Everson's news. A baby. A little Chase Junior.

I can seem him already, tow-headed, with blue eyes and an easy smile, running after me calling, Mama . . .

Mama?

Oh *no.*

I cup my hand over my abdomen as my breath hiccups. I can't be pregnant. We're going to Russia in less than twenty-four hours.

Overhead, the sky is blue, the birds chirruping, the weather warm, yet with the slightest tinge of autumn. Next to me a car pulls up, parks. The woman wrestles herself out and I see that she either had too many milkshakes or is also in a motherhood way. (Wait, does this mean I get to have milkshakes?) I watch her waddle into the clinic and something akin to dread passes over me. That's going to be me. Nine months from now, I'll be waddling.

But where? Down Main Street Gull Lake or through Red Square?

I touch my forehead to the steering wheel, hanging onto it with whitened hands. *Hey God, remember me, the Proverbs 31 wife? Did You not notice that I just gave all my furniture away?* A sweat slicks my hands. How will I tell Chase?

I pray that out of his glorious riches, he may strengthen you with power through his Spirit in your inner being. Yeah, me too. I'm not sure where I read that, but I know it's a Bible verse. And it thrums in my mind as I turn over the car engine and back out of the lot. I'm not sure just what is going on with my inner being (well, I now have a little more indication), but my outer part is sweaty and confused and close to tears.

I see two scenarios here:

1. I go home and break the happy news to Chase.
In all honesty, Chase will probably be thrilled that we're going to have a junior us. But what will it do to Chase and Josey, World Conquerors? We've been married less than two months. Not even long enough to figure out what side of the bed we'll each sleep on. How will we manage a baby?

In Russia?

2. I don't tell Chase and . . . when he finds out, hide out in Mongolia?.

I detour past the Cape Cod on Third Street on the way home. The For Sale sign is still in the yard, calling to me. But the house looks suddenly old and forlorn, the windows dark and gloomy. I notice now the slightly saggy porch, the fading paint from the clapboard siding.

I keep driving and stop at the Gull Lake Pharmacy, fill the prescription of prenatal vitamins Dr. Everson gave me. I don't know the cashier—some woman with an eastern European accent and the figure of a model—one of the foreign workers who flood our town in the summer, seeking employment. It strikes me as ironic that Chase and I are heading to Russia to help start small business when all the youth around the world flock to America to find their future. Not that I blame them, I mean, after all, this is the land of opportunity, but maybe if they had jobs in their own country...

I thank her, in Russian, and she smiles. *Spaceeba.* Yeah, I still got it. The thought gives me an odd sense of empowerment. Deep inside me, Lara Croft still lives.

Pregnant Lara Croft. I have an odd thought. What if... what if I went to Russia anyway?

No. I can't have a baby in Russia, can I?

Why not? Women in Russia have babies, don't they?

On a whim, I detour down the baby aisle. It's packed with paraphernalia. I had no idea how much stuff having a baby required until I saw Jasmine with Amelia. She takes a suitcase the size of Brazil with her every time she leaves the house.

And now I know what's in it.

Pacifiers, rattles, blankets, teething rings, wipes, diapers, Desitin, A+D Ointment, lotion, oil, baby food, baby spoon, formula, medicines. I wonder, is Russia abreast of the latest advances in baby formula?

I don't have to think hard to answer that question.

I pick up a package of tiny shoes and I get that feeling I have when I look at Amelia.

I'm having a *baby.*

Returning to the truck, I leave the parking lot, open the window, and let my arm hang out. The smell of hamburgers from the local Dairy Queen drifts in and turns my stomach into a writhing fish, and for the first time, ever, I can't stand the thought of food.

But instead of that thought thrilling me, all I can think is . . . it doesn't matter, I'll be fat anyway. Shoot. I motor through town, toward Berglund Acres. The sun kisses Gull Lake, the waves comb the shore, rhythmic, never ending. I'm struck that while my world has changed forever, everyone around me continues on without noticing. Hello, look at me, pregnant girl.

Pregnant. How overwhelming to think that inside me, right now, there is another life that I can't see or feel but that is my responsibility.

My *responsibility*.

I turn the truck around and head straight for the Hungry Wolf.

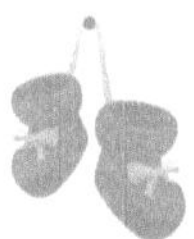

H's band is in full practice when I arrive. Two years ago, the bar changed hands and went from the Howlin' Wolf to the very original Hungry Wolf Saloon. By day, the place seems like a ramshackle roadhouse that should rightly be burned to the ground. But by night, it's the hot spot of Gull Lake. The roof vibrates off its rafters, the parking lot is crammed with dusty Chevy trucks and tricked-out Camaros. During a short stint the summer I turned twenty-one, I spent every summer evening shooting pool and generally cementing a reputation in this town that still makes me cringe. (And occasionally raises eyebrows as I march into the local church every Sunday. Yeah, that's me, the girl who graffitied the high school during homecoming the year after I graduated. Oh, whoops, nobody else knows that. The point is, if I can reform, anyone can.)

One night, as I was shooting pool, a tall, dark, and dangerous drifter sidled up for a game. Because my mouth had a mind of its own, it challenged him to a game. What I didn't figure out was that drifter had his thoughts on a different kind of game. We shot a round, I won. He challenged me to another match, and clobbered me. But I took round three when he sank the eight ball.

Which meant that he bought drinks. It's one of those memories that's hazy until the part where I'm in the parking lot, his hand braced against my car, effectively trapping me. During that era, I was all mouth and no action, and he evidently expected someone who could give him exactly what I was advertising.

In subsequent years, it's occurred to me that I don't deserve Chase. Because at too many pivotal times in our life he's gunned in on his motorcycle and plucked me from the clutches of disaster.

And it's not until the wind is in my hair, my arms around his waist, that I realize how close I came to living in a lopsided trailer, without running water or electricity, a single mom, barefoot and battered, wishing I didn't know how to play pool.

All I remember from that night is the sound of his bike, then Chase's voice as he asked me if I wanted to hop on, go for a ride. I also remember the snake-eyed stare he gave Drifter-boy. And how I ducked under the arms that held me captive and sprinted to freedom.

Chase is freedom and adventure and passion. He's Indiana Jones. Master Explorer Dirk Pitt (I told you he looks like Matthew). And I'm pregnant with his child.

It suddenly occurs to me that maybe he won't be happy at all. Maybe, in fact, he'll be angry. *We're not going to Russia if you're sick, Josey.* Those words reverberate through my brain to the beat I can hear from the Wolf's parking lot.

I am a Dream Killer.

Okay, so he had a part to play in all this, also. It's not like he wasn't . . . um . . . *there*. But I was the one bearing the birth control burden (of course). I'm suddenly flipping through my memories, trying to remember . . . with all the packing, could I have missed a day? Or two?

Or a week?

Okay, so I'm not exactly type A about taking my pills (although I think I get it now . . .)

I enter the Wolf and lift my hand to Lew Sulzbach, the bartender. He's gone from hosting parties in his parents' backyard to slinging beers just down the street. I think he discovered his gifting long before anyone else. H's band is banging out something indecipherable and damaging to my eardrums. I can't help it, I like country music. At least I can understand, and even relate to, the lyrics. And who doesn't like the earthy beauty of Keith Urban? He reminds me so much of Chase.

So every good-looking guy reminds me of Chase. I'm a newlywed, gimme a break.

Still, despite my distaste in punk music, I have to give H credit for following her dreams. And even for tattooing a monkey on her backside. That takes commitment. And a lot of vodka.

But so does being pregnant. (No, not the vodka part, although I'm sure many a child has been conceived via the help of vodka. Being pregnant takes *commitment*.) I smile at this, and even put one hand on my stomach, just to cover Junior's delicate and developing ears.

H nods to me, even as she's belting out the song. I perch on the end of a worn pool table, far from the speakers, and wait.

The music (noise) ends and she signals for a break. Her formerly-purple-now-orange-again hair is in a twirled mush today and she's wearing a dog collar with shiny spikes. It matches nicely with her nose ring. She's wearing a black tee and a pair of camouflage pants that end just below the knees, with leather ties at the bottom. Which just goes to show you that that everybody likes a good pair of capris, regardless of personal style.

"Hey," she says, sliding over to the pool table. Her boots make barely a sound on the spongy wooden floor. "What's up?"

"Did you get moved in?" I glance over to Rex. Tall and skinny, he has bleach-blond hair, gelled back and up, Elvis style, and is dressed in head-to-toe black. He lifts a drum stick to me in greeting.

"Yeah. Love your double bed, thanks for leaving that."

Oh, way over-sharing. But a good segue into what I have to tell her.

"H, I'm pregnant."

Her mouth gapes, and for a long, miraculously long second, nothing emerges. Then, "You're knocked up? That rocks!" She turns to Lew. "Hey, guess what, Josey's--"

I clamp my hand over her mouth before she can blurt it out.

"Nothing!" I add in the gaping silence. I lower my voice to a growl. "Nice way to put that, H."

She rounds on me, yanking my hand away. "What? Aren't you happy?"

I glance at Lew, who is staring at me like he did the night I poured a beer over his head—confused and more than a little shocked. (Well, someone should have kept his hands to himself.) I shrug and give him the "whoops" smile. I'm wondering if he's having the same flashback, because he shakes his head in a sort of dismay and turns away.

I drop my voice to dungeon levels. "I don't want everyone to know yet." Not that Lew or Rex or even H for that matter sees my mother or any of the Berglunds on a regular or even semi-regular basis. The only hope H has of running into my mother is when she's in the gas station convenience store picking up a pizza after the Wolf shuts down, while Mom is delivering her freshly baked, award-winning pastries.

I could use a pastry right now. Funny I should think that, with the smell of cigarette smoke invading every pore of my body. The good news is that I have my appetite back. Phew.

"Why don't you want anyone to know?" H asks, turning her back to Rex, the good secret keeper she is.

I give her the "c'mon, keep up" look. "We're going to Russia *tomorrow?*" I say, spelling it out.

"So?"

"So, if Chase knows, we won't go."

H has this look that always makes me wonder if I'm speaking English. I even roll the words back through my head to make sure. Yes. "He said he wouldn't go if I was sick."

"You're not sick. Pregnancy isn't an illness. It's a temporary condition." Her voice lowers further. "But let's just say now you have your out. Tell Chase, and the Cape Cod is yours." She opens her mouth and sticks her finger in, as if to emphasize just how she feels about that. Gross.

"Cut it out, H. I'm serious. Chase is thrilled about Russia, and frankly, I like him that way. I was even sorta . . . looking forward to going."

In fact, suddenly, all the things I could be missing rush through my head. The intoxicating chaos of the open market, with the mouth-watering smell of grilled shish kebabs. Subway surfing in the Moscow metro, that form of entertainment enjoyed only by expats. Learning a language that sounds like spitting and makes me feel like a Cold War spy. Drinking coffee *smolokom* at my favorite outdoor bistro. Chase and I walking hand in hand, bickering with vendors on Arbat Street, or attending the opera and shopping in the Moscow underground mall.

Moscow is alive and changing. It's white nights in summer, and fur coats and shopkas, your breath in the air in the winter.

It's challenge and victory. It's Josey and Chase, conquering the world together.

Josey and Chase and bumpkin.

"I don't know how to tell him."

H slips an arm around my shoulders. She smells like pineapple—probably from her hair goo. "You say, 'Chase, you scored, buddy.'"

I give her a nasty look. She shrugs. "Okay, so, how about, 'Chase, you're going to be a daddy'?"

I shake my head, look at my hands. "I can't tell him."

"You have to tell him. I think it's the law or something."

"No it's not."

She shrugs. "He's going to figure it out. I mean, I suppose you could hide it with sweatshirts—I'd stay away from velour leisure suits, but with the right army surplus jacket—"

"Focus, H. I don't intend to *never* tell him. Just to wait. Until we're—"

"Oh no, it's happening already!"

"What?"

H taps my head. "I hear that every pregnancy kills four billion brain cells. You're ahead of schedule."

"Stop. I'm just saying . . . women have babies in Russia all the time." Only, I was in a Russian state-run hospital once. Think 1940s America. Now add roaches. And cats. Bingo. I make a face.

H mimics it.

"So, what do I do?" I sink my head into my hands, feeling despair crest over me. Somehow, I didn't think that getting pregnant would elicit this response. During our engagement, I had conjured up this moment when I would tell Chase I was carrying his Junior. In my mind, I had a Hallmark card, maybe an outfit, definitely knitted booties. It would be this idealistic moment, if I knew how to knit. Again, my propensity to dream up another person's life.

"You have to tell him."

I nod. I have to tell him.

"You'll figure it out together. Isn't that what marriage is all about?" She casts a quick glance at Rex. Wait—H isn't wanting to get married, is she?

But a moment later, her gaze is back on me. I nod in answer to her question, regardless of how she wants to apply it. Marriage is about facing life together. Whatever it brings.

I put my hand on my stomach, look down. "I'm going to be fat."

H puts her hand on mine. "Think of it this way. You won't have to diet anymore."

So, there are some silver linings.

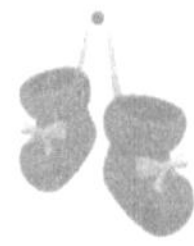

We'll work this out together.

We'll work this out together.

We'll work this out together.

The sun is sinking toward the Russia side of the world as I pull into Berglund Acres. My mother's Olds Cutlass is gone, as is my father's truck. I pull in, stop the engine. Sit in the cab, smelling Chase and everything about him, and screw up the courage to go in the house and drop a bomb.

Okay, so maybe I'm being melodramatic, but seriously, can you think of anything that rearranges a person's life more than a baby?

Didn't think so.

I climb out of the truck, slam the door. Our house was built in the 1950s and has a Mayberry RFD kind of charm. I climb up the porch, and the boards squeak. As does the screen door as I open it. I can hear Chase inside, humming. And something smells good, like garlic and cheese.

I pad through our front room, past the family pictures, my senior picture with my Jennifer Aniston hair (which I cut into a short bob in college, then again in Russia), and the chisel marks on the dining room hall that mark Jasmine's, Buddy's, and my growth.

Where will we mark Chase Junior's growth?

It's suddenly clear to me, we can't go to Russia. Not now. Because H is right—as soon as Chase gets the bug, he won't want to come back. And I'll be overseas washing out cloth nappies by hand in the bathtub.

They *do* have Pampers in Moscow, don't they? I search my memory . . . and come up with a big *nyet*. Or, at least, they might, but I don't remember because, well, I wasn't even married, let alone pregnant.

Pregnant. In *Russia.*

"Chase, I have something—"

I round the corner into the kitchen and there he is, my hero. Wearing an apron, and stirring something at the stove.

Is that Milton's apron?

It's definitely Chase, however, because I can recognize those jeans and that array of back muscles in a crowd of ten thousand apron-wearing Iron Chefs.

I stop short just as Chase turns. "Hey, GI. I have a surprise for you."

Uh, me too, I nearly say, but the sight of him cooking has me completely undone and all I can do is brace my arm on the doorjamb. He grins, and it's so cute, I'm glad I'm hanging on. "What are you doing?"

"I'm making shrimp and broccoli fettuccine."

He's making *what?*

"Remember our honeymoon, that Italian restaurant we found?"

With the cute wooden tables and the hurricane candles and the view overlooking Banff? Chase Junior probably wasn't conceived that night, but it's a distinct possibility. I nod, wordless.

He leans over and kisses me on the cheek. He's shaved, and smells like the cologne I got him for our wedding.

For a wild second, I wonder if Dr. Everson called. Thank you, thank you! Now I can act as disappointed as Chase will be. I won't be the destroyer! "What's the special occasion?" I ask in a sweet, innocent voice.

He wraps his arm around me, holds me close. "Tomorrow we go to Russia. I thought we should celebrate."

I smile, but my heart sinks. Especially when Chase twirls me around the kitchen, pins me for a second against the fridge, and kisses me.

Oh boy.

Then, with his lips against my neck he seals my fate. "Josey, I can't thank you enough for your courage and willingness to go overseas with me." He leans back and cups his hands to my face, running his thumbs over my cheeks. Yes, I feel tears forming. Shoot, shoot! I'm so putty in his hands! "I am constantly amazed at how God has blessed me with such an incredible, beautiful wife, and I want you to know that this will be the best year of our lives. You really know how to make my dreams come true."

What's a Proverbs 31 wife to do?

I smile at him, put my hands on his chest. He backs away, gives the sauce another stir. "Hey what did the doctor say? Why did they call you in?"

I shrug. "She gave me some vitamins . . . ."

He pours in the shrimp, starts to stir. "I didn't think anything was wrong. I figured you were just tired." He gives me a serious look, runs his finger down my cheek. "I know you, GI. You wouldn't keep anything from me."

No, of course not.

It's completely Chase's fault I'm in this mess. If he wasn't so cute, with charm leaking out of every smile, I probably wouldn't be pregnant. And hiding it. Why couldn't he have dangling nose hairs or burp in public? No, he has to be perfect, and because of his stupid perfection, I'm sneaking out the bedroom at midnight to repack my bags.

Because, well, clearly, size eight Gap jeans aren't in my future.

And, I'm going to need a *lot* more chocolate chips.

I'm going to tell him. I *am*. *After* we're safely in Russia. Didn't he say the WorldMar gig lasted nine months? If I'm doing my math right, we'll be boarding the plane right about the time I'm going to pop.

Yes, I know, I know, but he looked so . . . happy.

Besides, even if I don't make it home in time, women have babies in Russia all the time.

They *do*.

We're all going to be fine. *Really*.

I drag my suitcase from its spot in the living room to the bathroom down the hall. My parents are right across the hall, and I can hear my father's snores. Comforting, deep. Helpful. I used to lay in my bed in the room I shared with Jasmine right above them and calculate the exact moment when I could open my bedroom window and sneak out.

Something I will never, ever tell Junior.

Chase and I are occupying my old bedroom tonight—he's in Jas's old bed, I'm in mine. He suggested that we push the beds together, but there are simply some lines I have to draw.

No matter how much I love him, we're not . . . *you know* . . . with my parents sleeping below us. Regardless of how loudly my dad snores.

I shut the bathroom door, lock it, and open the bag.

I'll have to redo my list.

- sheepskin slippers—yes
- wool socks—without a doubt
- ~~5-lb~~ 10-lb bag popcorn
- all five seasons of *Alias*
- the first two seasons of *Lost*
- books (*and more books!*)
- pictures of Jasmine, Mom, Dad, and Amelia
- medicines—Ibuprofen, Acetaminophen (*can I have those?*), ~~1-5lb bag chocolate chips~~ all the chocolate chips I can find in the house
- toiletries
- Taz T-shirt
- no leather skirt (f*or potential embassy event*). Shoot.
- no leather pants (for second potential embassy event). Again, shoot.
- a year's supply of Tampax (*this could be a happy thing)*
- power converter (*for new hairdryer*)
- computer
- Gap jeans (*size ten and new size eight, just in case*)
- capris, black dress pants (*only because they have an adjustable waist*)
- underwear & socks (*new*)
- University of MN sweatshirt + any other sweatshirts I can rustle up
- my collection of tees
- my mules
- hiking boots
- slingback sandals

- black pumps—no
- black ankle boots—maybe, no
- black high boots—absolutely not (*Life is so unfair. Because what pregnant woman do you see walking around in heels? Must have something to do with balance, or lack of it. Oh, joy.*)
- Birkenstock sandals
- passport
- antacids—I remember this from Jasmine's pregnancy
- yoga pants (*because I have a feeling this is the only thing I'll fit into in a few months*)
- vitamins
- expectant mother handbook (*My mother gave it to Jasmine when she announced her happy news. I sneak out and take it from its current location—our family room bookshelf—where it's gathering dust. Apparently, Mom delivered all the knowledge of the book verbally to Jasmine, thereby negating the need for a book. Which I will now need. I'm wondering, perhaps, if having a baby far from home is suddenly a benefit?*)
- pickles?

I've never liked pickles, but doesn't every pregnant woman crave pickles? Just because I haven't craved pickles to this point doesn't mean I'm not going to crave them, right? What if my pickle craving doesn't kick in until I'm three months pregnant? What if I have to have pickles or die, and I send Chase out into the city to find pickles and he is mugged, or killed, and I'm left alone to raise this child?

All because I didn't have pickles.

I open the bathroom door, flick off the light, and tiptoe down the hall. My mother puts up pickles every year, and just because I don't like them doesn't mean they're not good. The

Minneapolis Star Tribune told me that they had a "distinctive crunch and tang that propels Myrna Berglund's pickles into a new category of taste." So, I feel I'm in good pickle hands.

I pull the dangling light cord to flick on the cellar light. The musty smell of dirt and cement rushes up at me. I spy a cobweb netting the floor joists and stifle a shiver.

"I double-dog dare you!"

My brother's squeaky seven-year-old voice slices through my memory as I stand at the top of the stairs—creaky old slats that groan and shake at every step.

"I'm eleven. I don't need to be *dared*." I am snarky back to him because apparently he's forgotten that I am the oldest, the bravest, the strongest. Besides, who invented the game in the first place?

"Don't go, Josey." Jasmine's hand is on my arm, and she has fear in those wide brown eyes.

We're in the middle of a quest, however, to sneak into the cave of Mt. Doom and retrieve the Treasure of the Saint Christopher (a name we dreamed up by driving by the Catholic Church every Sunday). Aka my mother's prized Macintosh apples.

I turn to Jasmine. "Don't worry, I'll be fine." But I don't believe my own words. Because Mandy Whittler watched *Nightmare on Elm Street* number four or five or fifteen last time she was here babysitting and when I heard screaming, I snuck out of my room, and I don't believe for a single second that Freddy is dead. I know he's just hiding out. In my basement. Under the stairs. Right next to the apples.

"She's chicken. She won't do it," Buddy says, and in case I don't get it, puts his hands under his arms and squawks. I'd like to make him squawk, but Mom is over at the restaurant and I'm in charge and if she has to "come back to the house one more time to stop a fight, you'll all be sorry!"

So I fight back with an emphatic, "Will too!"

"Will not!"

"Will too!"

"Not!"

"*Too!*"

He clamps his hands on his hips and grins and once again my mouth has taken me places my body doesn't want to follow. I glare at him, take a breath, and descend the stairs.

Of course, Freddy didn't live under the stairs. I figured out later that he lives in my father's dilapidated tool shed, but we agreed that I won't bother him if he doesn't bother me.

Little did I know that my brother had his own stash of St. Christopher jewels. It wasn't until my mother got a whiff of fermenting apples and found his pile of half-eaten cores that his deceit and false double-dog daring was revealed. I have to admit to smiling when Buddy found out how sorry Mom could make him.

That memory and others rush at me as I descend into the cellar. The floor is still packed dirt, the walls unpainted cement blocks. And along the back wall, on shelves, rows and rows of preserves. Canned tomatoes, pickles, relish, jams, jellies, peaches, pears, and applesauce. It's a sight to behold—color and texture and craftsmanship. Now I understand why my mother, after canning season every year, stands here admiring her work like a painter might regard a finished canvas.

I grab a jar of pickles, rearrange the shelves (so she won't know its missing and start asking questions), and tiptoe back upstairs. Where I grab a pair of Chase's black socks to wrap the jar in.

I slip it next to my wool socks, pad it with the yoga pants and one of Chase's old Gull Lake Gulls sweatshirts I dug out of the boxes in the spare room after dinner and hid in the bathroom closet. Returning to the kitchen, I open the pantry and empty the shelves of every package of chocolate chips, thanking Mom for her love of cookies. I also find another bag of popcorn—not the ten pounds I'd hoped for, but I'll take what I can get. Finally, I spy a jar of honey-roasted peanuts (Junior needs protein, right?) and a bag of white-chocolate-covered pretzels Mom got from a guest last Christmas. It's been far too long for a gift like that to go untouched.

I swipe it as well.

Sneaking back to the bathroom (and feeling a little like a thief, although after giving all my furniture away, I think I deserve a little mercy), I take out two more pairs of jeans and tuck my stash in their place.

A knock sounds lightly on the door. "Josey? Are you in there?"

Chase! Around me lies the debris of my rash decision—my jeans, the leather skirt, the Tampax. "Uh, yeah . . . ."

"Are you okay?"

I'm shoving the suitcase closed, zipping it. "I'm fine. I'll be right out." Picking it up, I plop it in the bathtub, pulling the curtain.

"Are you sure you're okay? You've been gone an awfully long time."

He's been timing me? What other things about me has he been watching? Panic reaches up to choke me. I can't hide this from him . . .

"Has the excitement of going upset your stomach again?"

I cringe as I say, "A little." *Sorry, Lord, I don't mean to lie.* I mean, yes, I guess I do, but I don't *want* to. Which should be factored in, don't you think? Is it still a lie if you're sacrificing yourself and doing it for the good of the other person?

I think this is an important universal question that bears scrutiny. Like, when H asks if her hair looks good. It's orange . . . what would you say? Then again, on her, it does look good, so I don't have to lie, which I guess makes it a bad example. Still, it's a good question.

"Do you need anything?"

Oh Chase, go away! I gather up my jeans, the bag of Tampax, the leather skirt and pants, and shove them all into the bottom drawer of the bathroom vanity, the one that used to belong to me. All that's left now is a few old Q-tips, a Band-Aid, a half-used tube of mascara, and strawberry flavored lip gel. And the remnants of my life before motherhood. The good thing is that my mother hasn't looked in this drawer for years. I think I'm safe.

"I'll be right out." I close the door and climb to my feet. And get a glimpse of myself in the mirror.

Florescence has never been my best lighting, but now I see myself differently. A mother to be. I turn to the profile view and pull out my jammies to create a tummy. A large tummy.

I'm going to be fat. And it doesn't matter what H says, I don't think fat is cute. I wonder if Chase will. When I tell him.

Which will be soon, I promise.

"Josey? Are you sure everything is all right?"

"Yes, Chase," I say as I open the door and walk out. He's in his sweatpants, bare-chested, wearing scruffy whiskers and the smell of sleep. He puts his arm around me, kisses me on the forehead. "Everything is going to be just fine," I say softly.

Now that certainly doesn't count as a lie, does it?

i am not a sherpa

. . .

From: "Josey Anderson"
Josey@netmail.moscow.ru
To: "H"
H.Henke@rr.mn
Subject: I'm going to, really

Dear H,

Before you ask, no. I didn't. But I will. As soon as Chase is settled into his job. It's been a busy twenty-four hours. And, in case I can't figure out how to delete this letter from the sent items box, let us call The Thing That Cannot Be Named (Yet) just . . . well, uh . . . maybe The Thing That Cannot Be Named (Yet).

First, I'm back! I didn't expect the rush of emotions as we landed at Sheremetyevo. The last time I stood in passport control, well, let's just say that my focus was on the breakfast I'd consumed on the airplane. And the fact that I'd neglected to use the restroom on board, a mistake I did *not* make this time. But more than being able to stand in the passport control line without doing the too-many-beers dance (you know, the one we did in the satellite line during Homecoming at the U of MN. By the way, have I ever apologized for leaving you there? How did you get home, anyway?), I had a sense that I, Josey Berglund Anderson, am savvy.

Savvy. Especially when Chase turned to *me* and asked *me* what line to get into, the red line or the green line. (Answer: Green.)

I'm so good for him.

I can't believe how much I missed Russia. The first time I arrived, I thought the country had been recently bombed, with the rubble and disrepair that hung over the city like a bad cold. But two years has changed Moscow. Outside the city, where once were dacha houses that looked more like Uncle Bert's chicken coop, are now palatial two-story homes. Moscow's version of Wisteria Lane.

And you'll never believe it—we have a driver! I felt like Condi or Brittany or someone special when we got through passport control and there, on the other side of the plexiglass barrier, I saw a sign—Mr. and Mrs. Chase Anderson. My attention was momentarily distracted by the customs official who wanted to open one of our bags. Because of my not telling you-know-who about The Thing That Cannot Be Named (Yet), I had to repack my bag, and well, let's just say the pickles might have raised some question. As it turns out, they did, but I'll get there.

I handed off Chase's bag to the customs guy and watched Chase's reaction as the man pawed through his things. Chase smiled when he saw the Scary Pants. I reminded him then that *someone* should have given me his extra bag of peanuts on the flight from Amsterdam. Because, well, I'm eating for . . . whoops! The Thing That Cannot Be Named (Yet).

Chase has many uses, one of the best is that he's a great bag schlepper. He carried both our suitcases *and* his duffel bag, leaving me with only our two backpacks (mine filled with two books I picked up at the Minneapolis Airport, a dozen bagels, and a book I stole from our family room last night. More on *that* later). Chase's was filled with one James Michener novel about the beginning of the world until now. I'm hoping the Canadian Bagel factory is still open in Moscow because if it's not, I only have enough bagels to last me a week. I figure it'll take me that long to chart my course from where we will live and the CB Factory. But wait, I have a driver!

His name is Igor. He's very thuggish—wide-shouldered and solemn and looks like he might also have served as one of Putin's henchmen in a previous life. (You *do* know who Putin is, right? Do the words KGB and President of Russia help at all?) His nose is off (as in off course), and he has an indentation in the center of his chin that looks suspiciously like a scar. Of course, he was wearing all black (because that's the official Russian color) and when he saw us, he crunched his cigarette right there in the middle of the airport, grabbed one of our bags, and for a long, scary couple of minutes we thought he was a thief (until Chase grabbed him by the back of the collar and nearly got flattened).

I have mixed feelings about our driver.

Especially after his driving. If I weren't already The Thing That Cannnot Be Named (Yet), my stomach would be roiling anyway, because along with a new highway through Moscow, there are forty billion more cars. And every driver thinks like Igor—that the Moscow highway is their own personal video game.

WorldMar has their own housing complex! Or at least their own apartments inside a gated complex. I felt like royalty or at least Angelina Jolie as the driver stopped at the double gates and showed our passports to the guard. He waved us through and we entered the Twilight Zone.

The apartment building is pink. With golden arches

above the door. And according to Igor, right below us lives the mayor of Moscow! Now, I'm confused. Because last time I lived in Russia, my roomie, who worked for an NGO, lived in a regular Russian flat (and hence, so did I), complete with roaches and a smelly elevator and a rickety wooden door that couldn't keep out a third grader. Apparently, Aid Workers' digs have changed in two years because when I opened the steel door (which I think they acquired from Alcatraz), I found our one-bedroom flat outfitted with a security system, a *real* leather overstuffed sofa and chair, wall-to-wall carpeting (although I once knew a missionary who had wall-to-wall carpeting), a large flat screen *with cable* (but no DVR, shoot), a dishwasher, fridge with water filter *and* icemaker (last time I was here, having ice in my Coke was a sort of national crime), and an electric stove. Finally, on the other side of the flat, we have a huge double bed with a matching armoire, a dresser, and night tables.

Where am I?

All of this glam was lost on Chase, who simply dropped our bags (and this is where I get back to the pickles), toed off his shoes, and fell onto the bed. Against my warnings.

I, on the other hand, thanked Igor and, seeing my opportunity to . . . let's just say, unpack . . . I opened my bag.

I had to wring out my wool socks, and I didn't even get a taste of the pickles due to the embedded shards of glass.

I won't need pickles anyway. Because I don't have any cravings. I'm probably one of those girls who won't get cravings when she's . . . The Thing That Cannot Be Named (Yet).

I hid the chocolate chips in the kitchen, in the cupboard, in a pot large enough to feed St. Paul. I poured the excess popcorn in a coffeepot (because, well, hello, I buy coffee, not make it), and put it in a cupboard over the refrigerator. As for the few extra food items I packed, I hid them under the bed.

(On which Chase was zonked out, which made me feel very Josey Bond.)

Then I unpacked both our bags. And paged through the first five chapters of the book I stole from Jasmine. And watched the sun set over Moscow. We're nine floors up and across the street from Gorky Park (the Russian version of Central Park), which means I can see over most of the other buildings, and nearly to the Volga River. The sunset is just as beautiful over the Volga as it is over Gull Lake.

You know that feeling you get when you've been up too long, and the whole world feels like it's operating behind a plate of glass, and yet your entire body seems to buzz, as if electrified? That's how I feel. Which I why I'm writing. But I know better than to go to sleep before bedtime. *Someone* is going to be *sorry* they didn't listen to me.

I have to admit, I can't wait until tomorrow. I can see now why God sent me to Moscow last year. He knew that I was going to marry Chase, and that WorldMar would need him, and he'd need a helpmate like me. Someone creative and smart and who knows Moscow.

I just know, when this year is over, it's not only going to be the best thing we did, but he'll be so thankful, he'll have no problem returning home and buying the Cape Cod. For *us* (and you know what I mean)!

I'm going to run myself a bath, but I wanted to tell you not to worry about *anything*.

Everything is going to be perfect.

Love you!

Josey

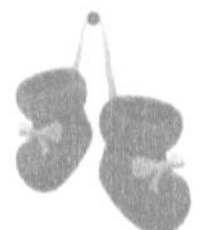

Stop the pain!

Like an electric current, the buzzing slices through my brain, past the darkness, and into that place that had been soft and happy and quiet.

Buzz!

My entire body vibrates as I'm yanked to consciousness.

Where am I? Outside a large window, lights blink like stars, a bright moon illuminates the dark room.

I'm cold. And sore. And the buzzing!

"What is that?" From the doorway, I see a form appear. Chase. He's in his underwear and stalking toward the door. Realization rushes at me.

Russia. I'm in *Russia*. Moscow.

I'm lying on a cold leather sofa.

And I feel like I've been run over by a herd of buffalo.

Behind the buzzing, I hear something. A trickling sound. It must be raining outside.

Pounding now threatens to take down the door. I leap from the sofa just as Chase reaches—

"*Stop!*"

He turns, wide-eyed.

"*Don't open that!*"

He's just staring at me, like I might be from the planet Vorgan.

"You don't know who's out there!"

"Calm down, I was just going to look through the peephole."

More pounding. And Russian words that don't sound very happy. Russian is sorta that way, though, even when the words are happy. Lots of guttural *khas*, and hissing *shhs*.

Chase peeks through the hole. "It's someone in his bathrobe." He reaches for the door.

I grab his arm. "You're in your underwear!"

He looks down, as if noticing this for the first time. Looks at me.

"Cover me," I say as I crack the door. I've been here before. I know how to handle strange Russian men at my door. But I leave the chain up, because, you know, those chains are invincible. I step back from the door, feeling Chase move behind me. "*Shto?*"

Now, I should interject here that I remember very little of my Russian. It took me six months just to learn hello (*zdrastvooyta*—yeah, I know, unfair), so I'm pretty impressed that *anything* Russian comes to mind at this moment. But it does.

Which also leads to the incorrect conclusion that I might understand even one word that emerges from our bathrobed visitor's mouth. Despite how fast or loud he might say it.

Over, and over, and over.

Funny, that background noise doesn't sound like rain, and with that thought something nudges the back of my mind. Something. I just can't—

"Just let me talk to him," Chase says, and steps past me to shut the door, unlock the chain, and open the door.

Sure Chase, have at it. Because I know that you're fluent in Angry Russian.

Maybe I should get a frying pan.

The man is stymied for a half-second at Chase's appearance. (I was also, but for different reasons.) Then he continues his barrage.

He's wearing a red bathrobe with leather slippers. About the height of Chase, Mr. Bathrobe has about fifty pounds on him, and smells slightly of vodka and cigarette smoke. And, the way he's gesturing, I'm thinking maybe someone isn't happy about the new neighbors.

He's pointing. Down. And now making those gestures a person might make in the eensy weensy spider song.

I always liked that song.

The eensy weensy spider goes up the water spout . . .

Down came the rain and washed the spi—

Washed!

"The tub!"

I turn and run to the bathroom. Water gushes from the closed door like a pretty Minnesotan stream.

I fling the door open. Inside, water stands ankle deep in the room as it runs over the sides of the overflowing tub. Oh no—I fell asleep! While running the tub!

Chase is a step behind me, followed by Bathrobe Man. I reach over, turn off the water, then plunge my arm deep and yank the plug.

The water gurgles out. And I stand there, dripping, and look over at our guest. I point downstairs. He nods grimly.

"*Izvenitya,*" I say quietly. See, that's another word I remember. Sorry.

Chase stands there in the warm water, running his hand through his hair, looking grim.

"*Menya zavoot* Josey," I say, and stick out my hand.

"Chase," Chase says. I am not sure how to say he's my husband. (Not having to have learned that the first time I was here. But suddenly it's a word I'd like to know oh-so very much.)

"Gregory Borisovich Franchuk," Bathrobe Man says. Chase pumps his hand, and I smile wryly, wondering if Chase realizes that he's meeting, in his underwear, the mayor of Moscow.

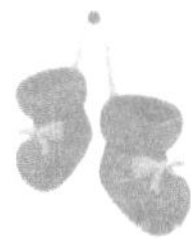

The next time we wake, some four hours after sopping up all the water from our bathroom floor with everything resembling a sheet, towel, or blanket in the flat (and then sleeping on a bare bed), the sun is just climbing unseen over the far side of the apartment buildings and gliding into the yard below. I open my eyes, immediately awake, my body humming.

Russia. I can hardly believe I'm here. Last time, I had unrealistic dreams about changing the world, or at least my corner of it, like some kind of Mother Theresa. At best, I helped a handful of students learn how to say, "Zis is a spoon," and witness in poor Russian my love for Jesus to a dying neighbor. I know, some missionary I was.

This time, however, I'm serious. I'm going to help Chase help the Russians help themselves. Like The Donald, I'll take fledging ideas and nurture them, bring them to life. God has given me a second chance to make a difference. And I'm up to the task. Because, deep inside, I'm still a missionary.

No, deep inside, I'm a *mother*.

That thought sweeps all others from my brain.

Chase is wrapped around me, one leg over mine, his hair crushed and tangled, wearing a speckled blonde and red five-hour—or would that be twenty-eight hour?—shadow. He's warm and smells like Chase, and a feeling of happiness so intense washes through me, I think maybe I can't breathe.

Or maybe that's just Chase's arm pressing on my stomach. A stomach that suddenly doesn't feel so good. I push his arm off and sit up. My head swirls. Or rather, the room swirls.

Chase stirs but I get up, cross the flat to the lagoon that used to be our bathroom, find the WC, open the door, and stand above the porcelain god. Waiting. Like Texas bracing for a hurricane.

Maybe I should eat something.

"Josey, you okay?"

I brace my arm against the wall, feel a slight sweat slick my body. Yeah, I'm swell.

The feeling passes, thankfully, and a moment later I return

to the bedroom. Chase is up and pulling on his jeans. "I don't suppose I dreamed that . . . incident . . . last night."

"Not unless someone left a giant spitwad in our bathtub," I answer, referring to the soggy everything that is starting to smell like rainwater.

"Any suggestions about what to do with it?"

"Not a clue." I head for the dresser, but Chase catches me and pulls me close. He knows how to distract me. And I like it. "We're in Russia," he says close to my ear. I love the feel of his arms around me, and I lay my head against his chest.

"*Da,*" I say. I can feel the blood start to heat in my veins. Chase always finds a way to steal my focus.

Or rather, find it.

He kisses me on the neck but lets me go before I can suggest anything, and heads out to the kitchen.

I am rummaging through the clothes that 1. Survived the last-minute pregnancy pillage and 2. Don't smell like pickle juice. I find a pair of black capris and a formerly crisp white peasant blouse. I'm pulling the blouse on as I walk to the kitchen.

Chase is standing with the fridge door open. The light and the smell of tomato and dill spill out. "There is a pot of soup in here."

I look over his shoulder. "I think that's called *borscht*. I wonder how long it's been here."

"Let's try it." He reaches for it but I put a hand on his arm. The voice of wisdom. Again. Wasn't it me that reminded him that he was in his drawers last night? "You don't know how long that's been there."

He gives me a frown. "We have no food."

"What about my bagels?"

He waggles his eyebrows and I swat him. "I brought a dozen bagels in my carry-on for just this occasion."

And that's how we find ourselves sitting in our family

room, sharing a couple of blueberry bagels, drinking leftover water from the plane (me, the Proverbs 31 woman, thinking ahead again). Chase and Josey, World Conquerors. Partners. I can't wait to get started on his NGO project, help him sort through ideas, present them to his Russian partners. I've already googled cottage industry ideas, and have a few cooking in the back of my brain. We are going to make such a great team.

Now is probably the time to tell him that we're taking on recruits. I can see his face already, the joy . . .

Chase must be reading my mind because he reaches across the table, touches my hand, smiles. "Do you know where my toothbrush is?"

Oh. Well. "In the bathroom."

He gets up. Shoot. I see my moment vanish, but it's okay. Because maybe today after we're done at WorldMar, we'll take the subway to Red Square. And find the bistro where I used to sit and daydream about Chase and our perfect life. I'll tell him there, with the twilight at our backs and the smell of fall in the air, with the jeweled leaves swirled at our feet. And he'll sweep me up in a hug, tell me—

"Did you bring my black suit pants?"

How did he ever live without me? "In the closet."

The doorbell rings. I get up to answer it as Chase dives into his dress clothes. Our thug driver is at the door.

"*Gatov?*" he asks.

Another Russian word. To which I nod, yes, we're ready.

See, this will be a cinch.

We ride down the elevator, which is oh-so much cleaner than any Russian elevator I remember. (They usually resemble a phone booth that has been well-used by the local canine population. This one is clean. Not a doggie treat in sight.)

We walk by a *doorman* (missed him last night) who nods at us, and find ourselves outside, where a dozen black cars line the sidewalk. Our thug opens the door to one of them, and Chase and I slide into the backseat.

I feel I must wave. To someone. So I wave at the doorman. He ignores me as we pull away and out the front gate.

Moscow is a different world. I remember the fashions from France, the well-dressed woman in Prada knock-offs and fake Gucci bags, but I don't remember the new sky-rises, the restaurants, and name-brand stores. Or maybe it's because I spent most of last time underground, riding the subway. Suddenly I miss it, the press of the crowd, the feeling of speed as humanity is sucked underground like turbo earthworms.

But I'm not complaining. Especially when Chase takes my hand. We drive past the McDonalds and Red Square, Moscow Underground, and finally to Volyachaevskaya Street to the WorldMar headquarters.

Which is located on the top floor of a *mall.* With escalators. And an ATM machine. And a movie theater and . . . get this . . . a *Baskin Robbins.* Thirty-one flavors!

Pinch me.

I walk through glass doors into WorldMar and the size two, age thirteen receptionist greets us in refined English. "I'm Olya," she says, and beeps Chase's new secretary. I glance over at Chase. He's beaming.

Methinks someone is enjoying this very, very much. Would like to wave his pink slip in *some* school administrator's face. As his secretary comes out, I take his hand.

Which is a good thing, because now I know he loves me. His pulse didn't even skip. Mine, however, went wild at her wool Ann Taylor suit and Prada knock-off slingbacks.

I need to go shopping.

One thing I failed to mention about Russia is that it is the capital of stolen designer wear. I figure, if I'm all the way over here, *sacrificing* for the good of others, I deserve to take advantage of the, let's just say, *uniqueness* of living in Moscow?

Except, well, these fashions won't fit for long, will they?

Shoot!

"Allo," Miss Well-Dressed says, and extends her hand. I see a manicure. "My name is Katrina." I also see how her gaze falls over Chase.

And then it hits me. Everywhere I look at WorldMar, I see shapely young Russian women. Now, yes, Russia has been extraordinarily blessed with shapely young women (and I happen to know that none of them between the ages of fourteen and fifty-one eat anything), but it seems that WorldMar has collected an inordinate amount of said shapely women. My radar (and you know what I'm talking about) is suddenly at red alert.

Chase shakes Katrina's hand. "This is my wife, Josey," he says. Good boy, Chasie. Keep saying that word—*wife*.

We follow the underfed Katrina and wiggle through the office to Chase's new digs. Which, for the shortest of moments, takes my breath away. It's pink, like our apartment building, which I think must be part of a giant Russian makeover, but the view makes up for the color. It overlooks the Kremlin, St. Basil's, and the Volga River.

Chase has a big black desk and a couple of bookcases, his own computer, and some black leather furniture. I think I'm seeing the same decorator's touch as in our flat.

"Wow," Chase says.

I smile up at him. He so deserves this, and he's going to be the best anthropologist-entrepreneur-consultant they've ever had. Katrina leaves, telling Chase she'll introduce him to the staff when he's ready. I'll just bet she will.

Just as Chase is taking me into his arms, again (I'm thinking for a little thank-you kiss), a knock at the door separates us.

An American enters. I pinpoint his nationality by his footwear (loafers) and the way he's dressed in colors—a blue polo and khaki pants. "Jim Wilkes," he says. "Chief of Party." He shakes our hands and I place him at mid-thirties, confident, with a sort of smart preppiness about him that I would associate with easterners. Or at least people from Wisconsin.

"I'm afraid your partner isn't here today, Chase. Bertha is out on a project but she'll be in later this week. I'd be happy to show you around the office, however."

Bertha?

I can't help it. A sigh of relief streaks through me. How much trouble can a Bertha be?

"It's nice to meet you, Josey," Jim says. He opens the door for Chase.

I'm baffled, because I know he's just offered to show Chase around, and it feels like he's asking me to . . . leave. And well, I'm Chase's partner too, aren't I?

I stand there and Chase just looks at me. And I look at him. And he says nothing.

Nothing.

And it's then I realize. Chase's idea and my idea of our life here just might be vastly different. I'm not the co-conquerer.

I am the baggage-toting Sherpa.

"Mz. Anderson?"

I hear the name through a fog of darkness and hard angles. Blinking, I frown, and it's a second or two before I realize that I've fallen asleep at Chase's desk. I sit up, and it's then I feel moisture, pooling at the corner of my mouth. Oh, gross.

I put my hand to my mouth to wipe it dry as I try and sort through my surroundings. Big window now reflecting a setting sun, black furnishings, cotton-candy walls—

"Mz. Anderson?"

I roll my eyes around to get them working again, feeling lines from the blotter on the desk embedded in my face. And yes, I see that damp spot. Underfed Katrina is standing before me, wearing raised eyebrows. She seems just a tad annoyed. "I'm sorry to disturb you, but your driver needs to know if you want a ride home."

Driver?

Oh yeah, our thug.

"I'll wait until Chase is finished."

I've been here all afternoon, right after I came back from my whirlwind shopping trip through the mall. Sherpas don't need clothing. Sherpas wear blankets and sheepskin shoes. Good thing I brought my wool socks.

"Mr. Anderson left with our Project Leader an hour ago. He told me to instruct your driver to bring you home when you awoke."

Chase left me?

Left me?

Her words erase all thought from my brain and my breath actually leaves my body as I blink at her. She waits, then finally raises one groomed eyebrow.

"I ah . . . I guess I'll go, then," I say. I stand and the room swims before my eyes. I feel like I'm walking through water—stiff and slow—as I stand up, move around the desk. My head is pounding. "When is he going to be back?"

"I don't know. They went to Gorkovich to visit the partner company."

I stare at her.

"The village where the project is."

Oh.

My stomach emits a growl. I put a hand over it. "I'm confused. Chase just left me here, with no word when he'll be back?"

She looks at me as if confused by my confusion.

"Fine." I smooth my formerly sorta pressed white blouse and brush past her. Thug is waiting in the hallway. He says nothing as I hit the elevator button.

But I feel a sort of pity radiate off him as we descend. Swell. Thug pity.

Darkness hovers over Moscow like a fog and by the time we pull into the pink palace, shadows have engulfed the courtyard. Thug escorts me up the elevator, which is a good thing because I don't have a key. Yet.

Tomorrow I will have my own key.

Tomorrow Chase will realize that he shouldn't leave me behind. That he needs me.

Because this is *my* town. I am the one who knows how to barter for bread (or a fake Kate Spade handbag, whatever be the case), I am the one who can negotiate the subway, and I am the one who used to have friends in this town.

I am not a Sherpa.

Thug opens the door for me, and I turn and hold out my hand. "*Klooch,*" I say, remembering the word for key. Oh, and I'm the one who can talk Russian.

Thug gives me the slightest smile as he takes it off his ring and hands it over. I nod. "*Das vadanya,*" I say. "*Spaceeba.*"

I close the door. The flat smells surprisingly fresh. I flick on the light. Draped across the family room on clotheslines that criss-cross the room are our bedclothes, sheets, and towels. What, did the Cleaning Fairy come while I was gone?

My skin crawls just a little as I tiptoe through the apartment. The Cleaning Fairy also made the bed. A large black blanket with a pink begonia. It's crowned at the head by two pink pillows.

Chase deserves all this pink. I think I'll find a nice pink stuffed teddy bear to put in the center.

I return to the kitchen to find the *borscht* gone. In its place is a pot of rice with meat.

Where am I?

The flat is quiet, darkness pressing the windows. Outside, I see the brightly colored Ferris wheel in the center of Gorky Park, turning round and round and round, moving, but never really going anywhere. Just watching the world.

I put my hand to my belly as tears film my eyes.

I am not a Sherpa.

lost

. . .

"OH, JOSEY, I'M SO SORRY!" CHASE'S VOICE DRIFTS OVER THE sound of birds and quiet conversations in Russian. I'm sitting outside, the sun on my face, leaves dancing at my feet and through the legs of the tables at Venetsia, my favorite little bistro I discovered during my missionary term in Moscow. I'm nursing an orange slushy and nibbling a cucumber sandwich and wearing my favorite pair of Gap, size 10 flair-leg jeans and a black tunic under a denim jacket. And a new pair of espadrilles. Which tells me this is a dream because I love those shoes and somehow I know I don't own them. Yet. Still, seeing Chase stroll up to me with a dozen red roses, kneel before me, and look up at me with those blue, melt-me-now eyes entices me to sink back into my dream.

Because, frankly, it's so much better than the reality, which is Chase arriving home late last night and slipping in bed beside me without a word. That's what I get for faking sleep.

"Sorry for what, Chase?" I smile, because while I know exactly why he should be groveling, it's good for him to admit it. I'm such a good, therapeutic wife.

"For not seeing that you are perfect, that I need you."

"You do need me," I say, but I'm magnanimous, because we're newlyweds, and one little mistake I can forgive. Okay, well, two mistakes counting that pink-slip omission. But I'm a forgiving person so I pull my feet off the chair and take the flowers. "I forgive you."

He grasps my hand. His hand is warm, as is his gaze. Which reminds me . . .

"I have something to tell you . . . I'm pregnant!"

His mouth opens and, just as I expected, his eyes fill with joy. He opens his mouth, probably to tell me how much he loves me—

"Josey, why do my socks smell like pickles?"

Nice Chase vanishes and in his place I open my eyes to snarly, red-eyed Chase holding his dark socks.

I sit up. The sun is slinking just over the windowsill, a clear indication that I'm up way too early.

A woman in my delicate condition needs her sleep.

And, something to eat. Because now that I'm vertical, my stomach has decided not to join me.

And that smell. I put my hand over my mouth as I climb out of bed. "What are you doing up so early?" I ask, pushing past him.

"I couldn't sleep. I thought I'd get to the office early today." Aside from the smell from his victimized socks, Chase is looking good, his hair wavy and semi-groomed. He's wearing a pair of black jeans and a pullover. Mr. GQ Anthropologist. I married a hottie. This cools my anger for him just a smidge.

"There are more socks in the top drawer," I say as I gesture to the bureau. "I'll wash those."

Because, you know, that's what I'm here for.

Chase opens the drawer and finds new socks.

"What are you going to do today?" Chase asks as he stands up.

Oh, I thought I'd scrub the kitchen floor, maybe iron the

sheets, and oh, bake some cookies right after I sew myself a new frock.

Stop, Josey, says a voice inside, the one that keeps me from bursting into tears.

I fold my arms, lean against the doorframe. Hitch a shoulder. He comes close and kisses me on the cheek. "Igor will drive you anywhere you want to go. And I changed money while I was out yesterday. I left it on the bureau."

Okay, now you can guess how that makes me feel.

"Igor said he'd take you shopping, if you want."

I'm not a Sherpa. I'm Pretty Woman. "I'll be fine, Chase."

Yet, as I stand there in my Taz T-shirt, feeling slightly woozy, seeing my man not only looking hot, but going off to his new life, I'm seeing the truth.

Chase is obviously going to have to be educated. I thought he'd recognize my surpassing noble qualities simply by my servanthood and ability to pack our lives into two fifty-five pound bags. (And a duffel. And two carry-ons). Especially, he should see it in my surrender of essential footwear.

Clearly, I'll have to be more proactive.

Which, I think is actually Biblical, if I were to take a deeper look at the Proverbs 31 wife. I mean, she doesn't exactly sit around the house, does she? How would she get all that flax for spinning, or buy the fields, or even clothe herself in fine linen and purple?

I wonder how I would look in purple?

One thing I know. Sherpas don't wear purple. Deep inside I know that God has a reason for my being here. Other than Chase's clean socks.

I grab him just as he's leaving and kiss him quickly. "When will you be home?" Oh, I hate that I just asked that. I'm hearing desperation in my tone. *That* will have to go.

He lifts a shoulder. "I don't know. I'll call you. Why don't you pick up a cell phone while you're out today?"

He lets himself out and I make myself three promises.

1. I will not let Igor drive me around town. I am a proficient subway surfer, and it's time to get back on the wave.
2. I will find something productive and useful and life-changing to do in Russia.
3. I will outfit myself with decent footwear.

The flat is instantly quiet but I refuse to let it sink into my bones as I grab a bagel and run a bath.

Because underneath the Josey Anderson exterior lives the woman who caused Chase to follow me halfway across the world.

He ain't seen nothin' yet.

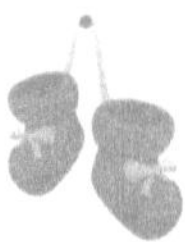

The sun is high and bright as I leave the flat. I see Thug (Igor) sitting outside in his thugmobile and I lift a hand as I stride past him. He frowns at me.

But I'm looking confident, so he must realize I don't need him. I am a seasoned Moscovite, and we in Moscow ride the subway.

The Moscow subway system was designed as a bomb shelter, located fifty-thousand leagues under the crust of the earth. With sculptured archways and ornately painted stations, the designers also hoped to make the average worker feel kingly. Bold.

Cultured.

Which is exactly how I will feel as soon as I get to GYM—pronounced Goom—the former state-run department store turned conglomerate of European and American chain stores—and buy some respectable footwear. (Because, you know, I got *paid.*)

Good thing I didn't spend *every* moment handing out Bibles last time I was in Moscow.

(Okay, I didn't spend *any* time handing out Bibles. Mostly, I taught English, but I *would* have handed out Bibles if I'd been asked.) On my way I'm going to stop by Moscow Bible Church—my old digs—and check into teaching classes.

Zis is a spoon. My old students fill my thoughts as I walk down the street, absorbing the smells of fall, the scent of greasy fried sandwiches, the enticing aroma of bread. I wonder if skinny Sergei who learned how to say I-ron is still attending school. *Zhozey.* His voice skims my memory and I smile. *Sergei* needed me.

I find the subway entrance a half-block down the street, next to an *apteka*—a pharmacy. I mental note it (not that I'd know how to buy even an aspirin, but still . . .) and descend the escalators that bring me into the bowels of Moscow. Standing at the brightly colored map, I chart my course.

The main line of the metro runs in a gold ring around the outskirts (or what used to be the outskirts) of Moscow. Bisecting the gold line and snaking inward toward the middle run multicolored lines—purple, red, brown . . . last year I lived on the green line. This time, I'm on the blue line.

I'll have to ride to the gold line, switch, and take the purple line to MBC. See how easy this is?

Standing on the platform, I check out the other passengers. Mostly babushkas with bags of lumpy potatoes and umbrellas, there are also a few very well-dressed ladies (the WorldMar variety) as well as mafia-dressed young men with high and tight haircuts. The Russian uniform is black, from the black leather jackets to the black pants to the squared-off shoes. I wonder how Chase would look in black.

Chase would look good in a paper bag.

I can hear the train coming a minute out—a rumble that fills the station, and then a whooshing sound that always sends shivers up my arms. I calculate the gulf between the platform and track and think . . . squish. Only, now that I've seen the Matrix, maybe I could jump out . . .

The train swooshes in and the doors open. Passengers exit and I enter, grabbing onto the overhead rail because I don't have my surfing legs yet.

Okay, I guess I should explain surfing. My friend Caleb, who turned out not only to be the most interesting Christian I'd ever met with his grunge attire and surprising knowledge of scripture, taught me to surf the first night I arrived in Moscow. Simply put, it's about balance and anticipation. And enjoying the little things.

Sorta Caleb's life philosophy.

But I don't surf. Instead I hang on and count the stops. When I get to the gold ring stop, I get out and follow the herd up the escalators to the next level, where the gold ring line attaches.

I'm on the next train before I know it, and it occurs to me that I forgot to confirm the number of stops to the purple line, and thus Moscow Bible Church. But I'm sensing the number three, so after three stops I get off, and again follow the masses, this time taking a left through the tunnels, and descend to the purple line.

I get on and surf one stop down then up the escalators to daylight.

Either Moscow Bible Church has turned into a Russian cathedral, or I exited too soon. Or too late.

I stand there, watching traffic whiz by, hearing the guttural Russian that used to scare me, and try to orient myself.

I descend again and get on the purple line.

Ride to the next stop. Getting out, I ride up to the surface.

I see a bookstore, an appliance store, and a sprawl of apartment buildings. No green-painted former-Komsomol-building-turned-church.

Shoot. Descending again, I ignore the accusing look of the subway lady. (Who always seems to appear to be the same woman, regardless of what line I'm on. I think they must have been bred to be gulag guards. Now they've had to find new occupations. Which gives you an insight on how it feels to go through the turnstiles, then down the escalators as they stand and watch.)

Feeling a little tired (and my feet hurt, just a little, which points to my need for better footwear), I get onto the subway again. Surf to the next stop.

I dispel a flock of pigeons waiting outside the subway entrance. That and two homeless women who follow me with sad eyes as I stand there, confused.

How can I be lost? This is my town. Only, it doesn't look like my town anymore. Not with the sleek black five-story buildings where there used to be (I think) green ramshackle flats without running water. I stand there, then drop rubles into the hands of the women as I re-enter the subway.

I am studying the map when I discover my problem. I am not on the purple line. Or even the gold line.

I'm on the red line. And near the end of it, if I am understanding the arrow that pinpoints my location.

Listen, no one has to know.

I get back on the train and am relieved when it doesn't empty one stop later, but continues on eight more stops toward the center of town. If I take it all the way in, I can connect to the purple line at the central station.

Mafia boys are staring at me. Well, I know I look out of place. Russian women dress 24/7 like they're going to the opera. I'm wearing a pair of jeans and my Birks with wool socks. So sue me. I'm a pregnant, angry American woman. I *dare* you to say anything to me.

I look away from them and meet the eye of a babuskha who is holding a nylon bag containing bread. She gives me a smile and then pats the seat next to her.

Isn't that sweet? I sit down and she nods.

Then pats her stomach.

My eyes widen. Is she psychic? Or am I showing *already?* Oh, kill me now.

Thrown, I say nothing as I get up and exit, beelining it to the surface.

Which doesn't resemble for a second the central station I was hoping for.

Where am I? To get my bearings, I exit to street level.

I'm expecting the center of the city, with its sweeping architecture, the Czarist buildings with the columns and adornment, the smell of history. Instead I smell shish kebab, which means I'm at least moderately close to an outside market. Concrete buildings overhauled in pastel colors hint at new owners, but none of it looks familiar.

Where am I?

The sun is high and traffic is heavy, honking and smelling of exhaust. I see schoolchildren in their uniforms crossing the street, which tells me that it's at least near noon.

As if on cue, Junior growls.

Hang in there, buddy. I'm trying to swallow my panic, but it fills my throat with an acrid taste.

How can I be lost? This is my town. I surfed my way around Moscow for a year, back and forth every day from Moscow Bible Church, to Red Square, GYM, Moscow's underground mall, and McDonalds.

I can't be lost.

I walk out to a small plaza, check out the ads on a

dilapidated kiosk. I see that the Rolling Stones were here in '98. And Swan Lake not long after that.

A woman walks by, pushing a pram. Inside, a baby peeks out from a snowsuit. I see adorable pink cheeks, but the woman is in a mini skirt and high heels. Cute slingbacks.

Maybe if I follow her, I'll find GYM. At least I'll have decent shoes when they find my starved and mugged body at the bottom of the Volga River.

I set off down the street, and pass a cell phone kiosk. In Russia, cell phones are purchased with cards that load minutes. I left my cell phone in Gull Lake. Suddenly Chase's number burns in my pocket.

But I will not call Chase.

Will not. I'd be in Siberia, freezing, as snow covered my emaciated body before I called Chase.

I walk farther. An orange bus passes me, burps out exhaust. I don't recognize the number pasted in the back window.

I'm lost. That thought thumps in my mind, and I walk another half-block before I listen.

I'm lost.

I'm *lost.*

I stand there and let Russia swirl around me, take me, overwhelm me. The sounds of foreign voices, the smells of dust and oil and grilled street food. The cool shadows of unfamiliar buildings, the wind that now tumbles leaves down the street.

It brings a chill that seeps through my jean jacket, and with it a despair that fills my throat. I blink back the prick of tears but I can't hold back the voice inside that says (in a slightly desperate tone, but I think it's appropriate at the moment), *Oh God, why did you bring me here? So I could fail, miserably?*

I look upward, as if for answers, and the sky is blue and blank . . . and golden. Golden . . . *arches.* They rise into the sky like some ethereal sign, behind a haze of buildings.

I stand there, disbelief swilling through me as I look both ways and cross the street. I nearly sprint the length of the block until I come out on the other side and the sight takes my breath away.

McDonalds.

The most beautiful golden arches this side of heaven. I can nearly taste my relief (and the salty fries and vanilla shakes) as I cross another street then fast-walk the length of two blocks.

I'm not lost!

And what's better, I know that across the street from McDonald's is Venetsia, my bistro. With the linen tablecloths and orange slushies. And Chase, delivering flowers. Someday.

I'm home!

I am nearly jogging, because I know that not much further is the architecture that I know and love—Red Square, the walls of the Kremlin. And across the plaza, GYM. There are boots in my near future.

All is right with the world.

Until I stop at the light and look across the street.

Where there used to be white tables with umbrellas scattered on the sidewalk, overflowing flower boxes, and a café that served sweet coffee, and tea, and cute cucumber or cheese sandwiches is a . . . Wallpaper World.

Wallpaper World! What happened to my Venetsia? The light changes but I can't move. Tears have filmed my eyes and I'm an idiot standing on the corner, seeing my past—and my future—turned into a home décor store.

This can't be.

I blame the next five minutes and the ensuing events entirely on Junior. And the fact that in my pregnancy book it clearly says, "You may feel a flux of emotions over the upcoming changes in your body."

I'm in full flux, tears dripping off my chin, standing there in my jean jacket, jeans, and Birkenstocks, enduring the stares of assorted babushki and mafia boys, when out of the blue I hear, "I can't believe it, Josey Berglund from Minnesota."

Now, I believe in Divine Providence, those God moments when things happen that are completely unexplainable without the God factor. Like the time my purse was stolen in inner-city Minneapolis, right outside the Caboose, and it appeared three weeks later on my doorstep in Gull Lake.

(Either that or the thief was Moose Collins, who I also saw at the Caboose that night, but I'm not pointing fingers or anything).

So, when I turn toward the voice and see none other than my grungy pal from two years ago, Caleb Gilstrap, I recognize a God moment.

"Caleb!"

And he looks good, too. His hair is shorter (which makes him nearly unrecognizable) and he's wearing a new piercing—an ear bar—but I recognize the army surplus attire, the Birkenstocks (I'm feeling very vogue suddenly), and the tie-dyed shirt. "I can't believe it!" he says and crunches me into a hug right there on the street.

Briefly, two years ago, I thought Caleb might have crushed on me. But he was first and foremost a gentleman, one who knew just the right thing to say, and was the one and only person who kept me from throwing my then-roommate over the balcony, so I hug him back, a little longer than normal.

I wipe my eyes when he releases me. "I can't believe I ran into you. Where are you going?"

He nods toward the golden arches. Oh, of course. Expat heaven. It's then I see the cute size-two blonde next to him. She's wearing a pair of hiking boots and a pink parka and a fluffy white scarf. And in a second I know she's not from around here.

"Hi," she says, holding out her hand. I take it, casting a look at Caleb. "I'm Daphne."

Then, as if in explanation, Caleb wraps his arm around her shoulders.

Oh. "Josey Anderson, but I used to be Berglund."

Caleb is only momentarily stymied, then he grins. "So he finally figured it out," he says cryptically.

But Daphne hasn't released my hand. "This is Josey?"

Caleb gives her a look, one I can't read. Then, he nods.

Her eyes widen and suddenly I feel like the main player in a torrid soap opera. Do tell, Caleb.

But he only nods toward McDonalds. "Want to join us for lunch?"

I glance at Daphne, but her eyes seem to shine, and she's nodding. "Okay." I say, hiding the relief that rushes through me, again grateful for the immediate welcome Caleb always seems to extend.

"When did you get back?" he asks as we cross the street. I notice he and Daphne are holding hands. Cute.

"Yesterday."

Caleb nearly stops, but he waits until we've crossed. "Where's Chase?"

Uh oh, I feel tears again. "Working. He got a job with WorldMar, helping start cottage industries. He's really busy."

Caleb and Daphne's hands are swinging between them, and I feel the slightest twinge of jealousy. Chase should be here, sharing this moment with me. But no, he's at WorldMar. With the women who don't eat.

"Are you still doing your computer consulting?" I ask Caleb as he holds the door open for me. Still the gentleman. We get in line, and the smell of fries has turned Junior into a full-fledged beast, complete with roars.

"Yes. But I'm working with Daphne, too."

I turn to Daphne, and ask the obvious question.

"I'm a nurse. I work with Operation: Home, an outreach program to the local orphanages designed to connect the children with adoptive parents. I oversee the volunteers from area churches."

A nurse? I have the sudden and nearly overpowering urge to spill my secret. But, well, I haven't told Chase yet, and since I already spilled to H, probably that's enough betrayal. For now.

"Are you teaching English again?" Caleb asks.

I turn and study the menu. Of course it's in Russian, but I can easily sound out cheeseburger in Cyrillic. It's my turn in line and I repeat that, ordering also, "*kartofily frees*" and "*maroshna*" (for shake).

Caleb pulls me aside as Daphne orders for both of them. Her Russian sounds poetic as it flows from her petite little body. Petite people have this uncanny knack of making everything sound light and airy.

"So, what are you going to be doing here? Are you working with Chase?" Caleb asks.

I don't look at him. What is it about Caleb that I'm with him for thirty-point-six seconds and he can zero in on the truth? "I don't know why I'm here, Caleb," I say, and I can't believe the words have left my mouth. Or that they feel as if I've ripped out my insides.

Caleb's brown eyes find mine, and he says nothing.

I look at the ground. "I thought God had a grand plan for me being here, but . . . " I sigh. "I thought I was coming here to help Chase. To be his partner and serve the Russian people with him." I shrug, fighting a sudden wave of emotion. "Now, I can't even find my way around town without getting lost. Worse, Chase doesn't need me."

Caleb is silent as our food order is filled. Then he takes our trays, the gentleman he is, and carries them upstairs to the deck.

I always love sitting on the second floor and watching the world enjoy McDonalds. Something about sharing the same food, despite the culture, is a universal bonding experience.

Daphne opens her hamburger, takes the patty off the bun and eats the meat with a fork and spoon. Sorry, that's not what I meant when I thought of bonding.

Caleb is diving into a double cheeseburger and large fries. Now *that* is what I'm talkin' about. Junior nearly cheers as I suck down my vanilla shake.

"Did it ever occur to you, Josey, that God sent you here not because Chase needs you, but because you need God?"

I am midbite, so I put my sandwich down. "I know I need God."

Caleb finishes off his burger. "I mean, you need God in a way you don't know you need Him yet."

I frown at him.

"We live in what I call ordinary grace. Everyday understanding of God's love for us." He opens his ketchup packets. "But what if God sent you here so you could get a glimpse of just how much He loves you?"

Of course God loves me. He gave me Chase, didn't He? But, if I search my heart, I have to agree that, well, I'm not feeling the love lately. In fact, I'm wondering, especially over the last few days, what I did to make God mad.

I'm still frowning. Caleb grabs a fry. "I'm just saying that when we're in over our heads, that's a great place for God to show us how much He loves us."

I take another sip of my shake. Out of the corner of my eye, I see Daphne grinning. She looks at Caleb, then back at me.

"What?" I put my shake down.

"I have an idea—a *great* idea." She leans close and puts her hand on my arm. "Come and work at the orphanage with me. Caleb told me you're a writer. We need someone who can write about our ministry and help us raise money." Her voice raises an octave, which is a real feat. "Just think of the little lives you'd be impacting."

It's true that the first time I was in Russia I had visions of being a sort of Mother Josey to a flock of devoted children. But I'm over that. Really.

"Where is the orphanage?"

"Gorkovich."

I'm seeing, suddenly, divine intervention. Would that be the *same* village that Chase is working in?

"Please, please, Josey? We could really use you."

They could *use* me. And *need* me. And *want* me. And I could learn about babies. Which, we all know would come in handy, wouldn't it?

I grab a fry, glance at Caleb, smile, and give a little shrug. "Okay."

Daphne launches herself from her chair and encircles me in her skinny arms. "Thank you, oh, thank you!"

What, exactly has Caleb told her about me? I extricate myself with the slightest of hugs and nod.

Daphne spends the next hour outlining the job and why, especially, I'll be perfect for it. Apparently, she's seeing divine intervention as well.

Caleb and Daphne and I part ways outside GYM where I spend the next three hours in shopping therapy. It's growing dark by the time I walk back to the central station, get on the purple line, then the gold line, then finally surf home on the blue line. Without getting lost once.

The air is brisk as I walk home. I nod to the gatekeeper. I don't see Thug, but I don't need him anymore, anyway. Doorman buzzes me in, and I take the elevator to the ninth floor and unlock the door.

Chase nearly tackles me as I enter, crushing me to his chest. He's breathing hard, and for a long moment I think maybe he's having an asthma attack or something. "Where have you been?"

I drop my bags on the floor and encircle his waist. "Shopping," I say. "I got some new boots." In fact, they're incredible boots—Italian, leather, with spike heels. Totally impractical. I love them.

“Shopping?” He puts me away from him, looking at me with those big blue Chase eyes. “Igor said you walked right by him this morning. He looked for you everywhere but couldn’t find you. I thought something happened to you!”

I frame his face in my hands, kiss him lightly. “No,” I say, “nothing happened to me. Everything’s just fine.”

In fact, everything’s going to be perfect.

the shoemaker and his elf

. . .

THERE ARE A FEW HABITS WE MISSIONARIES (OR FORMER missionaries) pick up while serving the Lord. We rise early. We find a quiet place. We read our Bibles and pray.

And most of the time it has nothing to do with the fact that *someone* has compelled us to get out of bed for early morning sustenance.

Or maybe it does.

Whatever the case, Junior turned my stomach into his own playground, something I didn't appreciate after having an excellent dinner of meat cutlets and mashed potatoes, so conveniently left in my fridge yesterday.

The case of the unseen cleaning-cooking fairy has been solved.

After three days of finding food in our fridge, Chase decided it was time for the shoemaker (or in this case, the anthropologist) and his wife to find out just who is our Housework Elf.

Oh, please, don't tell me you haven't heard the story of The Elves and the Shoemaker . . . you know the one, about the shoemaker who's in debt and can't pay his bills and only has enough leather for one more pair of shoes to sell. He lays out the leather on his workbench before he goes to bed, and the next morning there's a beautiful pair of shoes, ready for a buyer.

Hey, I'm suddenly seeing a need for little shoe elves in my life. Imagine having a new pair of shoes waiting every morning when I got up.

A reason to live.

So, to continue the story, after a few nights of repeats (and I would have let this go on for a couple of years), the shoemaker and his wife stay up to watch—and what do they see but a bunch of naked elves making the shoes. I always thought this story was a bit risqué, and remember feeling shocked (and somewhat naughty anyway) that my mother allowed us to listen to the cassette recording of the story.

Nevertheless, because they're so happy, the shoemaker and his wife make cute clothing for the elves and leave it out for the little guys the next night.

The elves make a last pair of shoes . . . and disappear forever, with the duds.

See, I would have let them remain naked. Seemed to me that if they wanted clothes, or at least shoes, they could have made them for themselves.

Which was my philosophy about the laundry-cooking-cleaning fairy. My argument (and a sound one at that) was, what if she was scary, with long nose hairs and gray hair down to her shins that she piles atop her head? Would I want to know that as I eat her mashed potatoes or blini?

See my dilemma? Food versus Facts.

Chase solved said dilemma by, well . . . ah, staying home late the morning after I scared him into appreciation. Long enough to catch our fairy.

Aka, Svetlana the Svelte. Oh yes. Size six (which is still two, or maybe three sizes less than me), shapely, bobbed brown hair, hazel eyes. And wearing a leather mini-skirt, knee-high boots, and a silk top.

Which she changed after she arrived into a pair of track pants and an old shirt.

She still looked great.

Through a series of grunts and gestures I discovered that she's employed by WorldMar. To care for our every need. (Don't go there.)

At least she doesn't have dangling nose hairs.

The thing is, after Chase left, and I Tonto-ed some basic Russian questions, I found out a few things. Like, she's a single mother of a six-month-old son. And she desperately needs this job after being fired from her previous employment. (I don't ask what that is.) And she's an exceptional cook.

God is on my side, after all.

This thought is on my mind as I creep into the main room and sit on the black sofa. The sun is just sliding through the courtyards and around the high rises, a golden river of light. For some reason, Caleb's words have me digging out my Bible, and I open it to Ephesians and the passages I was studying last time I saw the sun rise over Moscow.

I know, it's a lot. I find it easier to just focus on the phrases that pop out at me. Like, "rooted and established in love." It's also true that sometimes when I read the Bible it goes over my head. But suddenly, these verses hit home to me, in a new way. Established in love . . . like conceived? Like being formed? My hand goes to my stomach, to the secret there. And not to be gross or anything, but he's a part of me, too. Rooted, in a way.

So, is that what Paul is talking about here? That I might understand both my origins and my connectedness to God?

What if God sent you here so you could get a glimpse of just how much He loves you?

Caleb's voice in my head makes me turn that thought over.

I'm not sure I agree, but I'm willing to be wrong. I would like a fresh glimpse at how much God loves me. Because deep inside I think Caleb's right. I do live with a sorta everyday understanding of God's love. I don't let it change my world, not really.

Ready, God.

I close my Bible and hug it to my chest, just as Chase wanders out of the bedroom. He's wearing the Scary Pants and a rumpled Gull Lake Gulls T-shirt that makes him look about eighteen (with scrawny legs). "What are you doing out here?"

"Praying," I say. Because I'm the Proverbs 31 wife.

He gives me a smile. "You amaze me."

Surpass is the word you're searching for, pal. I hold out my hand. Now is the time. Right now, as the sunrise is gilding our room, and the room is quiet, to tell him about our future. About the love growing inside me, in a very tangible way.

Chase takes my hand, comes over, and sits on the sofa, then lays his head in my lap. So sweet. I twirl my fingers through his hair. He closes his eyes as I try and form the words to tell him how our life is changed, forever.

He beats me to the life-changing words. "I know I freaked out when I thought you went missing—I guess I forgot how capable you are." He reaches up and takes my hand, pulls it down, and kisses it. "I'm so glad you are comfortable here, GI." He blows out a breath and my chest tightens. "I'm not sure what I got us into. This is going to be harder than I thought. I met with Bertha yesterday. She's been on this project for a year, and between the mafia, the gangs, and the lack of business understanding, she's having a hard time fulfilling the grant. If we don't get a business going within the next six months, we'll lose the contract for next year for WorldMar."

He rolls over, looks up at me. "I'm so glad you have everything under control, because frankly, I don't think I can focus on one more thing outside WorldMar right now." He touches my cheek. "Except you, of course."

Of course. I swallow, smile, hating the tears that have edged into my eyes. His words are sweet, but I feel panic rise inside.

Panic and dread.

I wipe my fingers under my eyes as he reaches up and kisses me. "I'm sorry I overreacted. And I'm so glad you're working at the orphanage. You'll be a hit. Now I know I don't have to worry about you."

Nope, not me. Or Junior.

But he sees my tears and runs his thumb under my eye. "You okay, GI? You've been sorta . . . weepy lately."

"Yeah, Chase. I'm fine. Just . . . I love you." I wrap my arms around him, and for a long moment, all is well with the world. Or at least, I can talk myself into believing it.

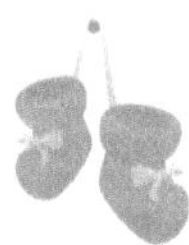

H's hours are very convenient to my current crisis. With her getting off at the Hungry Wolf at 3 a.m., and me sitting up late at night, the computer on my lap, we're able to message during our power hours.

Wildflower: You haven't told him yet? You've been there over two weeks already!

GI: You should have seen him! His hair all tousled, whiskers smattering his face. And he was wearing Scary Pants. That's his equivalent to a full bag of chocolate chips on the comfort needs category. I couldn't add to his stress level. And since then, well, it's only gotten worse. He's tired and worried and sometimes doesn't come home until late.

Wildflower: Didn't you say that every woman at WorldMar has that needy female pheromone? Are you sure Chase isn't . . .

GI: NO! Of course not. Besides, his partner is named Bertha. How much safer can you get?

Wildflower: Just don't fool yourself, Jose. Even Chase . . . well, you know.

GI: Listen, we're good. Yes, he's tired and working a lot, but that's going to get better. Everything's perfect.

Wildflower: Here's me pointing out that at least ONE thing isn't perfect. Is it possible he already knows about . . . The Thing That Cannot Be Named (Yet)? And is afraid to talk to you about it?

GI: Of course not. First, I'm not showing. I don't think, although twice now I've had babushkas make room for me on the metro, which makes me wonder. Secondly, Chase will be thrilled when he finds out.

Wildflower: Of course he will. Which is why you're SAVING the news.

GI: Waiting for the best time.

Wildflower: Not to point out the obvious or anything, but you can't hide it forever. Besides, what if you get sick, or have complications?

GI: I'm good. I feel great, I'm taking my vitamins, and I'm studying the book I stole from Jasmine. I'm right on track for the third month or thereabouts: fatigue, the need to use the biffy more frequently, nausea (which also adds to the biffy trips), and food cravings. (I'm out of bagels, and nearly through the chocolate chips. Thankfully, I've been graced with a now-named food fairy who delivers Russian food to my fridge every day like a personal chef. And unlike Thug, who waits outside our apartment building every day—I want to say, get a hint, pal, I don't need you!—I DO desperately need Sveta. Whose name means light and sunshine. Which I find apropos. The truth is, I can get used to having a chef. And a cleaning lady. She even got out the pickle juice.) Finally, I'm not the slightest bit irritable, which I guess is supposed to really be an issue this month.

Wildflower: You sound like a midwife. By the way, have you found a doctor?

GI: Better! I have my own personal nurse. Well, I will when I tell her. I'm volunteering with her at a local orphanage. It takes me about two hours to get there—I have to take the metro to the end of the red line, then get on a bus and ride forty-five minutes to a village outside Moscow. The orphanage is tucked just inside the town, a two-story building ringed with a rusty chain-link fence. Inside, the place is stark, with ancient furniture, but still, H, it's incredible. The teachers painted flowers on the walls, and there are about fifty kids, from babies to age five, and their huge eyes follow me everywhere I go. I'm supposed to raise money, so I took a bunch of pictures, but mostly I get on the ground with them and play games or go into the baby room and cuddle the babies. They're so adorable, I just want to take them all home.

Wildflower: You have your own souvenir.

GI: It's just that I can't help wishing they had parents. The orphanage is so poor, and they feed the babies with these huge spoons about seven times the size of their tiny mouths, and all they get is kasha and thin milk. They're all skinny and pale and weigh about as much as Amelia, even the five year olds.

Wildflower: That's horrible. By the way, I saw Jasmine and Amelia in the Red Rooster a few days ago.

GI: What were you doing in the Red Rooster? I thought you were a frozen-pizza-only girl.

Wildflower: Rex wanted lasagna.

. . .

. . .

. . .

Wildflower: Are you still there?

GI: Just getting a visual on you making lasagna. What's going on?

Wildflower: Nothing.

GI: I'm telling you, if you get married or something without telling me, I'll kill you.

Wildflower: Listen Queen Secret Keeper, I don't have anything on you.

GI: I'm serious, H. Marriage is for keeps, at least in my book. Are you ready for this?

Wildflower: I'm not ready to talk about this. But I think I love him.

GI: See how much trouble that gets us into?

Russia has stellar public transportation. Besides the metro, which stretches to all corners of the city, there is the trolley bus (attached to overhead cables), the *tramvai* (an above-ground train on tracks), and the regular old bus.

The big difference between the various forms of transportation is the ticketing process. For the metro, tickets are purchased at kiosks or machines and inserted into the turnstile or given to Gulag Woman. For the trolley, *tramvai*, and bus, money is collected by a woman I've come to call The Bus Lady. Usually a little down on her luck, The Bus Lady is normally dressed in the equivalent of Chase's Scary Pants, only in brown polyester. She wears an old dirty parka and slings a handbag from the 1970s over her shoulder in which she keeps both the money and a roll of tickets. She doesn't make eye contact as she collects the money and my heart goes out to her, just a tiny bit, every time I hand over my rubles.

I've had occasional nightmares that I'm somehow mistaken for The Bus Lady.

The one constant in all the forms of transportation is etiquette. Babushki in front, mafiosias in the back, students and children in the middle. And pregnant women any seat in the house. I see this played out as I sit with Daphne on our biweekly excursions to the orphanage in Gorkovich. A woman roughly the size of a wildebeest gets on the bus and the babushka sitting near the front practically beats a young man sitting nearby from his seat, barraging him with angry Russian until he rises and offers wildebeest woman his seat.

I think babushki were the most well-kept secret during the Cold War. I certainly would think twice about attacking a country filled with sixty-year-old women with hands and girth the size of Mike Tyson's. Add that spit, and I'm running for the border.

And when I'm eight months out and ready to pop, I'm going to line up behind the nearest available babushka and let them fight my battles.

I wonder if they rent out. Like when I deliver the news to Chase . . .

But no babushki notice me today, despite the fact that I'm holding a box of formula I found at the corner drugstore. I purchased the entire supply as well as a package of disposable diapers I stuffed in my backpack.

I'm feeling very matronly.

And not so very happy that this morning I couldn't button my jeans. I slipped into a pair of yoga pants, which then limited my footwear to a pair of hiking boots. I feel like a tourist.

A fat tourist.

A fat underdressed tourist. Because, when I walked outside today and waved to Thug, the brisk early November wind lifted the collar of my jacket and I realized something horrifying.

My parka, which adequately covered my body the last time I braved a Russian winter, doesn't have a prayer of covering my bulk this time around. I'm going to be a fat, underdressed, frozen tourist. With ugly footwear.

Beside me, Daphne is a chatterbox. In the month since we've started visiting the orphanages, or working at her offices at her mission headquarters (which are much poorer than

WorldMar), I've learned her life history, and more. An Iowa farm girl, Daphne went to nursing school at the University of Iowa, and graduated with honors. She came over originally with Mission to the World (my mission!) but switched to Operation: Home after she saw the predicament of the local orphanages. Her parents died when she was just a tot and she was raised by her grandparents, hence her affinity toward orphans. Her mission is to place the babies with the various adoption agencies that work out of western Russia.

I'm hoping to place every baby in the one room I've been assigned. Natasha, Pavel, Ryslan, Boris, and Sasha. Their skinny little bodies wiggle with joy when I come in the room, and their toothless grins turn me to mush. I wash them, try and soothe the cradle cap off their heads, feed them with normal-sized spoons (that I bring with me every visit), and generally just hold them. Most importantly, I pray over them.

I figure it's the best start I can give them.

Which has also propelled me to pray for Junior.

And myself. The Deceiver. *Please God, help me find a way to tell Chase!*

I like Daphne. She's petite and energetic, and she loves Caleb. Evidently, they met at a Bible study. She wears a lot of pink. Pink camouflage (which I think may be a contradiction in terms). Pink T-shirts. Pink jeans. And her hair is short and gelled.

I can't think of a better match for Caleb.

Apparently, Daphne can't either, because she's making a lot of plans.

Which, apparently, include me. Because as we're riding she suddenly goes quiet and twists her hands on her lap.

I hate long stretches of quiet, don't you? Makes me want to fill it. Usually with something stupid.

"Josey, will you mentor me?"

Methinks Daphne has the same propensity. "Mentor you?" I look over at her, and the meekness in her eyes throws me. Excuse me, but I'm like . . . three months older than her. Why would she think—

"You're already married, and I just want to be ready when—*if*—Caleb asks . . . " Her voice trails off. And there's that silence again.

"Um . . . what do you think I could teach you?" Because, while I might be an aspiring Proverbs 31 wife, currently I have a glitch in my resumé.

"I don't know. Patience? Maybe how to submit?"

Submit? I'm not exactly sure—

"I hope it's okay, but Caleb told me all about how you came over to Russia when you loved Chase and let God be in charge of your heart and your future, and I thought that probably you could teach me a few things about faith, and surrendering."

Uh, I think Caleb got the CliffsNotes version of my first tour of Moscow. Apparently I left out the part where *I ran away* from Chase and my love for him, how I dated a supermodel and for a long time thought I looked good in leather, and finally nearly lost Chase because of my inability to commit.

But, come to think of it, in the end, I did some good surrendering. Maybe I *could* teach her a few things.

After, of course, I clear up that little matter of our next of kin.

I offer a slight smile. "Sure, Daphne, I'd be . . . honored."

"Oh, thank you, Josey!" Daphne hugs me, again. Actually I'm getting used to this. Feels somewhat like having Jasmine around.

Jasmine! Right after I tell Chase, I'll have to tell her. I'm not sure who will be more angry. Guess I won't be getting any *kringle* care packages.

"Are you going to celebrate Thanksgiving?" Daphne says, changing the subject.

"Chase says that WorldMar is having a Thanksgiving dinner."

I can't help but notice the way her expression falls.

"What?"

She needs oh-so little encouragement to unload her every thought. First thing I teach her . . . how to keep secrets.

Or, maybe that's not a good trait. But isn't a little mystery good in a marriage?

Okay, yes, I know, I'm reaching, but I feel not only fat (and underdressed, with poor footwear), but also like pond scum. Every day, as Chase kisses me and heads off to work, there I am, smiling, me and Junior, hoping he doesn't look too closely at how I fill out the Taz T-shirt.

So far, he's also been too busy to . . . well, you know. Which means he hasn't seen me naked. I guess that's a good thing.

"Well," Daphne says, "I wanted to serve Caleb a nice dinner, but I've never cooked a turkey and I was hoping . . . " She clasps her hands together and peers up at me.

What? I stare at her, eyes wide. Memories of smoke and Chicken Kiev keep me silent.

Her smile fades. "That's okay. I understand. Of course, you want to spend it at WorldMar."

With the Underfed? Where I can stand out as the American Glutton? I thinketh Not-eth.

Besides, I, unlike Daphne, have reinforcements. Namely Jasmine. Maybe if I go to her for help, she'll be less likely to strangle me. And perhaps, with a turkey, stuffing, mashed potatoes, and gravy under his belt, Chase will be too full to chase me to Mongolia.

Oh, who am I kidding? As Chase's wife, I'm at least partially required to attend the Thanksgiving Day function. "How about I come over earlier, help you stuff it, and put it in the oven," I say. Because, after all, I am the Proverbs 31 wife. I can figure this out. Besides, even if Jasmine bails, I have all those *Martha* magazines. At the very least we can make our own nameplates, fold some stellar napkins, and make peppermints from scratch.

"Oh, Josey, Caleb's so right. You're terrific."

Yeah, I know.

you're wearing that?

. . .

Dear Josey,

I'm using e-mail! I'm at the library, and the librarian helped me set up an account, so I hope this e-mail address is right. Amelia is beside me, sleeping. I can't believe she's nearly four months old!

When Mom told me (through your friend you call H she saw at the pharmacy) that you wanted to know how to make turkey and stuffing, I nearly burst with pride. I knew that Berglund genes lurked inside you. First, some news!

Milton and I have decided to buy a house. It's super swell of Mom and Dad to let us stay above the restaurant, but we decided we need our own place. And, I found us the perfect house! You know that cute yellow Cape Cod across from the community church? The one with the red door? That's the one! The owner even dropped the price because it's been on the market so long. It's got the cutest little bedrooms upstairs for Amelia (and hopefully a brother someday), and we're going to update the kitchen with the money we saved on the price. And, I made friends with Carla, our realtor (remember her? She was in your class I think, but dropped out of school to have a child?), and she's started coming to church! We close on December 23, which is a horrible time to move, but will make me a super Christmas gift! And we don't have to do a thing to it—the previous owners painted the place a beautiful shade of salmon and both Milton and I love it so much, we're keeping it just as it is! Oh, by the way, Kathy, your landlord, says that your old apartment might be available when you get home. She says the current tenant is getting married?

Anyway, I wish you were going to be here for Thanksgiving, and especially Christmas. We're going to take a picture of Amelia on Santa's lap. But I know that you and Chase are following your adventurous hearts and having the time of your life. I just miss you, is all.

I put the instructions for how to cook the turkey at the bottom. It's super easy, I promise! And, if you want, I have a delicious Parker House roll recipe. Just let me know.

I love you,

Jas

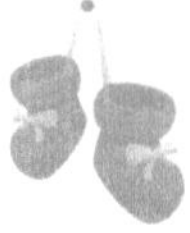

Here's the good news. I am no longer nauseated every second of the day. (Which should be decreasing my trips to the biffy. Sadly, no.) And, to make things even better, I hate food. Well, most food. You wouldn't have to tie me up and stick toothpicks under my nails to get me to eat a bagel. But basically, most food sorta turns my stomach. It's a condition I'd always secretly hoped for, but I have to say, the timing stinks.

Because I spent the morning (after scouring the city for two weeks trying to find a turkey) stuffing and cooking the most beautiful gobbler since Squanto's time, and the smells should have turned my appetite into overdrive. But all I could think about was the fact that I have to find something to wear to Chase's party tonight. And how I'm no longer a size . . . um, ten. In fact, I'm definitely pushing 12, or even 14, and I don't even feel pregnant.

I just feel fat.

I think I hate my life.

The upside is that I did Jasmine proud with the turkey, and Daphne thinks I'm some sort of kitchen diva, and when she hugged me (again), I felt as if at least someone knew I was alive.

Not Chase, of course. Who hasn't dragged in earlier than ten every night for the last two weeks, including Saturday. He even worked on Sunday, which forced me to attend Moscow Bible Church, my old stomping grounds, alone, with Caleb and Daphne. I kept an eye out for my friends Rebecca and Matthew Winneman, fellow missionaries. But when I asked about them, Caleb informed me that they were stateside. For counseling.

I'd like to go stateside. For counseling. And maybe a pizza with pepperoni and mushrooms and green peppers. (Bet that would turn my appetite back on.) Chase brought home a "pizza" the other night. Tuna pizza. With a hardboiled egg in the center. I tried to warn him when we moved here not to buy street pizza. Someone should listen to me if he doesn't want his wife to lock herself in the bathroom and cry for an hour.

I'm trying not to cry now as I stare at my closet. My suave Italian boots still fit, but my only pair of black slacks won't button, and I've suddenly grown Pamela Anderson breasts which, one would think, might make Chase pay more attention to me, but only serves to turn my white blouse into cheap thrills.

My choices:

- Yoga pants (which I've taken to wearing everywhere)
- Chase's Scary Pants

- A pair of Chase's dress pants
- Or, better yet, Chase's Levi's (the faded ones that hang so well on him), a tank top, and one of his dress shirts.

Think he'll notice?

When I was sixteen, I went through a creative dressing phase. Some of my more notable outfits included white shorts paired with black boots and a pink shirt tied at the waist. Yeah, I know, but I was young, and hopefully most people have forgotten by now.

But I'm feeling the call to get creative.

I grab Chase's favorite jeans, a white tank, and his white oxford dress shirt. Pulling the jeans on, I am overcome with relief that they are still way too big for me. The minute I surpass Chase (in size), I'm jumping.

The snugness in the hips suggests I might not need a belt to hold them up. All the same, I add my black belt.

Notching it on the largest hole.

I've decided that pregnancy is all about humiliation. Probably to get a girl ready for labor, and then spit-up and having to change diapers in public places. But today it's all about the fact that in three hours I have to face down Chase's sultry co-workers.

Good thing I hate food.

I tug on the tank, which barely covers my belly, slip on the oxford, and tie it in the front. If Sharon Stone can do it for the Oscars, so can I, right?

Apparently I'm not Sharon. Because I look like I have a big bow on my belly.

I untie it, smooth it down, button it just above Pamela Anderson, and let it drape. Better. But I still look like I've had one too many donuts.

Oh, wow, that sounds good right now. A donut. With lots of

sugar. Or covered in chocolate. So maybe I don't hate food. Just the food available in Russia.

I bet I'd love Gull Lake food. Especially eating it in my cute remodeled kitchen in a Cape Cod.

Rats, I wasn't going to go there. I wasn't.

Surveying myself in the mirror, I decide one thing. I'm going to have to focus on the hair.

It's grown longer over the past three months, and is now down to my shoulder blades. I never looked good in long and straight, and now I use my curling iron to flare out the ends. It's cute. And with the boots, well, I might live through my night.

I'm applying makeup when I hear the bolt on the front door and Chase enter. I turn just as he appears at the bathroom door.

He stops, and whatever was going to come from his lips (and I was looking more for action than words), morphs into opened-mouthed shock. And then a frown.

And then, "Is that what you're wearing tonight?"

Okay, note to all of the male persuasion. There are three things a man should *never* say to a woman, especially a pregnant woman.

1. Are you really going to eat all of that?
2. Pregnancy is not a disease. Deal.

And, the most important . . .

3. Is *that* what you're wearing?

I slam the door and lock myself in the bathroom. Which, I think, is a stellar alternative to the many, many options that run through my mind. Sinking down against the door, I lower my head into my hands. I can hear Chase outside sighing, loudly, and I picture him shaking his head, even running his hands through that tawny blonde hair.

"I'm sorry, Josey. It's just . . . well, all the rest of the women are dressing up . . ."

I'm sure they are. I fear the alternative to office wear they'll show up in tonight.

"I don't have anything to wear," I say, wishing I could tell him the truth, suddenly wanting to tell him how my iffy attire is all his fault and how he dragged me over here, a billon miles from home, where right now Milton and Jasmine are eating Mom's turkey and Jas's Parker House rolls, and probably apple pie made with Mom's Macintosh apples for dessert. How because of him, I've gained three million pounds, nothing tastes good, and I've lost my dream house to my I-Have-a-Perfect-Life sister.

And no, I don't want to talk about it.

"What about that black skirt you wore to the New Year's Eve party at your parents' last year?"

You mean the one I bought at Saks a few years ago and finally fit in after my first stint in Russia? The one currently wadded into a ball in my old toiletries drawer in Gull Lake? Thanks for paying attention, Chase.

"It's in America."

"Oh."

I can tell he's stymied. Ha! Now he knows how it feels. "Well, that outfit you wore the first day to WorldMar looked nice."

Yeah, that was probably the last time he took a good look at me.

"I know that you've put on a little weight over the past couple months, but surely it still fits."

Or maybe not. Apparently he *has* been looking. And now I know why he's not touching. For the first time since wedded bliss, a streak of what I think is hatred flashes through me.

"Go away."

He knocks on the door, and it takes me a second to realize it's his head, thumping over and over against the door. "I didn't say you were fat. It's just . . . well, I know you're home a lot, without any exercise, and . . . "

Excuse me? Thug has finished eighteen novels over the past few weeks, while I've been hoofing it all over Moscow and beyond. I'm more in shape than I've been since our wedding day. Notice *that.*

"You look great to me, I promise. I'm just saying that you don't have to dig into my closet to find something to wear."

And here I'd bought into the idea that a man likes it when his woman wears his clothes. Apparently, I'm disillusioned and confused as well as fat.

But not so much that I can't find the right response. "I like wearing your clothes. It makes me feel as if you're with me . . . you've been gone so much."

I grin in the ensuing silence. Wow, I'm good. Guilt, wrapped up in a compliment. My Norwegian ancestors would be so proud.

"Just come out of the bathroom, GI. I'm sorry I upset you . . . it's just that you seem so touchy these days."

Does he *want* me to go to this party with him? I stand up, yank the door open. He takes a step back, as if I've frightened him.

Yeah, pal, be afraid. Be very, very afraid. He so doesn't deserve to know about Junior. At least, not right at this moment.

"Listen, I *like* what I'm wearing. So either you take me as I am, or you go alone." My voice shakes a bit at the end, which lessens the impact, but I raise my chin and glare at him.

And for the longest moment, I see him debate. Every second that ticks by, I'm feeling something inside shatter.

Maybe it's my dream of Happily Ever After. Maybe it's us, and our future, and everything I'd believed about Chase.

Maybe it's my hopes that we'll make it through this, that I'll be able to tell him the truth without it destroying our lives, that he'll rise up, someday, and call me blessed.

He sighs, lifts a shoulder. "Whatever."

Yeah, sure. Whatever.

It's confirmed. I hate my life.

At our wedding, Chase and I invited my parents to choose verses from the Bible to give us wisdom on our marital journey. I was expecting something along the lines of, "And God blessed them, saying, "Be fruitful and multiply . . . " or an excerpt from the 1 Corinthians 13 love chapter. Instead, my mother pulled out Proverbs 14:1: "The wise woman builds her house, but the foolish pulls it down with her hands."

What's with that? At the time, I remember thinking . . . hey, what about Chase and *his* hands? But now, the verse seems appropriate, because my head is calling me an idiot but my body isn't listening as I surf the subway back to Daphne's flat while Thug drives Chase to the Thanksgiving shindig at WorldMar.

An entire herd of elephants, a deep-dish Chicago-style pizza, and a month's supply of M&Ms couldn't get me to attend that dinner tonight.

But a huge part of me feels like I'm tearing apart my life as I exit the subway, walk the half-block in the fading light, and climb the stairs to Daphne's fourth-floor flat. I can smell turkey from here, and wish I cared.

I lean on the bell and when Daphne opens the door, I'm

slightly shocked at her greeting—"Oh, thank the Lord, you're here!"

Now, *that's* what I'm talking about! She lets me in and gives me a tight squeeze. Eventually my Norwegian self is going to get used to all this affection. Really.

"You look so cute!" she says, giving me a quick survey. Thanks, Daphne, but we all know the truth. Besides, she's the cute one, in her pink yoga pants and a white tee. Looks like cotton candy.

"Hey, Josey," Caleb says, coming out of the main room. Daphne's flat is cute, like Daphne. The inside entry, just large enough for one person to toe off their boots, is wallpapered in a creamy pinkish swirl that extends to the main room, which has two overstuffed green couches. I helped Daphne set up her table in front of the couches to make a seating area conducive to romance. Which I'm destroying.

To the left, a galley kitchen the size of my mother's pantry is painted in a kelly green. The smell of turkey and stuffing is overpowering, but I'm sensing something amiss, because Daphne has her hands covering her face, sobbing. Caleb puts his arm around her and gives me a sad smile. "We're having turkey issues."

"Oh, Josey, everything was going great until a half-hour ago—the gas went out! And I still haven't flipped it onto its final side!"

There is a long beat of silence where I know she expects me to fill in with a ready remedy, but I'm completely blank.

I want my mother.

Only, my mother would probably quote Proverbs and tell me that I should be at WorldMar with Chase.

"Well, ah, maybe . . . did the little white thingie pop out?" Thankfully, we got an American turkey, with the self-thermometer. It cost about three thousand dollars at the International Food Store.

Her eyes widen. "No! Do you think it's ready?"

Well, according to my calculations, it was supposed to be ready two hours ago, but then again, we weren't sure what temperature registered in the oven due to the fact that it looked like a model that had been installed oh, about the time of Breshnev, with no external temperature indicator in sight. So I just put the flame at medium and said a little prayer.

See, people like me shouldn't be in charge of things like turkeys, dinner, or probably even motherhood.

I'm going to be the worst mother on the planet. We'll be lucky to have peanut butter and jelly sandwiches. Unless, of course, we live in Gull Lake. Then we can go over to Jasmine's cute Cape Cod and eat her four-course meal.

I feel a little like crying too.

"Let me take a look at the turkey," I say. Daphne practically pulls me into the kitchen, outfits me with hot mitts, and opens the oven door.

Steam and the smell of holidays rolls out. The bird looks delicious, crispy brown, with stuffing spilling out. I did this. I stuffed this turkey. I made Daphne look good.

The little white thingie hasn't popped out. But I do what I've seen my mother do every year—I wiggle the leg. Seems wiggly.

"Let's take it out."

I muscle the bird out and plop it on their tiny kitchen table. And, at that moment, the white thingie pops out. Daphne claps.

My mood is cheered as we scoop out the stuffing, slice the bird, and set it on the table. Daphne pulls up another chair. So far, she hasn't asked me once why I'm here and not at WorldMar. I'm not pointing any fingers, but *maybe* someone is a little too focused on her little pink self?

The table is overflowing with food. I recognize Russian black bread, and a jar of cranberry jam, and some unknown black spread, as well as pickles, mashed potatoes, and a cold carrot salad. I have to say, I'm a little impressed, and wondering who is mentoring whom here.

Caleb takes Daphne's hand as they slide onto the sofa. "It's a beautiful dinner, Daph," he says, and his brown eyes are shining.

I should be with Chase. That fact sweeps over me, and suddenly my throat tightens. What am I doing here, intruding on Caleb and Daphne, leaving my man to fight off the attentions of Underfed Katrina and her cohorts? I mean, it's not like they'll be eating. They'll need something to do. And here's hoping he'll be fighting them off, because after tonight . . . well . . .

"Josey, will you say the blessing?" Caleb asks.

Oh, sure. But the words feel stilted and sticky in my throat as I thank God for the many blessings He's given me. I'm surely not acting very thankful, am I?

Although, I do put my hand over Junior as I close with an Amen.

Daphne notices the gesture as Caleb reaches for the turkey. Her eyes widen. "Josey, are you—?"

"Chase doesn't know yet."

I don't know why I blurt that out, but suddenly I have to tell someone. And then, as if I might be a cask of fermenting wine, I explode with tears. "And he thinks I'm fat, and Jasmine has my house, and everyone is a size two, and Chase works late, and pretty soon all I'll have left to wear is scary pants!"

There is silence as Caleb and Daphne stare at me. Then, Daphne turns and gives me a hug.

See, I knew I'd get used to it.

bambi

• • •

I've finished off every chocolate chip, every bagel, every pretzel, every honey-roasted peanut, and I'm nearing the end of my popcorn stash.

Now, at least, I have a reason to be fat.

And I've discovered a new food. That black stuff on Daphne's table? Caviar! Black Caviar. Who knew it came in black?

I surprised her by scarfing down half the bowl. Little explosions of salty joy in my mouth, they also yanked the floodgates off my appetite.

I have a little addiction going. One that my cleaning lady noticed. Sveta Sunshine found the leftover caviar in the fridge (thanks to the doggy bag Daphne sent home with me) and introduced me to *ekra*—canned caviar.

I'm in heaven.

And growing. Even Chase's pants on me are tight. Not that he would notice, because he's spending even more time at work. And when he comes home, he climbs in bed and turns his back to me.

But, not to fear. I have a plan.

I am going to fix this.

I know, I know. The *truth* would be the first remedy. And that's exactly what I've planned.

On Christmas Day I'm going to serve up turkey (because my first one with Daphne turned out so well, I'm ready to solo), stuffing, rolls . . . and the truth.

Meanwhile, I've spent the last three weeks planning a Christmas event at the orphanage. Thanks to my fundraising letters, the orphanage was given a large gift by a church in Pennsylvania, and we're celebrating with presents for all the children.

Socks, sweaters, a piece of chocolate, and a small toy. My heart breaks as I wrap each gift, thinking of the overflow of presents underneath the Berglund tree every year.

I bend my rules and use Thug to drive out to the orphanage two days before Christmas. The sky is gray, and the air smells like snow. Bare trees against stark concrete buildings have turned Moscow gloomy. What's worse, they don't celebrate Christmas, so all the lights and trees and festivities won't show up until *after* the 25th. Just in time for New Year's Eve.

WorldMar is having a big New Year's Eve bash. Chase mentioned it, thinking I didn't care.

But, like I said, I'm fixing this. Daphne and I went shopping on Saturday and I found a pair of stretchy black velour pants and an extra-large white blouse. Yeah, I look like my gramma Netta, but at least they fit.

Even if my boots don't. I had to purchase a new pair, this time with a low, boring heel on account of a dizzy spell in the store. I tried to tell Daphne that I just needed a candy bar, or three, but she insisted on making me buy the boring boots.

The good news is that *after* I spring the news on Chase, I'll be able to wear something to the News Year's event.

And I'll have a *really* good reason to be wearing stretch, as well as consuming all the caviar and cheese in site.

"I hope they like the Nutella," Daphne says. She's holding a case of the chocolate hazelnut spread on her lap. I admit, the Nutella was my brainchild. Wanting to give the children a treat, I had to think economically—a little Nutella on brown bread will go a long way toward happy taste buds for children who subsist on kasha and potatoes.

"What kid doesn't like chocolate?" I know, because Junior loves chocolate. He's constantly telling me to buy it every time I walk by the *apteka* (which has won my eternal respect for stocking chocolate in a pharmacy).

We also have a monetary donation that should give the children a more substantial Christmas Day dinner. Maybe some meat in that potato soup.

The way Thug drives, it takes us about thirty minutes to get to Gorkovich, which is about six thousand people large. Every time we drive in, passing a chipped and ancient Lenin pointing to the center of the city, I wonder if Chase is here, and where he might be working. I know that he's been trying to increase production in a chicken canning factory and negotiating a contract with a lumberyard. But other than an occasional, "It's going okay," he's been rather quiet.

Makes a girl not want to ask. And feel a little like a mosquito.

We pull into the cracked and slightly icy orphanage parking lot. Snow has begun to drift downward, brushed easily aside by Thug's windshield wipers.

Thug helps us carry in the goodies. I've decided that even though I was slightly put off by Thug when we first met (okay, maybe that's an understatement, maybe he scared me out of my skin), Thug is okay. He opens doors. He carries things. He's even been known to follow me down the street to make sure I get to the subway without getting mugged. Sweet.

I purchased leather gloves for Thug for Christmas. I hope I'm not aiding and abetting some crime with this gift.

Thug follows Daphne and me into the main room, where the children aged eighteen months and over are sitting in a circle, singing. They look up at us and their faces shine. But, like obedient soldiers, they wait until their teacher gives them permission to greet us. What is it about thirty children hanging on my legs, saying Zhozey, that makes me go all soft and mushy inside?

Daphne and I hand out the gifts and then go to the kitchen, where we cut bread and make our little Christmas "snack."

"Reminds me of peanut butter," Daphne says. "I really miss peanut butter."

"Me too," I say, suddenly craving that now too. Thanks a lot, Daph.

"Seems to me that peanut butter would be a good thing to serve in an orphanage. All that protein. And it's pretty cheap."

"Not in Russia. I saw it at the International Food Store for about eight hundred dollars per kilo."

Daphne laughs.

"I s'pose if they made it locally . . . " I lick the butter knife and finish putting the bread on a tray. "I'm going to check out my room of babies. Can you handle this?"

Daphne nods as I exit.

The baby room is simply a room full of cribs. The nurse who tends the room—a woman who looks like she might have tended Stalin (which accounts for how he turned out)—is board thin, with dark eyes, pursed lips, and not a hint of a smile line. We met when she yelled at me for coddling the babies.

Is that possible? Really? To over-love a baby?

Her remedy to non-coddling is to prop bottles in their mouths four times a day and let them sleep soggy.

Mine is to pick up each baby and coo and play like I would with Amelia. It's when I'm with these babies that I believe I might have the remotest possibility of conquering this motherhood thing.

Today, Nurse Stalin looks up and sort of shakes her head, as if I'm beyond hope. I smile at her. Probably I should give her gloves too.

Or maybe a nice scarf. Warm her up a bit.

I enter my room, and am surprised to see another woman in the room. Wearing track pants and an old parka, she bears a resemblance to The Bus Lady. She is bending over Ryslan's crib. Ryslan is my adorable eight-month-old with dark hair and stunningly black eyes.

I'm about to ask this interloper who she is when she picks up Ryslan and turns around.

Silence fills the room as Sveta and I stare at each other. Apparently, she didn't expect me, because she not only doesn't look her sexy self, but she's quickly turning the color of *borscht*.

She is holding Ryslan over her shoulder and patting him like she knows him. He curls into her, sucking his thumb.

I'm feeling really weird. Like I've interrupted the movie at the best part. Like I shouldn't see her here.

"*Prevyet,*" I say. My 'hi' falls flat as Sveta bursts into tears. Turning, she lays Ryslan in his crib then, holding her hand to her mouth, brushes past me and out of the room.

Ryslan is crying, which has started Boris crying. Sasha is soon to follow. She cries at everything.

I turn to follow Sveta, but she's gone.

Striding up to Nurse Stalin, I ask, in my broken Russian, "*Kto?*" Who was that?

And, for the first time since I met her, Stalin's stoic exterior cracks. She sighs, and her eyes look past me, down the corridor where Sveta has vanished.

"*Mot* Ryslana," she says.

Ryslan's mother.

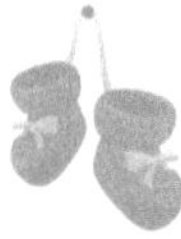

"She probably didn't have enough money to take care of the baby." Daphne is sitting beside me as Thug drives us home. The snow is heavier on the windshield, and for once, I'm grateful not to have to take public transportation.

"So she leaves him in an orphanage?"

"Mothers have up to two years to claim their child. After that, the state can sever rights, if they so choose."

"So Sveta could lose her baby if she can't provide for him?" I'm suddenly wondering if her size six is from not eating. (Well, I know it's from not eating, but I mean *starving*.) I feel ill for consuming all that caviar in front of her.

Daphne nods.

I sit back, my hand on Junior. I couldn't imagine leaving him behind in an orphanage, seeing him only when I can take two hours out of my day, knowing that I might lose him forever.

"What if someone wants to adopt him?"

"He won't be adopted unless her rights are severed."

"Which means he could sit in limbo for two years, growing up in the orphanage, while Sveta tries to make a life."

"Or struggles with letting him go. By that time, he's two or three or even five, and his chances of adoption decrease each year."

But to lose your child because you can't feed him? I remember stories of the Great Depression, of parents selling their children into servitude. In fact, I know it happens today in Cambodia, and India, and even Burma. But to see it up close, well, I suddenly have a mission.

Sveta *will* get her child back. I have enough Lara Croft in me to guarantee that.

Daphne and I swing by the market, and since Thug is

driving, I pick up potatoes, carrots, and a hunk of what looks like pork.

Tonight, Chase and I will have a nice dinner. And I will tell him what I discovered at the orphanage. And we will make up. And then Chase and I will solve this problem.

Oh, and I'll tell him the truth. Because even though tomorrow is Christmas Eve, it's time he found out about Junior. Really.

Thug drops off Daphne and then helps me upstairs with the food. As he's leaving my flat (which is clean, with a pile of fresh blini in the fridge—what, did she *run* back here?), I hand him the package of gloves.

I'm expecting him to nod or something and simply walk out the door. I mean, it's not like we're deep friends or anything. But he stares at the package. Then looks up at me, and in crisp, clear English, says, "Zank you."

Huh. "You're welcome," I say.

Can it be that Thug understands English? He smiles and opens the door to leave.

Methinks I need to watch what I say in the car with Thuggie.

I wash the pork, peel the potatoes and carrots, put it all in a pan, light the oven, and set everything cooking.

You have to admit, I've got this cooking thing down.

The flat is already clean, but I pull out the table, set it, adding candles. Then I wrap the cute little shoes I found at the *apteka* that I've been saving just for this event.

Enough is enough. I love Chase. He loves me.

At least, I think he loves me. He did agree to love me in sickness and health, for better or worse. And while I'm not sick, I have been better. So here's hoping he's a promise keeper.

I can see Chase's face when I tell him the happy news. *Chase, I'm not moody, I'm not fat. I'm carrying your child. Your son. (Or daughter, I'm flexible.)*

Josey, I'm so sorry I've been ignoring you! Why didn't I see this sooner? I'm sorry I've been so blind! He'll drop to his knees and hug me and tell me that I'm the best thing that's ever happened to him, the perfect wife.

He'll rise up (from his knees!) and call me blessed.

I need to be looking my best, so I run a mineral bath. An hour later, the flat smells delicious and my makeup is on, and I'm smelling clean and my hair is done and I've lit candles, and where is Chase?

I look out the window. It's dark, but if I flick off the lights, I see an eerie orange glow outside. Snow falls past my window and I see that it's accumulating quickly outside.

I flick back on the lights, grab the phone.

Chase isn't picking up his cell.

I call WorldMar.

"Allo?" Answers a perky Underfed.

Glancing at the clock, I'm a little surprised to hear someone at work this late.

"I'm looking for Chase. Is he there?"

There's a muffle, then a pause. Then, "*Nyet*. He and Bertha are in the village."

"Oh."

"There is a snowstorm. They called to say they are staying there for the night."

Oh. I don't know why, because you know, I *trust* Chase, but I feel weak. And I sit, hard, on my sofa. "They called?"

"About an hour ago."

I was in the tub, but, still didn't hear the phone ringing off the hook.

"If he calls, will you tell him to call home?"

"*Konyeshna*," she says and hangs up. She said "of course" like I call all the time, bothering them. Bothering Chase.

It suddenly occurs to me that perhaps they need to hear from The Wife more often.

Or maybe, The Wife needs to take her role more seriously. Maybe I need to remind Chase exactly why he should make it home for dinner. Because his wife and his baby love him.

I set the phone back on the cradle. Turn out the lights. Blow out the candle. Take the shoes and set them on my belly.

Watch the snow drift from the eerie orange sky and wonder where my husband is sleeping tonight.

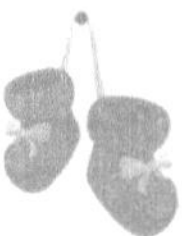

Forgiveness happens in Russia with every new snowfall. Redemptive white covers the blemishes, turns a bleak landscape into a snow globe, complete with hope and life and new beginnings.

I'm sitting on my bed, my knees drawn up under the covers, as I watch white flakes drift from the gray sky. The sun has been up for hours, as have I, listening to my heart thumping, asking how I let things go this far. How I tore down my house with my own hands.

I actually searched for that verse in my Bible, and while I couldn't find that, I did find a Psalm that spoke to the moan in my heart. *"Blessed is he whose transgressions are forgiven, whose sins are covered."*

Covered, like snow covers the trash, and broken pipes, and cracked pavement, the gray sidewalks and weeds that overgrow the dry flowers. I put my hand over my stomach, wondering if God can cover my sin. My lies.

"When I kept silent, my bones wasted away through my groaning all day long."

If I were to put one word to my marriage, my relationship with Chase, it would be groaning. A pain that seems to only deepen with each day.

And it's seeped into my bones. I palm the empty place beside me on the bed, my breath short at the gulf between us.

"Many are the woes of the wicked, but the Lord's unfailing love surrounds the man (or woman) who trusts in him."

I'm not a wicked person. (Well, if you don't count the time I "borrowed" my parents' car one Friday night only to crash it into a light pole. But that wasn't exactly my fault. Jenny Franklin saw Mike Killman crossing the street right in front of the Red Rooster, and leaped across the driver's seat to wave at him, causing me to push her away and thus jerk the steering wheel hard right, causing the car to plow into the light. I explained this to my father many times over, but apparently he couldn't grasp my innocence. I was sentenced to a month's hard time, cleaning the Berglund cabins. Which I suppose makes me ever more sympathetic to Sveta's plight, and can be used by God for good, now. See, I still have a smidgen of that missionary thinking inside me.) But I'm not sure I've exactly trusted in God. I suppose that's clear due to the fact that if I trusted God then I wouldn't have lied to Chase for three months.

I close my Bible, aware that the morning is drawing out and I haven't yet talked to Chase, or even Sveta, who I thought might be here by now.

I get up and go into the kitchen. My roast turned out perfectly, but I can't bear to eat it without Chase, so I turn to Sveta's stack of blini. I put a little butter and sugar on one, roll it up, and like how it crunches in my mouth.

What I wouldn't give for a microwave.

Sveta hasn't shown up yet, an absence that I'm not sure has to do with the weather or with humiliation. Aside from the fact that I've gotten way too used to having a cleaning and laundry lady (attested by the stack of dishes I've piled in the sink, hoping, waiting . . .), I can't wait to tell Sveta that things will be okay.

Of course, I have to tell that to myself, first.

I pad over to the window and am staring out into the snow-covered courtyard and it hits me. It's Christmas Eve.

The night God revealed His truth to the world. The night He showed us just how far He'd go to love us and make us a part of His family.

I miss my family. Sometime in the next twenty-four hours they'll gather around my mother's table, eating Swedish meatballs and snowflake pudding and homemade Berglund cinnamon buns.

I'm eating a cold blini.

I close my eyes as I lean my forehead against the cold window pane. "Lord, I really screwed up. I should have never lied to Chase. Please, forgive me. And if it's possible . . . please fix this."

I stand there a moment longer, letting the quiet seep through me. And that's when I feel it. A flutter, like a feather, inside me.

Junior?

I put my hand on my stomach and feel it again.

Junior.

I'm engulfed by the sudden rush of emotion. Junior is in there, moving around, making himself comfy. He's in the little world God made for him, surrounded by warmth.

Surrounded by love.

I wonder if this is what Paul meant in Ephesians when he said we might grasp how wide and long and high and deep God's love is. That God's love surrounds me, on every side, even in the midst of my sin. I can't escape it.

I'm reveling in this when the phone rings.

I sweep it up.

"Josey?"

Can Chase hear the relief in my voice? "How are you? Are you okay?"

"Yeah. We got stranded in the village, and I just got back to the office." Fatigue layers his tone. "I'm sorry I didn't call."

He didn't call.

He didn't call.

I'm trying not to let that fact hollow me out, but it's not working. My voice turns frosty. "That's okay."

Silence. I can sense him turning his back to me, like he does when he gets into bed. *Please, God, help me not to tear down my house!* "Really, Chase, I know it's hard to call from the village."

He waits a beat, and then, to my relief, "I missed you."

Tears mist my eyes. "Me too."

"I'll be home tonight. And I'll go in late tomorrow."

I frown a little at this, but manage to find my nice voice. "Today is Christmas Eve."

Silence pulses through the line.

"You knew that, right? Tomorrow is Christmas?"

Again silence, then, "GI, I totally forgot—not about Christmas, but I thought it was in a few more days. I totally lost track of the dates. And with the entire country not celebrating––"

"That's okay, Chase." Just come home. Please. "I'll make us a nice Christmas, I promise." And I will. With superb gifts. Better than gloves.

"You're the greatest, GI."

Oh, how I want to be. "See you soon, Chase."

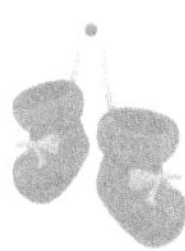

Why couldn't I have been born with the Berglund gene for pastry making? My sister can take a handful of flour, a pinch of baking powder, give it a wink, and turn it into award-winning biscuits.

I can spend three hours reading a cookbook, measure meticulously, and still I'm staring at a lump of unleavened bread that would have lasted for the forty-year wanderings.

However, the kitchen smells of baking poultry, and I managed to follow the directions on a pack of Jello (I mean, really, how hard is it to dissolve sugar in water?), and made a banana pudding for dessert. Most importantly, there are no flames.

Well, at least not coming from the turkey. But the fat girl in the room can't wait for her man to come home. To relight the smoldering, nearly cold embers between us.

I've dressed up the apartment in twinkly lights I found at the *apteka*, and am dressed in my new holiday attire—the black velour pants and sparkly shirt. I know Martha would make some sort of homemade wreath, or mint candles or something, but—she doesn't live in Russia, does she?

The most important decoration sits in the middle of the table, where a tree should be—a tiny, wrapped box containing the cutest shoes on the planet. I can't wait until Chase opens it.

Oh Josey, why didn't you tell me? His eyes will light up, and he'll wrap his arms around me. He'll be wearing his jeans and smelling of soap, and as he pulls me inside the cocoon of his arms, I'll know that all is well.

Because I didn't want to put more pressure on you, make your life harder, I'll say.

His eyes will turn soft with understanding. *Don't you know that you're the reason I get up in the morning? You could never make my life harder.*

Then he'll kiss me, ever so gently, like he does, and I'll beg him for forgiveness, but he'll already be offering it, and then he'll put his hands on my tiny (okay, not so tiny anymore) belly and we'll be a family.

I'm nearly as excited as I was on our wedding day. Then again, that day didn't play out exactly how I intended, but I won't complain about the end result. Anything with me in Chase's embrace is a perfect ending in my book.

I finish setting the table for two, and am just lighting the candles when I hear the lock turning at the door.

I turn, and my heart jumps, seeing Chase. He looks tired and snowy, his hair in curls, his leather jacket shiny from the cold. "Hey, GI," he says with a hesitant grin. And then, to my shock, he drags in behind him . . . a tree.

A Christmas tree! "Oh, Chase, I love it! Where did you find it?"

"The corner market," he says, and leans over to kiss me. "I think I got first pick."

I hug him around the neck, smelling his two-day cologne, rumpled cotton, even pine. A wave of regret nearly overwhelms me. How could I have kept the truth from this man I love?

"Chase, I have to tell you—"

"Is this Josey?"

I hear the voice, without an accent, right behind the tree, and I move the branches aside to discover . . . Carmen Electra.

No, not really, but she could be her sister, with the caramel-colored hair that curls just below her shoulders, the kiss-me-now lips, the curves that no man can ignore. Even hidden under her black suit and open wool dress coat, I see plenty of cleavage.

I'll bet Chase has noticed it too. I blink at her, wordless. She looks classy. And successful. And gorgeous. Chase has Bambi for a partner.

I'll bet she surpasses.

Oh please, don't let her surpass. Not with Chase. My pregnancy nausea is returning, in spades.

She holds out her hand, and I see a French manicure. "Bertha Schultz. Chase's partner."

Of course. I take her hand, but I'm a fish grip, and I'm still scraping up words when she looks me up and down, and I see a strange expression—surprise, delight?—flash across her face.

"Oh, Chase," she says, looking over at him, her perfect lips pouty. Why does it suddenly burn me, the way she uses his name? "Why didn't you tell me Josey is pregnant?"

My world stops, and although it's snowing outside, there's a blizzard in my soul. Cold, terrifying. Because Chase turns and looks at me, disbelief and not a little anger on his face.

I nod, my hand moving over Junior. Protectively.

Hopefully.

Then, as my world turns to Siberia around me, Chase turns, marches past Bambi, gets in the elevator, and leaves.

the world poker champ

• • •

I MET CHASE ON THE FIRST DAY OF KINDERGARTEN. HIS FAMILY had just moved in down the road, and we met at the conglomeration of mailboxes, where Steve, our bus driver would pick us up. Chase made a snide remark about my Care Bears lunchbox (for which I gave him a whack over the head) and I noticed he had only a soggy paper-bag lunch. He told me his father was a Ninja, I informed him that mine played goalie for the North Stars.

It was a match made in heaven. We began to spend every hour in competition/courtship. Crafting castles and tunnels in his sandbox. Racing on our bikes down Bloomquist Mountain, making tree forts. And gradually, we began to unveil the truth. Like how I always wanted to be a cowgirl, but since we didn't have a horse, I had to ride the ponies down at the yearly county fair. And he told me how he didn't really get hit in the face with a baseball to cause his shiner.

But I guess, despite all this time learning each other's secrets, we're still lying to each other, at least a little. Because it's clear to me that I'm not the only one hiding pertinent information.

If I worked with, say, Orlando Bloom, or Matthew McConaughey, wouldn't I owe it to Chase to at least mention that? C'mon, even happily married women aren't that blind.

The truth is, I never gave the idea of Chase cheating on me much significant play in my imagination. Not that Chase isn't a red-blooded American male, but frankly, he'd been chasing *me* my entire life. After all that commitment, he didn't seem the type to get sidetracked.

Until today.

As I sit in our quiet, dark flat, watching the candles burn to a nub, my mind is stuck on two things:

1. The way Bambi said *Chase*, like she knew him better than I did.
2. The betrayal on Chase's face when he realized I'd been hiding from him his child.

I could be in big trouble here.

But I'm pregnant. Clearly I wasn't thinking with all my zeros and ones—and that's normal, according to H. Remember—four billion brain cells lost with each pregnancy. I think I'm due a little slack here, with all those brain cells dying each day. I plead pregnancy as my defense.

I set up the tree using a pot I found in the cabinet that could make soup for fifty. Then I drape it with the twinkly lights. Finally, I sit on the sofa in the darkness, waiting for the lock to turn.

Hoping the lock will turn.

Please, God, don't let him be with Bambi . . . er Bertha.

I pull a blanket up over my body, tuck my nose down inside it, put my hands over Junior, and wish I'd never left Gull Lake. Never left my Cape Cod, my Denali, my office at the *Gull Lake Gazette*, Jasmine's *kringle*, my mother, who, despite her devices to drive me crazy, has been a mother for nearly twenty-five years with some success. I'll bet she can teach me a few things.

My thoughts return to the day Jasmine birthed Amelia (which also happened to be my wedding day). To the look on Jasmine's face when Milton wrapped his arms around her, around their daughter. Her expression spoke of peace. Contentment.

My throat burns. What was I thinking? That I was doing Chase a *favor* by lying to him?

We're going to be *parents*.

As the dark seeps into the windows, the night lit by only the twinkle lights, my thoughts go to Mary and Joseph. And a thought occurs to me—Mary was in my shoes, exactly. She didn't know how to tell Joseph that she was divinely pregnant, knowing he might not be exactly thrilled. In fact, she went on holiday to her cousin Elizabeth's, leaving God to sort out the situation with Joe.

And just when Joseph (who really wasn't a bad guy but planned to be merciful to the betrothed who he thought had betrayed him), was going to break it off with Mary, God intervened and set Joseph straight.

I think I need a little God intervention here.

What am I thinking—I need *total* God intervention here, because I've done a stellar job of screwing up our first year of marriage.

I close my burning eyes and let the tears drip.

I awaken to the sun on my skin, warming me. I'm on the sofa, curled into a ball, still wearing the velour pants, the blouse. The lights still burning on the tree. The flat no longer smells of turkey, or even banana pudding, but pine. I stand up and pad to the bedroom, my heart thumping.

I'm alone.

On Christmas morning.

But, as I feel a tickle inside me, I realize . . . .not quite alone.

You are my hiding place, you will protect me from trouble and surround me with songs of deliverance. The Psalm I read yesterday rises from the ashes of my hopes and fills my mind.

I will instruct you and teach you the way you should go. I will counsel you and watch over you.

Even in Russia? Even after I've made a mess of everything?

For some reason, as I stand there, feeling Junior awakening, staring at my empty life, I'm not afraid.

God *can* fix this.

Just like he fixed Mary's problem. Here's hoping Chase got a midnight visitation—a *divine* visitation.

"Lord," I say aloud. "I'm sorry I didn't listen to You. That I tried to do things my way. From now on, You're in charge. I trust You."

The doorbell buzzing makes me jump. Sveta. Although she has her own key, we agreed she'd buzz first. Thus alerting me before she entered, in case I was standing in my underwear, staring at my closet, hoping my clothing had magically expanded overnight.

"Come in," I say, with a rush of relief. Now, at least, the dishes will get done.

I hear the lock turn, and decide to retrieve my blanket from the sofa, because, well, I can help clean a little, right?

"Josey?"

His voice stops me cold, and I turn. My throat fills.

Chase.

And he's looking rough. His hair in spikes, his cheeks chapped, blondish red whiskers across his chin, his eyes reddened.

"Chase," I whisper.

He nods, comes in, and shuts the door behind him. He's holding his briefcase and sets it down as he shrugs out of his jacket.

He's staying.

But I can't ask him where he's been. I can't, because what if—"Where were you?"

Oh shoot! Someday I'm going to make my mouth obey me.

"WorldMar. I slept on my sofa."

Somehow I keep from asking, "Alone?" Instead I give a little nod then turn to fold the blanket. But tears blind me and all I can do is stand there, biting my lip, not wanting to make a noise.

I feel his hands on my shoulders. Warm, comforting. Strong. "Josey, I've spent the night thinking about the past three months."

I nod. Me too.

"I am such a jerk."

Huh? I look up, turn, and meet his gaze. His eyes are red, and glossy. He puts his hands on my arms, runs them down to catch my hands.

"Chase you're not––"

"I've been thinking only of myself since we got married. You gave up your job, your family—"

My Cape Cod, the dog—

"Everything that you worked so hard for."

I didn't work so hard for the job. Mildred wanted to retire. I was willing to work for ten bucks an hour. It was a perfect match. Even so, I can't speak. A tear runs down my face, and he catches it with his thumb.

"You found out you were pregnant when you went to the doctor in Gull Lake, didn't you?"

I narrow my eyes at him. Just because he's an anthropologist doesn't mean he can read my mind. "Yeah . . . "

"I knew it! You had the strangest look on your face, and I thought it was because I was making dinner. But later that night you disappeared––"

"I was repacking."

The slightest grin edges up his face. “Pickles. You packed pickles.”

I give a shrug.

“You didn’t tell me, because you didn’t want me to say we couldn’t go, didn’t you?”

Wow. He *is* good. Probably he should work for Dr. Phil or something.

“And that’s why you’ve been so moody, and distant––”

Listen, Bub—

“And . . . rounder.” He takes his hands from mine and runs them down my body. “Wow.”

That’s a good wow. I can tell, because his blue eyes are lit up with a hue I’ve never seen before. And he’s holding me ever so gently. Then, he swallows, and I can hear it reverberating through my soul.

“I thought you were angry at me for bringing you to Russia. And with the job . . . not working out, I took all my anger out on you. I didn’t even *try* to understand.” He tightens his jaw and swallows again. His voice has turned ragged. “Can you ever forgive me for . . . for not knowing?”

Oh, Chase. “I should have told you. But you were so busy, and then we got into that fight, and I was mad, and I can’t believe I didn’t tell you. I’m sick about it. Can you forgive me?”

Chase’s hand goes around my neck, and his expression tells me that he already has. He swallows again, and then very slowly, very sweetly, kisses me.

I could live forever in Chase’s embrace. I kiss him back, and it’s a moment before he moves away, breathing just a little bit harder, desire in his eyes.

Just call me The Firestarter.

“I got you something,” I say, moving out of his embrace. I retrieve the little box from under the tree, hand it to him.

He gives me that scoundrel grin that makes my heart do backflips, and opens the package. He’s speechless for a long time, his chest rising and falling as he takes out the little blue shoes.

"They're for—"

"I know what they're for, GI," he says softly. He looks up at me and oh boy, he's going to turn me into a pile of mush here. And, as if sensing the moment, Junior wakes up.

"Oh!" I can't help it, the feeling still catches me off guard. Concern flashes across Chase's face.

"What is it?"

I put my hands on my tummy. "Junior. He moved."

Chase's mouth opens. And then, he leaves me breathless as he crouches before me, putting both hands on my belly. "Hey there, little guy. It's your daddy."

His daddy. *Oh, Lord, thank You.* I tangle my hands in Chase's hair. "He's very, very glad to meet you."

Chase looks up at me, eyes shining. Then, "I got you something too." He stands up and goes to his briefcase. From it he takes two envelopes. He's written Merry Christmas on both. Gesturing me to sit, he joins me on the sofa.

"It's sorta an either-or gift."

I frown at him.

"Just open them."

I work my thumb under the lip of the first envelope and rip it open. Inside is a folded piece of paper.

Reservations for two plane tickets. Back to Minnesota. I stare at, feeling a stone fall through my heart, and settle in my gut. Oh no.

Or . . . not? Isn't this what I wanted? To go home, start over? To be around pickles and take-out, and decent prenatal care, and my mother? To start our life as parents surrounded by the people we love?

I'll be sure to take caviar with me.

When I look up at Chase, his smile has faded. He takes my

hand. "I love you, GI. More than I love this job. We can leave tomorrow, be home for New Year's Eve."

I can't speak.

"Open the other envelope." Chase hands it to me, and I feel something heavy inside. I tear it open, and a key slides into my palm.

"It's to my office, at WorldMar. Our office."

I frown at him, not connecting the dots. Remember, four billion brain cells, buddy. Spell it out.

Chase takes my hand. "It's not working, Jose. Every idea I come up with stinks or has already been tried, and I'm completely in over my head." He runs his thumb over my hand. "I should have asked before." He shakes his head. "No, I should have told them that you were my partner. That we were a package deal." Looking up, he's wearing the expression he did the time he asked me not to go to Russia. I didn't give in then, but I'm ready to now. Because my man needs me. "Either we go home, or you come to WorldMar and help me. What do you think, Jose?"

I think a decision of this magnitude shouldn't be made by a woman with shrinking brain cells. Even if she is a Proverbs 31 wife.

I have choices here. Aside from the obvious two, the others are . . . who to call for advice?

1. Daphne. Who thinks of me as Martha (I know, she's so confused, but really, that's okay).
2. H. Who thinks I'm not dealing with a full deck, or at least all my brain cells.

3. Jasmine. Who will kill me for not telling her I'm pregnant, and possibly cut off my *kringle* care-package supply.

I dial my mother.

When she picks up, it sounds like she's in the next room, and a rush of emotion engulfs me. I can hardly speak. "Merry Christmas, Mom," I say.

"Josey, is that you?"

No, it's your other daughter three thousand miles away calling you mother. "Yeah. How are you?"

I can hear the phone muffled on the other side as she covers the receiver and hollers for my father. I bought them a new telephone for Christmas last year, a cordless with a mute button. My mother refuses to read instructions, hence why the time-bake function on her oven has never been used, along with the convection feature on her microwave as well as the speaker and mute functions on her phone. I'm thinking Mom would be happy with a woodstove and a tin can on a string.

"Mom, I gotta talk to you," I say, hoping I have time before my father picks up. "I'm . . . pregnant."

I wince, because I know what my mother thinks about us living in Russia. You were there—she wasn't exactly doing the hula. And I don't blame her. Despite all the reforms, she's still reliving the air-raid drills she grew up with during the Cold War. That has to scar a kid's psyche.

"Oh . . . Josey!" But instead of the dread in her voice, I hear . . . joy? "That's wonderful, honey! Congratulations!"

"What time is it there, Mom? Did I wake you up? This isn't a dream."

"It's six a.m., I've been up for an hour, for Pete's sake!"

Of course she has. "Well, I just . . . I wanted to tell you." Go figure, my mother isn't fazed! "And I need your advice." I squint one eye with that word. Because, well, Mom's advice has generally fallen on deaf ears. Until now. When I see the need for a parent.

I'm not going to say it, but I want my mommy.

"I . . . I don't know what to do, Mom."

She pauses, and I can hear her confusion over the line. "About what, honey?"

"About being pregnant . . . in Russia."

I can imagine her in the kitchen, her yellow apron about her waist, her blonde hair cut short. She's thin and tall and up to her wrists in flour. The house is clean and the turkey stuffed for Christmas dinner, and soon the house will fill with Buddy and Jasmine and Milton. And Amelia. Grandchild number one.

"Are there doctors in Russia?"

"Yeah, I suppose."

"Well, then, go to a doctor."

I grimace. Chase is sitting next to me on the sofa. I haven't given him my answer yet, because, well, I don't know. I can't make decisions on an empty stomach.

"I will . . . the thing is, Mom, Chase says we can come home if I want." I glance at him. His expression doesn't betray an inkling of what he hopes I might say. Shoot! He picks now to become a World Poker champ?

Mom is quiet. I hear water running, like she might be doing the dishes. "You'll be home by the time the baby comes, right?"

Oh, please, Lord, I hope so. The idea of having a baby in Russia . . . I go a little cold and reach for Chase's hand. "Yeah. It's due the end of June."

Mom is quiet for a long moment, probably doing the math. She's a whiz, having spent her entire life adding and subtracting measurements in two systems. (Norway, where Mom gets many of her prize-winning recipes, is a believer in the metric system like the rest of the world.)

I can hear a chair sliding out from our ancient kitchen table. "Sweetheart, how far along are you?"

"I felt the baby move today."

I can hear her concern from here.

"First thing you need to do is find a doctor. If he thinks you're fine, I see no reason to cut your trip short. As long as you're eating right, getting plenty of protein and calcium, and taking care of yourself, you should be fine for the next few months. However, it's up to you, Josey."

Rats, that's what Chase said too. I was half hoping Mom would make this decision for me. Chase gets up, moves away from me. Pads into the kitchen, his hands combing back his hair.

I did this. I got us into this sticky place. And now I gotta figure out how to get us out.

Wait—didn't I, just an hour or so ago, agree to let God make the decisions? And just like that, it's clear. I prayed for God to fix this, to do a miracle and smooth out my bumpy marriage. And He did. And Chase didn't marry me for my propensity to quit.

This is my town. And not only that, I have the most magnificent of ideas.

"Thanks, Mom. Give Dad and Jas a kiss for me."

"You guys doing okay otherwise, honey?"

I glance at Chase. He looks at me, a frown on his face. But I smile. "We're perfect."

As I hang up, Chase comes back and gathers me in his arms. They're strong and safe, and inside them, I am his bundle of yuletide joy.

Merry Christmas to us.

i've been bambied

. . .

I HAVE DECIDED THAT RUSSIA THROWS THE BEST NEW YEAR'S EVE parties on the planet. Case in point—two years ago I spent New Year's Eve at Spaso House, at a *ball* with the ambassador to Russia. There was an orchestra and fireworks.

Whereas, last year I spent New Year's Eve fighting my mother for puzzle pieces. (She won't admit it, but every year, she takes one piece and puts it in her pocket, only to Voilá! find it after the puzzle is near completion. I don't understand this mentality—I steal the pieces openly, without any of the covert antics.) It if weren't for Chase talking me into taking a midnight stroll through the snow, and later shooting off some private fireworks with a kiss under our old tree fort, well, I might have gone to bed at ten with a good book.

But this year, I'm back in action. Not only is Chase on my arm, but I'm looking hot. Well, as hot as a nearly five-month pregnant woman can look. Because in a rare act of husbandly kindness, he took me shopping.

At a maternity store. Can you believe they have leather pants with stretchy tummies? And I found a sleeveless black sequin top and a pair of knock-off Prada pumps.

Not only that, but we received an embossed invitation for a "Private Party at the Galeria" for New Year's Eve. I, for one, know that Putin had a party at the Galeria not six months ago.

I am a happily married woman with a hot man on my arm. Chase is looking very mafia in a pair of black pants and a matching black shirt. Against his blonde hair and blue eyes, well, eat your heart out, Underfed Women of WorldMar.

We use Thug, who is wearing his new gloves, to ride to WorldMar. It's okay to utilize the help for special occasions, and especially since I gave Chase remedial surfing lessons during our shopping trip.

Chase is in full reparation mode. He took me out for dinner at the American Bar and Grill, where we knocked up a hundred-dollar bill just for a couple burgers and shakes, then attended Moscow Bible Church with me. Sitting there, next to Caleb and Daphne, my man trying to decipher Russian next to me, I felt a wave of happiness that I can only attribute to hormones. Because it can't be that I'm actually content, can it?

He also took a week off of work, or rather worked at home while we put our heads together and I unveiled my master plan.

Peanut Butter.

I know, it shouldn't be that easy. But that Nutella thing sat in my brain like . . . peanut butter, and I couldn't get past the fact that Russians need something besides Nutella and caviar to put on their bread.

With a little online research I discovered that peanut butter is easy to make. And perfect for cottage industries. Chase and I tracked down a peanut butter press online, and a supplier from Georgia (not Atlanta).

I am Chase's favorite person. His blessed and surpassing wife.

WorldMar has rented out a room at the Galeria Restaurant, just off Red Square. Russia has dressed up (finally!) for the season, and Red Square is alive with lighted ice sculptures, rides for the children, and a giant tree. As we pull up we can hear music pulsing from the ornate building—Machina Vreminya, and Pugacheva, Russian pop-music icons.

The Galeria is two stories of New Russian glamor. Building on the past, the owner revitalized the former residence of some Russian aristocrat and turned the place into a club.

As we enter, an elderly woman dressed in velvet and wearing a brooch at her cleavage takes our coats. I shrug out of my parka, hating the fact that it barely buttons, and hand it to her. It's okay if she wants to get my coat mixed up with one of the minks she hangs it next to.

Chase takes my arm and leads me into the great hall. Along the sides of the room, giant pillars stretch up to the second story, which is bordered by a balcony overlooking the room. The place is packed, the lights dim, the air heavy with smoke and the redolence of vodka, and alive with women who are dressed like it might be July. I've never seen so many belly piercings in one place. That, and sultry looks aimed at my husband.

In the middle of the room, a woman wearing the regalia of a harem girl belly dances on a platform. I stand there mesmerized for a moment. How exactly does she—

Chase leads me up a staircase like he might know exactly where he's going.

"Have you been here before?" I ask as we walk along the balcony and toward a private room.

"Once," he says, but offers nothing more.

Hmm.

We enter a brightly lit room decorated with faux palm trees with twinkle lights and a New Year's tree at the far end. Around the room, tables encircle a dance floor. And it's packed, mostly with skinny women and old men who are as mesmerized by the Underfeds as I was by Miss Belly Dancer.

I feel yucky, suddenly wishing for my puzzle pieces and a walk in the snow.

"Chase!"

I turn at the voice and see Bambi headed for us. She's wearing a gold V-neck lamé top, and a pair of black stretch pants that leave nothing to the imagination.

She hugs Chase then pops him with a kiss on each cheek. "And you brought Josey!"

Surprise, surprise.

She turns to me and before I know it, she's planted two puckers on my cheeks also. I've been Bambied.

"Come and get something to eat." She hooks her arm around Chase's free arm, and we're a Congo line headed to the food table.

Maybe there's hope for this evening after all. Smoked salmon, crab salads, *peroshkie*, black bread, cheeses, cutlets, potatoes with dill, and best of all . . . caviar! I grab a plate.

"Chase!" Katrina greets him with a hug and two more cheek kisses. Hmm. She turns to me, and with a smile that doesn't meet her eyes, "Oh, and you brought Zhozhey."

What is this, show and tell? Get used to it, girls!

I smile at her. She reaches out and puts her hand on my belly.

Hello, that's attached to my body, honey.

"I love babies," she says, and her gaze falls back to Chase. He smiles at her.

Okay, what is it with men who can't see when a woman is putting out "I'm yours" signals? Slug her, Chase!

But, no. "You look lovely tonight, Katrina."

Oh, please. I put the plate back down, my appetite gone. Chase turns to the table and dishes himself up a plate of food. Meanwhile, I see Katrina return to her band of thieves and deliver important reconnaissance information. Yes, Chase is here. Yes, he brought the *wife*. Yes, she's really pregnant.

"Wanna dance?" I ask him. I'm not holding out a remote hope that I can gyrate like WorldMars Underfeds, but maybe a reminder that I still got it would—

"I don't like to dance," Chase says, wrinkling his nose. "Can we not?"

I sigh, and nod. Then, "I want to go home." Rats, I didn't mean to blurt that out. But suddenly this New Year has turned lurid and gross and unromantic.

He turns, scowls at me. I can see him weighing my words, as well as the last three months. He swallows, then glances around. "Okay. I just want to say hi to my boss, okay?"

Oh Chase, I love you.

I follow his gaze where it's landed on a normal-size woman sitting at a table. She's wearing a black, sleeveless dress and is propping her head up with one hand while turning the stem of her cocktail glass with the other. "That's Jim's wife, Janet."

I follow Chase through the crowd, moving to avoid being poked by boney women, and join him at the table. "Hello, Janet," he says. "Is Jim around?"

She looks at him, and I see age on her face, despite the heavy makeup, the red lips, the dark eye shadow. Her eyes are a bit glazed. "He's around, Chase."

Chase turns to me, and I come to the rescue, sitting down in a chair next to the woman. "I'll wait here."

He sets down his food and I eye the caviar as I turn to the woman. "My name's Josey—I'm Chase's wife."

"Janet Wilkes." She holds out a hand, and it's sorta like shaking a walleye—clammy and limp. "Glad to meet you," she slurs.

Maybe one bite of caviar would be wise, just to tide me over till we get home. I pick up a fork. "This is quite a party, huh?"

"Just wait until they start the champagne showers. It's a hoot."

Somehow, by the look she's giving me, I'm not so sure she's lying. "Champagne showers?"

She lifts a shoulder. "Last year, the girls made themselves into human ice cream sundaes."

"You've got to be kidding."

Janet raises one groomed eyebrow. "Look around you and then ask yourself if I could be remotely kidding."

Okay, Chase, we're leaving, right *now*.

"How long have you been in Russia?" I ask, scanning the crowd for Chase. If I see him even near ice cream . . .

She sighs, and her gaze falls off me, onto the dancers "I just got back."

I don't spot Chase, but I see Bambi center dance floor, wearing a wreath around her neck, holding a champagne glass in the air. She must have taken lessons from Belly Dancer. Nice. "From where?"

She takes a drink. "Connecticut."

"Just in time for New Year's Eve, huh? Did you have Christmas with your family?"

She looks at me again, and this time there's an edge to her gaze. "I was stateside for medical reasons."

Why do I feel like there's more to that story? The former missionary in me suddenly feels something heavy in her spirit. I put down my fork. "I'm sorry. Are you okay?"

She shrugs a shoulder. "Depends on how you define okay. Will I live? Yes." She lifts her glass. "Nothing a little Prozac and vodka won't cure."

My mouth opens a second before I have the good sense to shut it.

Janet gives me a wicked smile. "Who did you say your husband was?"

"Chase. He's working in Gorkovich with the cottage industry program."

"Oh," she says, and I hear a chuckle. "He's the one."

"He's the one?" I mean, yes, I know that, but I think her The One is meant in an entirely different context than my The One.

"He's the one who took Bob's spot."

Information is slowly clicking into place. Like the fact that Bob had to go home. Suddenly.

"What happened with Bob, Janet?" I lower my voice, and the music, the surroundings, and the fact that I have my fork in a bowl of caviar, make this all seem very KGB and Cold War. I'm ready to slip her a few rubles under her plate.

She takes a long drink, puts her glass down. Signals a waiter for more. I'm thinking I need to intercept him. She takes the glass the waiter hands her and slips a hundred-ruble note into his hand. He winks at her.

Please, God, don't let this be my future.

"Bob had a little . . . extra-curricular activity going on in the village."

She's got me right where she wants me. My mind is swirling with ideas—a maple sugar factory? A vodka processing plant?

"Let's just say that his hard work was focused in one place." She smiles wickedly and her voice carries a bitterness that can only come from personal experience.

"Don't tell me . . . he had an affair?" I glance around again, looking for Chase. My heart hiccups a moment when I see him talking to Bambi. She has her arm draped over his shoulder, and is whispering into his ear. He catches my eye and smiles at me.

Good boy, Chasie.

"Bingo."

I turn back to Janet and see that she's missed her mouth, her vodka dribbling down the front of her blouse. She doesn't even notice. As she puts the glass down, I right it before it falls over. "And it looks like your boy Chase is next in line."

Huh? I glance again at Chase, and notice that Underfed Katrina has joined Bambi. They're trying to get him to contra dance. "He's just . . . .getting into the New Year spirit," I say hollowly.

"Yeah. Well, I'm sure that's what Ginny Martin thought when she caught Bob in the horizontal contra in his office." She gives a laugh. It's sloppy and makes my skin crawl.

But I have to ask. "Who was he with?"

Her eyes turn to fire and she fixes her gaze on Chase as she answers. "His secretary. Chase's new partner. Bertha Schultz."

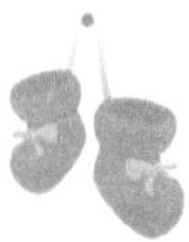

Wildflower: Are you sure it was Bertha?

GI: I'm telling you, a woman that schnokered couldn't lie if she wanted to. And the way she was eyeing Bambi, if Janet were Clark Kent, Bambi would be a pile of ash. As it was, Bambi was smoldering, leaving her perfume all over my husband like creosote. I threw his clothes into the pile of laundry in the bathroom. Which is starting to overflow because Sveta still hasn't returned. (And the fact that Sveta still hasn't shown up since before Christmas has made me not only nervous—because somebody is going to have to do those dishes!—but sorta sad. And worried about Ryslan.)

Wildflower: Your cleaning lady? Join the rest of the human race, Josey—the people who have to do our own laundry.

GI: Not by hand in the bathtub. (Although I have to say, even in college I had my washing-by-hand days. Or nights. Usually at a party. And it involved one too many beers.) Besides, I can't bend over. Much. I deserve a cleaning lady.

Wildflower: Whatever. Do you seriously think Chase is the kind of guy who would cheat on you? Honey, I'm going to say this gently. It's all in your head. Get a grip.

GI: It's not all in my head! He line-danced for an hour! And this is the guy who has, before this moment, repeatedly refused to give the slightest wiggle on the dance floor.

Wildflower: I'm sure it was the mood of the party.

GI: It better not have been the mood of anything else. (I can't help it. I rode home in fuming silence next to Twinkle Toes. And when he tried to two-step with me later than night, I wrinkled my nose and said, "Can we not?" Okay, I know, not so Proverbs 31, but, well, can you blame me?) I don't know, H. What if Chase isn't attracted to me anymore? I don't feel very romantic. Pregnancy seems to have sapped me of every romantic bone in my body. Not only that, but my ankles are fat. My ankles! I can't help but think Chase isn't so thrilled with having a fat and hormonal wife.

Wildflower: I guess I shouldn't tell you then that Rex composed his own song and sang it to me as the clock struck twelve, asking me to marry him.

GI: You're engaged?

Wildflower: Can you believe it? Will you be back for the wedding? We're going to have it in July, during the 10,000 Lakes Festival in Detroit Lakes. The Sugar Monkeys are playing, and we'll have it during the concert.

GI: I'll be back, I hope. (Please, let me be back. Because by that time I'll be a month overdue, and as God is my witness I am not having this baby in Russia.)

Wildflower: Good, because you're my matron of honor, okay?

GI: (I hate that word, matron. And trying to envision just what a bridesmaid dress made from green Army surplus might look like.) Of course. I can't believe you're getting married. Are you sure you're ready?

Wildflower: Yeah, it'll be fun.

GI: (If H has heard nothing of my tirades over the past three months, I thought she'd learn that marriage is not . . . .fun. Okay, maybe it is. But not five months pregnant. With a closet Baryshnikov.) As long as you're ready. It's a big commitment.

Wildflower: Think of the rent we'll save! And we can share the gig money.

GI: (Methinks I'm not getting through to her.) Did I tell you my new venture?

Wildflower: Besides the orphans? How did they like their Christmas party?"

GI: Loved it. Which led me to an idea to save Fred Astaire's tutu. I'm going to make peanut butter!

Wildflower: You're kidding. I thought you hated peanut butter.

GI: That was only because my mother fed us peanut butter and jelly every single day of my life for twelve years. I think she deliberately packed the sandwich under the apple.

Wildflower: Some people like their sandwiches that way.

GI: Some people also like fluffernutters. Yuck. Marshmallow and peanut butter on bread.

Wildflower: Hey now, don't be disrespectful.

GI: I love peanut butter, appropriately utilized. Like in brownies, or cookies, or even on Thai noodles. The thing is, Russians have a plethora of toppings for their brown bread—Nutella, jam, honey, apricot preserves, and caviar. I think peanut butter would be a perfect fit. There's just one problem.

Wildflower: Peanut butter makes you nauseous?

GI: Bambi hates the idea, of course. She thinks it's a waste of time, that Russians won't know how to eat it. I have this sick feeling she's going to sabotage the idea.

Wildflower: What does Bambi know?

GI: She knows a good-looking man when she sees one.

Wildflower: Calm down. I can hear hysteria when I read it. Listen. First off, you know Russia just as well as Bambi, and if you think it'll work, it'll work. Secondly, Chase loves you. Since the beginning of time. Thirdly, I happen to know you have your yellow belt. You can take her.

GI: I do have my yellow belt, don't I? (Here's to the Kenpo classes I took the summer between junior and senior years of college. Never knew it would come in handy to learn a front snap kick. Okay, yes, I used it once, but Lew had it coming, and I was just practicing, really.)

Wildflower: You'll see, everything's going to work out just fine. What's the word you used . . . surprise?

GI: Surpass. I hope so H. I really hope so.

luka

. . .

I HAVE BEEN TO THE RUSSIAN DOCTOR. AND SURVIVED.

This, in itself, should qualify me for some sort of award. I did discover two important things at the doctor's.

1. If I have five children in Russia, I get a medal.
2. And, if I have to give birth in a Russian hospital, I'll kill myself.

It started out innocently enough. There I was, remembering the time I went with Jasmine to her doctor's appointment. We entered the clinic to a room full of baby toys (for those on number two or three or beyond), a beautifully appointed waiting room with comfortable seating. A receptionist greeted us with a smile, asked her to sign in. I got a mint.

Music played—soothing music. When the nurse came to get Jasmine, she was weighed (and of course, gained a perfect half pound per week), then led to her room where she stayed in her own clothes, and they took her blood pressure. I got to hear Amelia's heartbeat. There were smiles, and happy moments.

Not me. Not here.

Chase asked the Underfeds and found a clinic near our house, connected to the *apteka* (pharmacy). Since the International Clinic is located four subway lines and two buses from my flat, I weighed my options and, since I wasn't actually giving birth here, figured that a half-block jaunt versus a three-hour journey might be a better alternative for my bladder. I recruited Daphne because she's already a nurse and might have some inclination as to whether I should be worried at the doctor's facial expressions.

I briefly considered asking Thug to accompany me since he knows English. But, uh, no. Unless the doctor gives me any trouble...

And the only other person I could think of was Katrina. For obvious reasons, Daph and I opt to go it alone.

We enter the clinic and I know enough to stop by the counter. Where a woman who looks a close relative to the Gulag Women barks at me. Not sure what she says, I point to my stomach (which is roughly the size of a twelve-pound turkey), and say, "*vrach*." Which means, appropriately, "doctor."

She points down the hall where I see a row of what looks like old vinyl chairs. As Daphne and I draw closer, we confirm our location via the other patients—namely, pregnant women. All wearing bathrobes and slippers.

The fact I didn't get slippers when I checked in registers in my mind. However, not sure what the protocol might be, I sit down next to a woman who looks about my size. She has red floral slippers.

She looks at me, at my belly, then gives me a "misery loves company" look.

Sorta sends a little chill up my spine.

The doctors resemble pastry chefs. Roughly the size of my uncle Bert, they wear tall, straight hats and white lab coats. They could be decorating cakes back in the labyrinth of rooms beyond the pebbled glass doors where the other women keep disappearing.

And not returning.

I sit for twenty minutes, not sure if I should have made an appointment. According to my research, one doesn't make an appointment in the Russian medical system. One shows up. And waits.

And waits.

Finally, a dark-haired man who looks about my age appears in the hall. I can't help but notice that he looks a little like Luka. You know, Luka. Hot, Slavic, ER-television show doc with melt-me eyes and a sardonic smile.

Then again, perhaps all Russian doctors in a lab coat and with a Slavic accent resemble Luka. I'm not sure if I should be thinking *run* or . . . jackpot!

"*Potcheemoo tee zdes?*" he asks, his blue eyes in mine.

Why am I here? Is it not obvious? I point to my stomach. The universal sign language for expecting.

He nods and motions me beyond the pebbled doors.

As I enter the inner sanctum, I can't help but notice that the exam room doors are open. Which means I get the oh-so lovely view of the activities in these exam rooms.

Keeping my eyes ahead, I feel myself go a little weak.

That is way too much information for me.

Luka opens the door, motions me into a room that looks too much like a torture chamber. Metal table with two paint-chipped stirrups, a cement floor, and the smell of antiseptic.

And, running across the table, a roach.

I grab Daphne's hand.

"*Rasdeyvaietsa*," Luka says.

Undress. Ha. In his wildest dreams. Or maybe not, because I am as big as Ohio, but still. Not happening.

He stands there. I stand there. I keep thinking, so this is how the Cold War felt.

Finally, he folds his arms and quirks an eyebrow. Yes, definitely Luka.

"I think he wants you to undress and get on the table," Daphne says quietly.

Ya think? "I'm not undressing, especially in front of him, without a gown or something."

And (bing!) suddenly I understand the need for a bathrobe and slippers.

"Maybe we can just ask him to listen for the baby's heartbeat. Maybe take your blood pressure?"

I am still staring down Dr. Luka. I see exasperation on his face, but I know that I present something of a novel situation for him. I can imagine him sitting around with his pals drinking vodka, talking about the stubborn pregnant American woman.

Who refused to get undressed. That's right pal, it ain't happening.

Now, Russians are known for their patience. Queuing up all those years for bread or shoes or cheese or even apartments has taught them how to wait.

And wait.

"I think you should just do what he wants," Daphne whispers.

I narrow my eyes at him.

He narrows them back.

I fold my arms.

He shrugs.

"You have to find out how you're doing, Jose."

"Fine. But he has to leave. And I need a blanket or something." I can already feel my face heating.

But Luka smiles.

It's the smile that does it. "*Nyet,*" I snarl. I point to my belly. "*Ya hachoo slishet tserstoo.*"

I just want to listen to the heartbeat! Because, otherwise, I feel fine. Jasmine carried Amelia without a glitch, and Berglund woman have a history of normal pregnancies. Not only that, but my grandma Netta baled hay the day my dad was born.

I slide onto the table. Lift my shirt just above my belly button and look at Luka.

His smile vanishes.

But he steps forward and motions me to lie down on the table. I try to erase the vision of the roach running down my back, avoid the stirrups, and lean back.

Luka takes my pulse, then my blood pressure. Daphne writes down the information. Then, he pulls what looks like my mother's custard cup press out of his pocket. Wooden, about ten inches long, it has a curved bell on both sides.

He presses the larger of the two bells to my stomach. Puts his ear against the other side.

"He's got to be kidding," I say to Daphne.

"*Tiha!*" Luka snaps.

Sorry, I didn't mean to interrupt his game of telephone. "What is he doing?"

Daphne's eyes are wide as she watches. "I've heard of these, but I've never seen one."

"What is it?"

"*Tiha!*"

"It's an old stethoscope. Dates back to the eighteen hundreds. But a lot of doctors still use them, especially in countries where supplies are limited."

Did we go through a time warp? What's next—blood-letting? No, wait, we are in a Dr. Zhivago movie. I stare at this young, seemingly intelligent man with the pastry hat, and something inside me snaps.

"That's it!" I sit up from the table, knocking Luka in the face. He gasps and jumps back, dropping his . . . ancient medical tool, and puts his hand over his nose. I see blood as I swing my legs down from the table.

"Josey where––"

"I'm finding a real doctor!"

"But he is a real doctor."

I look at Luka, at him pinching his bloody nose, ready to dispute that, when I see an expression pass over him. Hurt?

Or, concern?

At once, the fact he's been trying to listen for my baby's heartbeat hits me, and I reach out for the table. Swallow. "*Izvenita,*" I say meekly. I'm sorry.

Luka considers me for a moment. Then, nodding, he takes a piece of cotton and shoves it up his nose. Nice.

"*Poedozhdee*," he says and disappears from the office. Wait? For what? Bad news? I can barely breathe, let alone sit there. Americans, unlike Russians, are *not* known for their patience.

I put my hands over my stomach, feeling sick. "What if he didn't hear anything? What if there's something wrong with Junior?" Why, oh why didn't I listen to my gut that told me to stay home? Why did I think I could come here without decent prenatal care?

Luka returns. Carrying a stethoscope. A *real* stethoscope. Now, was that so hard?

I slide back onto the table, my heart pounding. Lean back.

And then, my throat feeling tight, I close my eyes. "Please God, let the baby be okay."

I feel the cold bell on my skin, and then to my surprise, Luka puts his hand on my shoulder. "*Na*," he says.

I open my eyes and see that he is handing me the earpieces.

Trembling, I put them on.

And hear, for the first time, the heartbeat inside me. The one separate from my own. Alive and swishing.

Junior.

I can barely find my voice, but I manage a breathy, choked, "*Spaceeba*," as I meet Luka's eyes.

He smiles down at me. "*Pazhalusta*." You're welcome. He takes the stethoscope back, curls it up, and puts it in his pocket.

"*Sledooshay maysitsza?*"

I nod, blinking back my tears. I'll see him next month. In a new bathrobe and slippers.

This is getting out of hand.

I think this while staring at the mound of dishes in my sink.

It's been nearly a month since Christmas (and before you get your knickers in a knot, I *did* the dishes—twice) and Sveta still hasn't shown.

Chase nearly had to wear Scary Pants to work today. I did a quick save by unearthing his jeans and sweater, spritzing them with cologne and telling him he looked great.

But even I can't wear my yoga pants one day longer.

I need Sveta.

And in order to get her back, I also need Thug. Because deep down, I know Thug can find things out.

Like where, perhaps, to buy a hijacked copy of the new Gerard Butler movie. Or lay my hands on a Keith Urban soundtrack. (Sadly, Russians aren't big on country music. Not sure why.)

Most importantly, he can track down Sveta's whereabouts. I don't need to know how. I just want results.

I slip into the backseat and nearly startle Thug out of his black leather jacket and beret. He turns, quirks a dark eyebrow at me.

"You know my housekeeper, Sveta, right?"

He blinks at me.

Oh, don't play dumb, Thug. We all know you can speak English. I stare him down and Thug finally lifts a shoulder. Atta boy.

"I want to find her."

Thug considers me a long moment, and I can see him sorting through his loyalties. Does he side with the collective Russian pride and prohibit me from seeing how Sveta lives? Or, does he surrender to the moody fat lady (who gave him some very lovely winter gloves)?

Thug nods and, to my surprise, gets out of the car. I watch as he goes inside my building. It's cold out today. Minus twenty on my Celsius scale. I'm wearing my parka, but it doesn't button around me, so I'm making do with one of Chase's sweatshirts (although that is tight also, just shoot me) and a big scarf I bought at the market.

I clap my hands and pull my wool hat down further over my ears. Being from Minnesota, you'd think I'd be used to below-zero chills in January. But we in Minnesota have a secret. We go from our heated house to our heated car to our heated offices, churches, schools, and grocery stores. The occasional brave few who actually like to leave their homes and get out into the frigid white are equipped with enough artic gear to outfit a sled dog driver mushing the Iditarod.

I'm forming breath rings in the air when Thug returns. He looks back at me, nodding, and I'm feeling like a kingpin. Do my bidding, Thug.

That thought is silenced as Thug nearly takes me out more than once on the highways of Moscow. My stomach is in my throat, and I know this is payback. The Bolshevik class revolting.

We pull into the northern section of town, a poorer section, where two- and three-room shanty-houses still comprise the majority of the neighborhoods. Where New Russians haven't yet bought up and overhauled the land, creating suburbs and sidewalks and cafes and art galleries. I see a central pump in the middle of the dirt street as we drive past the fences with their little square number plaques near the entrances. The houses are painted green or blue, most of them pumping out black coal from the crooked chimneys. A few places have livestock. Cows or pigs. Chickens.

Thug stops in front of a blue house with ornate windows. I did research on the architecture of Russia during my stint here and discovered that the ornate windows were designed to ward off evil spirits. Like the kind that would break a woman and convince her to give up her child, whom she so obviously loves?

I get out and notice that Thug does too. He leads the way up the steps, watching to make sure I don't fall. My hero.

As Thug knocks on the door, my heart fills my throat and I suddenly wonder if this is a good idea after all. Am I prying?

Don't answer that.

The door cracks, and I'm surprised to see Sveta's face. She has a wide face for someone so thin and today her pretty brown hair is tied back in a white handkerchief of some sort. She glances at me and I see panic streak across her face.

"Please, tell her I mean her no harm. I just want to talk."

I hear Thug translate, and Sveta's face relaxes. I smile and she reluctantly opens her door.

The inside of her tiny house smells of mold and coal soot. The walls are wallpapered in tiny red roses. In the entryway, I move to take off my shoes, as is custom, but Sveta reaches out to stop me. "*Nyet*," she says.

I take off the parka and hang it next to a shiny leather jacket and a padded canvas work coat. The disparity between the outside and inside life of a Russian peasant.

Sveta is wearing her own version of scary pants and a bulky sweater that looks homemade. Motioning me into the kitchen (with Thug at my heels), she goes to the stove, as if to prepare tea. Tea is the answer for everything in Russia. Medicinal, social, it provides one something to do when they don't want to face a problem head-on. I think tea consumption might be what got the collective population through seventy years of communism.

"Sveta," I say, glancing at Thug, who has kept his boots, his coat, his hat, and his gloves on, looking like a proper thug. "Can I talk to you?"

Thug translates, and Sveta glances at me over her shoulder. "I just want to help."

Sveta sighs and scoots up a chair, motioning me to sit opposite her at the round table.

"I know about Ryslan," I say. I reach out to cover her hand with mine and find it cold and chapped. "What happened?"

Sveta takes her hand away, folds her arms across her chest. I see pain flash across her pretty face. She glances at Thug, then away and doesn't look at me as she speaks.

I look at Thug for translation.

His voice is low. "She says zat she had no choice. She said zat ven Ryslan vas born, she had to move in here, vith her mother. Her mother is sick, and she needs to spend all her money on medicine. Her mother can't take care of Ryslan, and she can't take him to vork vith her. So she had to take him to zee orphanage."

"Is she planning on getting him back?" My words are soft, and I hope Thug conveys them this way.

He asks, and she answers with a shrug that I feel all the way through my chest. My throat tightens.

"Is she thinking of giving him up?" My gaze doesn't leave Sveta as Thug translates. She closes her eyes as she answers.

"She says zat she can't give him a good home. Zat if a family in America vants him . . . " Thug stops, purses his lips.

And here I thought I had it bad. My husband spending nearly every waking moment in the company of Bambi the

Beautiful. At least, at the end of the day, Chase comes home to me. And Junior.

"What about Ryslan's father? Is he in the picture?"

Thug translates, and for the first time, I see a spark of life in Sveta's eyes. Thug's jaw muscle tightens for a millisecond as she answers him. I see him put his hands in his pockets and fist them.

Interesting.

When he turns to me, his voice is clipped. "She vas married. But her husband left her for another voman during her pregnancy."

Silence thuds between us like an anvil. I hear my own heartbeat and in it, my own fears. I swallow hard, and meet Sveta's eyes.

They are dry. And hard. Refusing to bend. Oh-so Russian. I nod in silent understanding.

"Tell her that I'd like her to come back to work. That I want to help her get her son back. And that I understand."

Thug meets my gaze a moment before he translates. In it, I see something shift, much like the night I gave him the gloves, only this is deeper, more profound.

Sveta lets a beat pass before she answers. "*Ladna*," she says. Okay.

But it's not okay. Because my future has just flashed before my eyes.

run, daphne, run

. . .

I AM THE PROVERBS 31 WOMAN. THE WIFE OF NOBLE Character.

I am worth far more than an entire crate of caviar.

And I'm not even showing my brain cell loss. Much.

I select woolen socks at the market. And type with eager hands. (Helping H plan her wedding from overseas is a daunting and time-consuming task, but that's what we matrons do.)

I am as big as a merchant ship, and bring home food from afar. (Like the International Food Store, which is located two hours away—three subway lines and a bus ride from my house, but it has . . . Oreos! Life is good.)

I get up while it's still dark to go to the bathroom. Again, and again, and again, and then sleep until eleven a.m.

I provide portions . . . er, rations, for my servant girl. (I figure if she cooks for me, she can bring home half for herself, right?)

I consider a field (or at least house plans for our home that will be built on the field including color schemes for Junior's room, and where to put the furniture), and buy it. (Did you know you can apply for an IKEA credit card online? And just because I'm not there doesn't mean I can't ship it home to my parents' basement.)

I set about my work vigorously. Well, maybe not quite vigorously . . . okay, yes, I have a few power naps in my day, but all that online shopping wears a girl out!

My arms are strong for the task. And getting stronger. Or maybe just larger.

When it snows I have no fear of staying home for a week in front of the heater (and a stack of Russian-dubbed movies).

I am clothed with strength and dignity and can laugh—hysterically, the kind that just might get me committed.

I speak with wisdom, like, "Chase, maybe I should accompany you to dinner tonight with Bertha," or "Would you like me to bring you supper?"

Most of all, I do noble things, like bring a plate of peanut butter brownies (thanks to a pre-mixed box Jasmine sent in my pregnancy survival care package) to the mayor of Moscow, in an about-time apology for flooding his apartment. Or hijack Sveta from work and take her out to the orphanage for some sweet time with Ryslan.

In short, I surpass.

Thankfully, *someone* has noticed. Sadly, not Chase yet, but Daphne remarked last week as we visited Luka, again (this time with fluffy white slippers and a hundred-dollar terry robe), that she was amazed at all I do, and she didn't think she'd ever be able to be like me.

Well, you know. Few people can.

Especially since today is February fourteenth . . . and I've decided to surprise Chase with a home-cooked meal.

Yes, I know, fire and smoke. But really, I have this all handled. Might I say . . . *turkey*? That's right. That's me. Turkey Cook.

I can handle pancakes.

When Chase was eight years old, we found him one

Saturday morning sitting outside on our back stoop. I remember seeing him shivering in the early morning frost in his flimsy jean jacket and baseball hat. I wondered why he was over so early. After all, we'd agreed to go biking after lunch, but I had to clean my room first. And we both knew I hadn't a prayer of finishing my side anytime soon. (Whereas Jasmine, of course, lived in a pristine state of cleanliness. I threw laundry on her side just to see her go apoplectic. Isn't that what siblings are for?)

"Why are you here?" I barked as I wrenched open the door.

But when he turned, my words vanished. He had been crying, I saw that much. And hosted a neat shiner. He gave a sort of sad grin.

I opened the door. "We're having pancakes."

He stuck his hands in his pockets as he brushed by me into the kitchen. "I love pancakes," he said. Later, in my teen years, I wondered if he might have meant more by that statement. Now I am sure of it.

Which is why I'm standing at the stove, trying to translate the various baking goods I picked up at the market. Thankfully, I was able to download a recipe, but everything is in metric. I need a hundred millileters of oil. Which is . . . ? Yeah, see, not so easy, is it?

And, to top off my surpass-ity, I found . . . maple syrup! I can't wait to give Chase a touch of Gull Lake.

Probably, he'll bring home roses, because he knows what Valentine's Day means to me. Two years ago, he sent me a package on Valentine's Day all the way from Gull Lake to Moscow, and then surprised me by showing up at my doorstep a few weeks later. But Chase has a history of surprising romantic moments. Like the time he drove five hundred miles to show up for my graduation from college. Or the time he sent me a DVD of *The Princess Bride* (because I became fluent in Bride-Speak and for a long time required everyone to allow me to talk to them in dialogue) for my birthday.

It's not Chase's fault the peanut butter idea is a great hit and keeping him busy. (It's mine, if I can recall correctly.) He's embraced it, diving into the marketing and production and training of peanut butter manufacturers. Yes, he's been gone most nights. And spent a few in the village.

But he's working.

Hard.

Really.

I measure the flour, the salt, the eggs, the oil, and what I assume is the baking powder. But remember, I don't have the Berglund genes, so as I whip it up, I notice small bubbles aren't appearing like they do in Jasmine's pancakes.

Maybe I need more powder? I add more. Sufficiently frothy, I heat the pan with oil and pour in the batter.

A perfectly cooked pancake is a thing of joy and beauty. I flip and stack and soon I have an entire plateful of pancakes. Glancing at the clock, I see it's nearly six-thirty, but Chase is normally late.

It's just a phase. After he found out about the baby, he came home early every night for two weeks. And the fact that it's getting more difficult to see my toes has nothing to do with his sixty-hour weeks.

The sunset over the far-off buildings is glorious tonight. Purple, with streaks of deep-blue and red. I stop for a moment, my hand on Junior. He's taken to moving toward my hand, kicking me as if telling me he knows I'm out here. And I've taken to talking to him. Because, you know, he can't argue with me.

I'm setting the table when the doorbell rings. I have to laugh—the man forgot his key, again.

But it's Caleb. And, from the scowl on his face, I'm sensing all is not well.

"What have you done?" he asks as he brushes by me.

Excuse me? I'm scrounging up an answer—made pancakes, done the dishes?—Yes, I know!— when he rounds on me.

"Daphne broke up with me!"

And this is my fault, how?

Caleb is wearing black hiking boots, cargo pants, and a black parka. Sorta suave for grunge-boy. Although he's been keeping his hair short and frankly looks more like New-York-boy these days. Especially when he paces and runs his hands through said short hair like he's doing now.

"She broke up with you?" I close the door behind him. "Why? And how's that pacing going for you, because you're making me seasick."

He gives me a look and plops down on the sofa, shaking his head. "She says she can't do it."

I'm stymied for a long moment because I don't think he means what I think he means, but still, it sorta sounds like it. *Shame on you, Caleb*. "Well, maybe you should be glad that one of you––"

He gives me a look of disgust. Okay, well, newlywed pregnant woman here with rampaging hormones. Sadly, my romantic moments consist of a jar of caviar and reruns of *Lost*. (All the ones of Kate and Sawyer. I just love the way he calls her Freckles!)

"She says she can't be like you."

Huh? I stare at him, and it's one of those rare times when the words are sucked completely out of my mouth. I know Chase longs for these moments. Again I glance at the clock. 6:45.

"What does she mean, she can't be like me?" I say finally and sit down opposite Caleb.

Caleb shakes his head. "When I told her you were amazing, I didn't mean for her to take it to heart."

Hey! Why not?

"I mean, you are, but she's completely freaked out." He gets up, paces to the window. "She says that if I expect her to be like you, I'll be sorely disappointed and that she can't do that to her, or me. So she broke up with me."

Wait. Let me get this straight. Daphne broke up with Caleb because I'm so awesome? Because I surpass?

Wow. I can't help the grin that emerges from me. I know, I should be feeling Caleb's pain, but really, I knew I liked that Daphne. I recover quickly and put on my compassionate side. Because, you know, I surpass.

"I'm so sorry, Caleb," I say, coming up behind him and patting his shoulder. "I'm sure she's just overwhelmed with . . . well, whatever she thinks you might be thinking."

He turns to me. "I want to marry her. I was going to propose tonight. Valentine's Day." His expression is so wounded I want to give him a little hug.

"Would you like me to talk to her?" I say. I'm such a good mentor. We'll talk, I'll tell her how wonderful marriage is, how incredible it is to be pregnant, what a great future Chase and I have, and she'll sprint back to Caleb's arms.

"Please, Josey, that would be great."

He glances at the phone, and I'm suddenly thinking he wants me to do this right now. I give him a smile. Look pointedly at my stack of pancakes and the two candles.

"Oh," he says. "You're waiting for Chase."

I nod, in a sort of maternal way. (Because I'm practicing.) "He'll be home any moment."

Caleb nods and gives me the most forlorn expression I've ever seen on him. My heart suddenly turns for him. "I'll call her as soon as I can."

"Thanks, Josey," he says. He heads for the door.

The flat is quiet after he leaves. I sit on the sofa and watch the clock. The sun has now set beyond the apartment buildings, and the room is darkening. I lie down, put my hands over Junior. Sometimes I get so tired.

It's nine when I open my eyes again. The flat is dark. Lights from other apartment buildings twinkle like stars. I sit up, my heart thumping in my chest.

And realize the truth. Chase has forgotten Valentine's Day. I rub my eyes, trying to dispel the sleep. Getting up, I sit at the dark table, take a cold pancake, roll it, and dip it in the cold maple syrup.

I nearly gag. It's so salty, I have to run to the fridge and grab a glass of cold water. Whatever I added, it wasn't baking power.

I slump against the fridge, fighting tears as the phone rings. I pick it up on the second ring.

"Hello?"

"Hi, honey," Chase says. "I'm sorry I'm not home yet. Bertha and I had to work late."

Of course you did. I can see him sitting at his desk, his shirt rumpled, his hair mussed. And in my pregnancy-induced thoughts, Bertha is perched on the corner of his desk. Listening. Smirking.

"I'll be home in an hour," he says.

"Don't bother," is on my lips. But the thought right before it is . . . if he doesn't spend the night here, where exactly will he sleep?

"I'll be here," I say, hating myself. When did I turn into a doormat? He hangs up and I cradle the phone to my chest.

I know I should call Daphne. But right now, all I would say is . . . *run*.

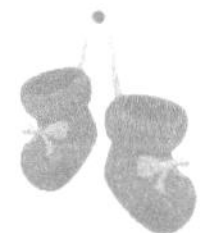

The ride to the Gorkovich orphanage is long. And quiet. Thug in the front seat has more cheer than Daphne.

She won't talk to me. At least not about Caleb. She's been avoiding me for weeks, and if it weren't for the fact that I made Thug drive me to her flat to force her to go to the orphanage, I think she might simply barricade herself in her apartment and eat popcorn.

Now who would do something like that?

I've tried calling. (Especially when I'm in a magnanimous mood.) She simply refuses to talk to me about him, or her, or even me. Especially about me. And how Proverbs 31 I am. A Wife of Noble Character.

I could use some talk about me right now. Because I feel sorta like the weather. Gray. Overcast. March.

Like march right back home to Gull Lake.

I sit back against the seat of Thug's car. He has a little crown air freshener on his dash—very New York cabbie, and it fills the car with a cologne that smells exotic and rich. Thug seems different lately . . . dressing better, clean shaven. It's not like he's skipping or anything, but I've seen a certain jaunt in his demeanor.

Sorta makes me wonder if Thug might have a Thugette in his life.

At least *someone* is getting some romance.

I put my hand on my ever-increasing belly and try not to let it bother me that Chase treats me as if I have the Ebola virus that can be contracted by kisses longer than two point three seconds. The other night I grabbed his hand to put it over Junior, and he yanked it away like I might burn him.

Watch me.

Worse, Chase seems even more distant. Yes, he calls me every day, usually before he's heading home, but it feels as if we're suddenly roommates.

It's not because I'm fat. Or that I can barely tie my shoes. Or that I am wearing the only two pair of yoga pants that fit me. Since January I've ballooned like I might have an entire platoon of little soldiers inside me, and sometimes it feels that way. Marching here and there, over my bladder, up my spine, jockeying for space. And just shoot me, I have over three months left!

Maybe Daphne is onto something with the hiding and popcorn and even the no-men rule.

I glance at her.

"Daph, please, can't we talk about Caleb? He's so heartbroken."

She folds her arms over her chest and looks the other way out the window. "How's the peanut butter thing going?"

Oh, she thinks she's so good. Because I'm bound by my Minnesota nice to answer her. "We're having the kick-off unveiling in a couple weeks. Chase is planning a big party. I'll invite you." I take a breath and dive in again. "Caleb told me why you broke up with him."

She glances at me, her shoulders slumping. "He shouldn't have. He had no right."

"He knows me better than you do. He knows I'm not the person you think I am."

She lifts her gaze to mine, and it's forlorn. "See, you're even humble."

Humble? Okay, maybe a little.

I touch her hand. "You will be a great wife and . . . if you want, mother. You'll do it your way, and Caleb will think you're incredible."

She takes my hand, squeezes it, but doesn't look at me. "But what if Caleb ends up working as much as Chase? What if I'm all by myself, visiting the doctor, or sitting at home making pancakes? I just don't think I could do it." She glances at me. "You're so patient."

Or stupid.

I swallow. "Marriage doesn't have to look like Chase's and mine." In fact, I wish it wouldn't. I wish that Chase would see that this will never happen again—me being pregnant with his child, and him missing it. "It'll look like yours and Caleb's marriage and it'll be perfect." Suddenly, that word—perfect—makes my throat burn. What is perfect, anyway? I turn away.

The car is quiet.

Thug finally turns on the radio. Pugacheva is playing, and in my mind I see Chase at the New Year's Eve party, dancing.

Have I mentioned how ugly March is, with the gray melting snow, the frosty winds that pick up dirt and trash and rancid odors?

We pull into the orphanage parking lot and I pry myself out of the car, ducking into the wind. I can't wait to see my babies.

Daphne heads into the big room with the toddlers while I beeline past Nurse Stalin and into the baby room.

I'm stunned to see three couples, all leaning over the beds of, or holding, my little bundles of joy. I stand there, staring at a woman who looks like she might be my long-lost cousin from Duluth. Short blonde hair, blue eyes, she's all grins as she holds . . . Ryslan?

"Hi," I say, with a hitch in my voice. "Uh . . . who are you?"

"Oh, I'm so glad! Finally, someone who speaks English!" Blondie grins at me then up at the man beside her. He looks like he might play guard for the Timberwolves.

"Clay," he says to me. "And this is my wife, Debbie." He puts his hands on her shoulders. Oh, how sweet. I ignore the gesture and focus on Ryslan.

"Nice to meet you," I say (because, like I mentioned earlier, Minnesotans are bred from birth to respond with some modicum of politeness). "Can I ask what you're doing with Ryslan?" I pronounce it the Russian way, rolling the *r*, turning the *a* into an *ah* sound. Because, you know, he *is* Russian.

"Is that how you pronounce his name?" Debbie wrinkles

her nose. "I don't like it. We thought it was like Reece, plus Aslan, you know, the Narnia lion?"

Debbie dear still hasn't explained how she knows my, or at least Sveta's Ryslan, and her time on this earth is running short. "It's Ryslan. After his father." Which I found out. Poor Sveta. If Chase left me, the last thing I'd ever name Junior would be . . . well, Junior. Something like Peter, or David, something solid and vastly remote from Chase.

Debbie goes white. "You know his father?" Her voice has dropped, and I notice that the two other couples in the room have turned, staring at me like I just told them that I was CIA, undercover.

"No," I say, looking around, sliding a protective hand over Junior. Why do I suddenly feel like I'm treading through a mine field? "I know his mother."

"His mother!" Debbie opens her mouth, and if Clay hadn't been there, she might have completely dropped Ryslan. "How?"

"She's my . . . " Oops. Calling her my cleaning lady suddenly seems so bourgeois, I just can't bear it. " . . . friend."

Debbie's eyes are pinned to me. "You mean you know Ryslan's mother?"

I'm confused, because I thought that's what I just said. But maybe I've lost more brain cells than I think. "Yeah. And she comes once a week to visit her son. I nearly brought her with me today." I don't know why I said that. Maybe it's because I'm feeling hormonal. And Debbie looks about a size four.

Debbie looks at her husband. "Clay, don't let her––"

"I don't think that's a good idea," Clay says to me, towering, suddenly.

I'm not intimidated. (Especially with Thug right outside.) "Yeah, why?" (I'm so having flashbacks of old Godfather movies.)

"Because we don't want Ryslan getting too attached to his mother before we come to get him."

"Come to get him?" My voice has shrilled. But I don't care. Little Sasha in the next crib starts to cry. "What are you talking about?"

Debbie wraps her arm around Ryslan, who's started to wiggle. It's apparent she doesn't know how he likes to be held. "We're his adoptive parents."

Over my pregnant body. (Which makes an impressive barricade, if I do have to say so myself.)

"I think there's been some mistake," I say, but my voice is light, and shaky, and I'm feeling the need to sit down. As if I haven't eaten in an hour. "Ryslan isn't available for adoption."

Clay looks past me, and I follow his gaze. It lands on Nurse Stalin. "Not according to her."

watch josey surpass

. . .

"You don't understand, Chase. There are Americans, here, right now, ready to adopt Ryslan!"

I'm in the hallway of the orphanage, pacing, my cell phone to my ear, trying (although not very hard, I admit it) to keep my voice down. But even Junior is panicked. I can feel him pacing also.

"I just don't know what I can do about it right now."

Okay, here's the thing about male-female communication. Mostly, a woman just wants to hear an, "Oh no, really?" on the other end. We don't actually expect the man to solve the problem. We'll do that ourselves. Eventually. We just want horror, anger. Someone to feel our pain.

"Did you hear me? They want to adopt Ryslan! Sveta's Ryslan!"

"Sveta, our cleaning lady?"

I sigh. One would think that Chase doesn't know much about our life. Then again, Sveta is sort of an ethereal being to him. For all he knows, I could be making her up in my brain-cell-deprived brain. I school my voice. "Yes, Chase, our cleaning lady." I slowly remind him of her situation and how I found her when she disappeared, and then cajoled her to continue to work for us, slipping her extra meals, money, medicines, and the hope that we'd figure out a way to get Ryslan back. "And now it looks like she's going to lose Ryslan anyway!"

I can hear Chase pause, and wonder if he's resting his elbow on his desk, rubbing his eyes with his finger and thumb. "Maybe it's for the best. If someone doesn't want to be a parent, they shouldn't be forced to."

My breath hiccups. What? "She wants to be a mother, Chase. She was *forced* to give Ryslan to the orphanage because her shyster husband left her for another woman!"

"Okay, just . . . keep your voice down. I don't like you getting upset."

Upset? *Upset?* If he wants to see upset, he should have been with me at the last doctor's appointment when I stepped on the scale. Good thing it's in kilograms. "Oh no, Chase, why would I be upset? They're only *stealing* her child––"

"They're not stealing Ryslan. She had to sign papers––"

"Haven't you ever heard of coercion? Adoptions bring in big money for orphanages. Who knows but someone didn't get to her, talk her into trading her baby for money––"

"Listen to yourself. Do you seriously think Sveta was extorted into handing over her child?"

I don't know. Nothing, not even an entire tribe of machete-wielding Mongols, could separate me from Junior.

Then again, I don't have a sick mother to care for. Or a husband who isn't in the picture.

Not yet. I swallow, and again I get that lightheaded feeling. Bracing my hand against the wall, I lower my voice. "I'm sorry I called. I just . . . " needed to talk to someone. "I'll see you when you get home."

"Josey, really, I'm––"

I hang up. Because, well, his words are reverberating through my mind.

If someone doesn't want to be a parent, they shouldn't be forced to.

Like Chase, perhaps?

I swallow hard and lean against the wall, watching the American parents send me surreptitious glances through the window of the baby room. Yeah, I'm probably a little prone to hormonal attacks, but there is something desperately wrong with this situation, and I'm getting to the bottom of it.

I turn and march outside. Thug looks up from book number 517. I motion to him to join me. Which he does. He's such a good Thug.

"Will you translate for me?"

Thug smiles and nods. Finally, a little compassion!

We march in and I arrow straight for Stalin. She's looking especially Communist Dictator today with her dark eyes, the pursed lips, not a hint of flexibility in her stoic expression. She raises one eyebrow.

"Please ask her why Ryslan is up for adoption."

I put my hands on my non-existent hips while Thug glances over at me, a frown on his face. Is he weighing who could hurt him more? I raise an eyebrow to match Stalin's.

Finally, he translates.

Stalin meets my dark gaze and answers. I get some of it. Mother. Six months. Money.

"She says zat all children left hereh by zeir mozers have to pay a small stipend for zeir care. Sveta iz monz behind in her payments. Alzough she hasn't signed zee papers yet, zee director says zat in six monzs, Sveta vill be so far behind, she'll have no choice but to stop her rights. And she vants Ryslan to have a home."

"I thought that the babies could stay here free." I can't ignore the sense of panic burning my throat. Sorta feels like a credit card payment that skyrockets with interest charges each month until the holder is buried in debt.

Only Sveta would be buried in grief.

"The orphanage is so—how to say—vif out money zat zey had to start charging zee parents of zose children kho's rights haven't been terminated by zee state. It's zee only vay zey can feed zee children."

"There are more mothers like Sveta?" I can't help my tone, I'm completely hollowed out.

Thug translates, and for the first time I see humanity in Nurse Stalin's eyes. I understand her answer perfectly. Too many.

I'm speechless for a long moment. (Probably to Thug's great relief.) There are more mothers like Sveta? Who are losing their children because they can't feed them?

I hear a baby cry in the baby room. One of the mothers is trying to soothe Sasha. I swallow the burn in my throat. *Please, Lord, fix this!*

"If we're able to pay Sveta's bill, then Ryslan won't be adopted, right?"

Stalin nods. "Da."

But what about the other women, the other babies? I look at the adoptive parents, and my heart breaks for the longing on both sides of the ocean.

The ride is again long and quiet, even after we drop Daphne off at her flat. Thug seems more pensive than usual, a darkness about his demeanor that is beyond his usual Thugness.

"You okay, um . . . Igor?"

He glances at me in the rearview mirror. I see in his eyes the caring I'd hoped to find in Chase's voice. Hmm.

The flat is dark and quiet when I let myself in. Sveta has been here, evident by the laundry hanging across the living room. In a future life, I will have a dryer. Something that doesn't make my clothes feel like paper as I pry myself into them.

I open the fridge and see cabbage rolls. A wave of

camaraderie rolls over me. Sveta was here, taking care of me and Junior, while I was in Gorkovich, fighting her battles.

However, it seems as if only one of us is going to win. Because, even if I empty my bank account ($5,437.23), it still isn't going to solve Sveta's long-term problems.

I eat a plate of cabbage rolls, then stretch out on my lonely bed, watching Junior move. At first when I saw my skin ripple, as if an arm or leg were pressing against it, my hair stood on end. Now I trace the movement with my hand. "Hey there, little buddy," I say.

If someone doesn't want to be a parent, they shouldn't be forced to.

Chase's mother got pregnant in high school. His father would have made for the state line if it weren't for his father-in-law, who hunted him down and supervised the proverbial shotgun wedding. Chase's dad, who until that time had gone to state twice in track, eked out a living down at the gas company, cleaning tanks and driving trucks. And hating Chase's mother until the day she died.

If someone doesn't want to be a parent, they shouldn't be forced to.

Chaz Anderson Sr. turned to his buddy Jack, as in Daniels, to solve his problems. Chase swore to me when he was about twelve that he'd never drink. Ever. And to my knowledge, he's kept that promise. But I'm wondering, suddenly, if his commitment to WorldMar, his late nights, his sixty-plus-hour weeks might be about something other than making his project succeed. His own method of self-medication.

Tears fill my eyes and I let them flow. I'm not ready for parenthood either. But I wouldn't even consider walking away. (Remember the Mongol horde?) But maybe the initial surprise passed, and reality has taken root. Is there a reason Chase hasn't bonded with Junior? A reason he won't even put his hand on my stomach?

If someone doesn't want to be a parent, they shouldn't be forced to.

Oh no.

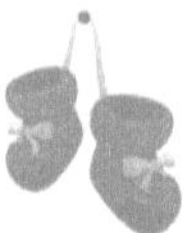

Peanut Butter is not difficult to make. Not that I'm whipping up batches of the stuff at home or anything (I'll leave that to Jasmine), but it's basically peanuts, oil, and varying amounts of sugar, ground together. The tricky parts are roasting the peanuts to the right consistency, and storage.

But even those problems have been solved by my husband extraordinaire. With a smidgen of help from his wife. After three months of waiting, the peanut mill arrived, and, with a "gift" of a couple crates of vodka, made it through customs. In the meantime, Chase and Bambi, er, Bertha, designed labels and formed a marketing plan. They trained the Russian project managers. They procured and designed and remodeled production and storage facilities. And they refined the recipe. (Again, with my help.)

And tonight is our so-called coming-out party. I suggested we hold it somewhere with a lot of children (for example, a school?), but Bertha decided to glam up the event and host it at the Galeria.

I'm already ill as I pull on a tent-dress I found at the maternity shop. There is nothing I can do to make myself look better. I have to simply surrender to the fact that I resemble a rhino. But my mood isn't rhino-like. In fact, I can barely contain my excitement. Especially since Chase came home early, carrying a huge bouquet of red roses.

"You did this," he said to me as he backed me into the corner. And I saw the twinkle in his eye a second before he put both hands on the wall, over my shoulders, trapping me, and kissing me like he did on our honeymoon.

I think I might have been reading too much into Chase's coldness. Because he certainly wasn't cold . . . er, I guess that's too much information. If my instincts are right he's going to be a great dad. *Please let me be right, Lord!*

"Josey, do you know where my new tie is?"

Chase pokes his head into the bathroom and I see that he looks incredible. We went shopping last weekend and found a black suit with a steel-gray dress shirt and a silver silk tie that gives him the suave mafia look without being scary. His hair has decided to betray him, however, and lies in rumpled curls.

"On the bed." Or at least it was. "Maybe under the bed."

"Great." He gives me a wink and I feel something flutter inside me that has nothing to do with Junior.

I finish putting the last curl in my hair, dab on some lipstick, and resign myself to the hard, cold truth that I'm not going to be able to hide in the Congo line. I just hope I don't hear any "I think she's been over-sampling the peanut butter" comments.

Thug drives us. We haven't talked much in the last week since my discovering Sveta's newest dilemma. And when I asked Sveta about it, she simply burst into tears. I sent her home and did the dishes myself.

Moscow is still gray and dull, but here and there, grass is starting to peek through the grimy snow. Overhead, the sky is cloudless and the setting sun over the Kremlin turns Red Square to fire. I'm mesmerized as we drive by, and remember the first time I saw Red Square—a week after I'd arrived in Russia that first time. I found the plaza on my own and congratulated myself on my brilliance.

But that pales in comparison to the Great Peanut Butter Adventure. Chase and I have introduced a new food group to the former Soviet Union! I sit back in the seat and reach for Chase's hand. He squeezes mine and gives me a smile.

The Galeria is again pulsing with pop music, but at least this time it isn't wall-to-wall Russians ogling a gyrating belly dancer.

Instead, it's a few Russians grimacing as I waddle inside and gyrate up the stairs.

Keep your head up, Josey. The fact that I had to ask Chase to help me put on my shoes doesn't have to wreck my evening.

The party is already starting down the hall. Music filters out—American pop, which clashes nicely with the Russian rock downstairs. As we enter, I hear someone shout Chase's name. Bambi is looking smart and curvy in a simple black dress.

"Josey!" she says, air-kissing me. Where, exactly, did she learn that? Because we don't do that in America. Or at least middle-Minnesota America. And Bertha is from Illinois. Which is close enough. "So nice to see you!"

Then she drapes herself around Chase, hanging onto him, laughing. "We did it!"

Um, *we?*

She disentangles herself from Chase, and he again takes my hand as we enter the room to rounds of applause. Bertha, I notice, takes Chase's other hand and bows playfully.

What is it about WorldMar parties that makes me long to leave five minutes after arriving?

At the central table, jars filled with peanut butter are on display, red labels that say, "*Arekhnaya Masla.*" Not a great translation from Skippy, but at least it gets to the point. Butter made from peanuts.

Waiters carrying open-faced peanut butter sandwiches circle the room, and each table is stacked with make-your-own sandwich options—jars of peanut butter and various kinds of breads.

And not one bowl of caviar in sight.

On a far table, an ice sculpture in the shape of a peanut catches the light glinting off the disco ball over the dance floor, which is packed with a gaggle of Underfeds.

Chase catches the eye of his boss and leads me to his table. I see Janet and am surprised that she looks clear-eyed and focused. "Hi," I say, holding out my hand to her. "We met at the New Year's party. Josey Berglund."

She looks at me, frowns. "I'm afraid I don't remember meeting you," she says. Her gaze falls on Jim and Chase, talking together. "You're Chase's wife?"

I nod.

"He did a fabulous job with this peanut butter idea. What a brainstorm. He told me that it was yours?"

I smile at her. "It was mostly Chase's idea." Somehow saying it makes me feel good, but the fact that Chase bragged me up, well, I just might go home with him tonight.

My attention falls on Chase, on the way he's glad-handing the crowd, smiling, occasionally looking back at me. I'm so happy for him I want to sing, or maybe just sit here and quietly hum. But after his hard work, he so deserves this night to be a success.

I hear an announcer, and turn to see Katrina emceeing the event. Cameras flash, and there is at least one shoulder-held camcorder.

"Is that a reporter?" I ask Janet.

"The room is full of them," she says. A waiter walks by and she motions to him. He hands her a glass of champagne.

Uh, maybe that's not such a good . . .

As she takes it, she glances at me. One side of her mouth lifts up. "My last glass of bubbly in Russia. We're leaving next week."

"Oh?" I quirk an eyebrow, one eye on Chase, who's been drawn to the stage with Bertha.

"Jim is being assigned stateside."

I see relief on her face, and I relate to it so well it takes my breath away.

I thought I liked it here.

But, as I see Chase wave to his admiring audience, I know I'm just enduring. Counting the days.

"Congratulations," I say.

She nods. "If Chase's peanut butter idea takes off, they'll probably renew his contract."

Oh, joy.

Thankfully, even if Chase's contract is renewed, we have one very good, and tonight very lively, reason for going stateside in two and a half months. And living there happily ever after. In a two-story colonial I saw online at Carla's realty company.

The clapping has subsided, and I see a waiter bringing a tray with a bowl of peanut butter, a spoon, and bread to the podium. The first taste test!

This is why I came to Russia. To be a noble wife, to see my husband respected and applauded. And in a moment he'll turn to me with those baby blues and in them I'll see the gratitude, the love.

I hold my breath as Katrina takes the spoon. However, instead of scooping it out onto her bread, she plops it in her mouth. Smiling, she looks up at Chase.

And starts to gag.

Her smile vanishes, she drops the microphone, grabs her throat with one hand, Chase with the other.

A few titters ripple through the crowd, but as Katrina tries to swallow, her mouth opening to no noise, the audience begins to gasp.

And when she collapses into my husband's arms, to a storm of flashing lights and Russian garble, I see Chase look up at me, a stricken look on his face.

Woman Killed by Peanut Butter.
Now, you have to admit, I can really surpass.

From: "Josey Anderson"
Josey@netmail.moscow.ru
To: Jasmine Snodbrecher
MJSnodbrecher@rr.mn
Subject: I miss you

Dear Jasmine,

Well, I've done it. Remember when I said I understood God's wisdom in putting me with Chase and sending me to Russia?

Well, not so much, anymore.

First, let me tell you that spring has arrived in Moscow, complete with early lilacs (I'm starting to miss that tree in our yard under our bedroom window), and the occasional crocuses. I can smell the return of life in the air—the fragrances of grass, flowers, even street vendors cooking up fried grease sandwiches, called *Chiboriki*. (We'll work out the recipe when I get home—I'm telling you, there is nothing better than a hot *Chiboiriki!* Well, with the exception of one of your homemade lamb pasties.) All this spring air has made the last month bearable.

Slightly.

First, I look like a hippo. Seriously. And to confirm it, the only time I feel good is in the bath, where I float. On land, I can't see my feet, my back hurts all the time, I can't walk down the street without losing my breath, I sleep about twenty minutes at a pop (in between bathroom breaks), and I think I have varicose veins! I don't get it. We have the same genes, the same body type (almost. Okay, I wish. I don't think "bigger boned" is a nice thing to say about someone), and generally the same eating habits. I mean, you ate *kringle* when you were pregnant, right? Maybe not ten all in one sitting, but still, over time, you consumed the same portion. So why do I look like I'm carrying Hippo Baby? I'm telling you, this kid must be fifteen pounds. I'm humongous. Even Luka (my very hot ER doc) seemed surprised last week at my doctor's appointment. Of course, his solution was to cut down to potatoes and tea.

Just tell me I'm not giving birth to a *Guinness Book* baby. My fear is that they'll measure me when I get on the plane and even if my papers say I'm only eight months along, they'll give me the boot and I'll end up having this baby on an eighteenth-century delivery table in front of half of Moscow, being offered a shot of vodka as pain control.

I wanna go home.

Which brings me back to the Peanut Butter Fiasco. I told you about my/our brilliant idea, right? We had an unveiling party two weeks ago, including press and bigwigs, and wouldn't you know it, but the taste tester was allergic to peanuts! Nearly choked to death in front of a hundred people. She collapsed on stage as her throat swelled and *The Moscow Times* got a great shot of Chase giving her mouth to mouth resuscitation. (That was my favorite part.) Thankfully, one of the Americans—actually, Chase's boss's wife, Janet—carries an EpiPen. Which bought the Peanut Choker enough time for the paramedics to get there. (Good thing she wasn't *dying* or anything. Seems to me that an hour for a fast response team isn't so fast.)

We made every paper in Moscow, plus one in St. Pete, and even the television news for the next two days.

The best part is that Chase's order of two tons of peanuts arrived the very next day. Ready for massive distribution.

No, wait, the best part is that Bertha, to crown the event, told Chase that she thought the idea was a bad one all along and that if he's wise, he'll cut his losses (probably meaning me) and spend every waking moment the next two months coming up with a new idea. (Which, I'm sure she hopes includes sleeping at WorldMar . . .)

Chase, of course, isn't thrilled with this new set of events/adventure/challenges. And although he doesn't blame me, I can see defeat in his eyes. He's mentioned returning to Gull Lake twice and once asked me how hard it might be to clean a pool. Watching my man break before me and not being able to help him is worse than the fact I can only eat a spoonful of caviar in one sitting before getting heartburn. And, deep inside, I have this fear that Chase thinks he'll never be able to support his wife and soon-to-be family. That he'll end up like his father, hating his life.

I have to admit, he's not the only one thinking that thought.

Meanwhile, the orphanage I'm working at (and trying unsuccessfully to raise funding for) has begun a baby-stealing program, and my friend Sveta is one of the victims. And my coworker Daphne thinks I'm so wonderful she's broken up with her boyfriend. (Okay, that didn't make much sense, did it? Well, just to set you straight, Daphne thinks I'm the Proverbs 31 wife, which is so far from the truth it can send me into fits of hysterical, sobbing, get-me-committed laughter. But she can't see it.)

I mentioned hooking up with my ex-grunge friend Caleb again, didn't I? (Daphne's brokenhearted ex-boyfriend who doesn't let a week go by without calling me to tell me just how brokenhearted he is.) Well, the first week I was here, he asked me if God might have sent me to Russia to teach me how much He loves me. Which has me thinking now . . . where's the love?

I've been reading in Ephesians this year, and of late I've been stuck particularly on one line. . . . *to grasp how wide and long and high and deep is the love of Christ, and to know this love that surpasses knowledge . . .*

What does it mean to know a type of love that surpasses knowledge? Does it mean to feel it in our hearts, not just know it in our brains? Because I'm not feeling it. In fact, right now I'm reduced to the Jesus-loves-me-this-I-know-because-the-Bible-tells-me-so kind of thinking.

I don't expect you to have the answers. I've spent a lot of time asking God these questions (in between pleading for Him to fix all this). I just wanted to tell you that I miss you. I wish I were home. Or I wish you were here. Whatever.

Love,

Josey the Hippo

i can fix this

. . .

My life as I know it is over. Because today I discovered that I like Chase's Scary Pants.

Namely, because they are the only thing left that fits me. Scary Pants and an oversized gray T-shirt with Gull Lake Gas and Oil written on the front. But somehow, wearing them makes me feel as if Chase is with me. Sorta. To accentuate my stellar appearance, the hot water has been turned off for the entire city (now that winter is over, so is bathing, apparently) while the Moscow plumbing department works on the pipes. (Little known fact: All utilities—gas, water, sewer, electricity, heat—are run by the city and flow out from one central location. Which means that when the heat or hot water goes off, we all suffer en masse. You can imagine how fun it is to ride public transportation during these times of the year.) I haven't been able to wash my hair this morning (due to the freezing take-my-scalp-off temperature of the cold water). So, I comb back my hair and put on a baseball cap. It's black and white and says Gull Lake Gulls.

At least I'm thematic—Gull Lake Bum. Thankfully, I only have to go out to the International Food Store, where I'm going to scrounge up some Jello for the WorldMar May 9th picnic. May 9th is Russia's "We beat the Fascist Nazis" victory day. I tried once to point out that maybe there might have been a few other countries involved in that world event—for example, England and America. But it fell on deaf ears.

The good news is that the event is *not* being held at the Galeria, but at Gorky Park. During the day. And I'm bringing a Jello salad. With bananas and pineapple. The recipe is on the back of the orange Jello box (and mistakenly listed as dessert), which I read when I bought the red Jello at Christmas. Now, just because half my Jello turned out runny and the other half rock hard doesn't mean I can't make a good Jello salad. I was under stress. I had a turkey to bake (which turned out well, even if we did eat it cold). I can do orange Jello.

The only thing I don't love about this day's activities (aside from my attire) is the fact that every time I go to the International Food Store, not only do I spend about three months' salary (on such things as Lucky Charms, Oreos, and Doritos), but I have to enter through the gauntlet of begging gray-eyed babushki or young children, clothed in the grime of the street. I'd like to give each of them enough to buy bread, but I never seem to have enough rubles to go around.

I slip on my Birkenstocks, which seem to be the only footwear that fit my elephant feet, and ride the elevator down. It'll be a quick ride to the international store with Thug, and in my disguise, no one will even see me. In the meantime, I've run a bath and plugged in the heating coil, draping it in the tub to heat the water. Don't panic—it's supposed to work this way (although yes, I have to admit, the concept does sound contrary to everything I've heard about electricity and water).

I get outside and raise my face to the sun. The sky is blue beyond the high-rises, and I feel a hint of summer in the warm breeze. Only five weeks until we head home, two weeks after Memorial Day weekend. And then another two weeks or a month and Junior is born. What Chase doesn't know is that I contacted Carla and she found us the cutest rental in town, a two-bedroom bungalow overlooking the lake (the colonial was taken). And, I wrote Myrtle, who will let me write freelance from home. Even the pool has an opening, according to the online *Gull Lake Gazette* Want Ads.

And I'm saving this for last—if Chase turns down the pool job, my dad has offered him a job maintaining the grounds at Berglund Acres.

See, everything's going to be just fine. Me, again, surpassing.

I look around for Thug in the lineup of black sedans along the sidewalk. Everyone in the building seems to have a driver today—everyone except me.

Where is Thug? I walk the length of the row. (Okay, I waddle the length of the row. To a few smirks. I'd like to dare one of those men to spend even one day in my body. Then we'll see who's smirking.)

No Thug.

Where is he? Yes, it's not like I've been traveling to and fro much these days. A bi-weekly trip to the orphanage. Another to Daphne's office, although I do a lot of my fundraising letter writing at home. Maybe a trip to the *apteka*, and the clinic (although it's embarrassing to ask Thug to drive a half-block. Okay, maybe not so much), and sometimes to the market.

But today I need him! Then again, how much does a box of Jello weigh? Probably, I can do this. Probably, I need the exercise.

Shoot. I hate opportunities that involve exercise. Casting one last look along the row of cars, I waddle off down the street and descend to the subway.

This time of day, the subway isn't crowded, and I find a seat without a problem. Getting off at the gold ring, I surf over to the purple line, take that to the green line, then get off, walk a half block, and get on a bus.

It's crowded. And hot. And I stand at the back, surrounded by men in short-sleeved shirts holding the overhead bar. Yeah, you get the picture. After the first stop I spot an empty seat. It's a high seat in the back. I beeline toward it, pulling myself up and tucking my bag at my side, since my lap hasn't made an appearance in the last three months.

The bus fills again, and we ride one more stop and pick up more men with short-sleeved shirts.

As the bus takes off again (and I'm about to asphyxiate), one of the men turns to me.

And hands me money.

I stare at it, blinking, confused. I look up at him, at his unshaven face, the sharp scent of vodka . . . and comprehension washes over me.

He thinks I'm The Bus Lady.

Can't he tell that I'm *pregnant*? He might be a bit drunk, and a man, but certainly . . .

"Na," he says, thrusting the money my direction. The bus rolls to a stop, the doors open. He's looking at the door, nearly frantic.

Fine. I swipe the money from his hand and he dashes off the bus.

I am staring at the five-hundred-ruble note (about fifty cents in real money), when another man hands me his fare.

I'm suddenly seeing the golden lining. By the time we reach my stop, I've collected roughly two thousand rubles.

I exit the bus and head down the street to the international store. Lined up outside is the collection of beggars. I gladly fill their outstretched hands with the windfall of the day.

Entering the food store, I have just enough left in my pocket for the Jello and maybe a package of Oreos. Pulling my cap down low (because the official attire of the IFS is a mink jacket, black pants, spike heels, and the aroma of mafia money), I shuffle down the French food aisle. Where, of course, the Jello is shelved.

Finding the package (they've helped the average international consumer by pasting Russian directions over the French, which probably attributed to my less-than-successful attempt at Christmas), I am beelining to the cookie aisle when I pass a display. Of watermelon.

Watermelon! I have yet to see a watermelon in Moscow. Ever. And they're on sale! Watermelon is summer and beaches and barbeques and Gull Lake and Chase and I having a seed-spitting contest, recapturing our youth.

Without a second thought, I grab a watermelon and head to checkout. I have just enough left for bus and subway fare. But the watermelon won't fit into my bag, so I have to heave it under my arm as I trudge back to the bus.

I get on the bus at the front this time, and the crowd separates like the Red Sea for me and my watermelon. A young lad arises (not to call me blessed, sadly) to give me his seat. I have to cradle the watermelon in my arms until we reach the subway stop.

The waning afternoon hours have brought out the crowds, and the subway is full as I surf back to the purple line, then the gold line. By the time we've reached the blue line, I hate the watermelon. It is the bane of my existence, with its propensity to want to rocket out of my arms at every stop, and I swear it's gained ten pounds (that's less than five kilos, though, which sounds a lot better at the doctor's office) since leaving the store. I wonder if it's pregnant?

But no one will be allergic to watermelon (I hope) and frankly, now that I'm committed, *I* need the watermelon. I need normalcy and fun and a reason to drag my body out of bed. I might be just a little addicted to food for happiness, but right now, food is all I have.

It's my friend.

It doesn't stay out late, or embarrass me by dancing with other women. It doesn't decide to disappear (unless I choose so) when I need it, and it would never mistake me for a bus lady. In fact, it fights my battles (case in point, Katrina's near-death experience. Let that be a lesson!).

I will get this watermelon home if I have to drag it and my exhausted body down every street in Moscow.

I exit the subway, holding the watermelon in front of me like a load of wood. Get on the escalator. Three thousand stories later, we reach street level. I fix my eyes on the pink apartment building set before me and trudge home.

Kids are out of school. They race by, laughing, jostling each other. If even *one* of them bumps me . . .

A car lays on its horn beside me and I jump, nearly upsetting my package. But I'm too quick, too steady. A dog leaps at me and its owner pulls it back on its leash. I smile and nod at her. Nice try, honey.

Sweat runs down my back, which is shooting pain from my tailbone out to every cell in my body. I nod to the gatekeeper, who barely looks up from his paper. No, don't help the fat bus lady.

Crossing the parking lot, I am home free. I glance once more to see if Thug has returned. No.

And, as I look back, I misjudge the obscured step below me.

The watermelon flies from my grasp as I brace myself for the fall. I hear the sickening sound of fruit splatter as I go down on my hip, saving Junior, spraining my hand and rolling to my back.

I hate my life.

I lay there a long moment, looking up at the sky, reeling, checking to see how many places hurt. A shadow slants over me. "Zhozhsy?"

I blink, and recognize my neighbor, the mayor of Moscow. He holds out his hand. Wiping a tear that's escaped, I take his hand and he pulls me (with some effort and unnecessary grunting) to my feet.

"*Fso normalna?*"

No, everything's not okay! Don't you see the broken dreams splattered in pink and green and black all over the sidewalk? My arms are trembling and I can't speak as more tears form. I shrug.

"*Eedee soodah*," he says, his eyes kind. Come this way.

Broken, I head inside, up the elevator, and let him usher me to his flat. Mrs. Mayor greets me at the door. "*Shto sluchilas?*"

I tell her what happened. I fell. With a watermelon. But Mayor is already explaining that to her. She gives me a sympathetic look. Points to the baby. "Maybe . . . doctor?"

So relieved to hear English, I get my hopes up. "No, I'm okay, I went to the doctor last week. I think––"

She's wearing a glazed look.

"*Fso normalna*," I say. Everything's just fine.

She smiles. And then disappears into the kitchen, returning with my baking pan. Oh yeah, the peanut butter brownies. "*Vkoosna*," she says. Tasty.

"*Spaceeba*," I say back. See, peanut butter. It's an all-around happy thing, for people who know how to use it.

Who know how to use it? Hmm . . .

The Mayors let me out, and I climb the stairs to my flat. Inside, the place is quiet and clean. I check the fridge. Sveta has left a cucumber salad and salmon cakes.

Dumping my purse on the counter, I head for the bathroom. Unplug the heater. Test the water. It's a perfect temperature.

This day may end okay after all. I swirl the water to combine all the temperatures then go to my room for my robe. Undressing, I throw Scary Pants in a corner, strip off the shirt, and grab a towel. It covers roughly half of me.

Heading back to the bathroom, I stop by the kitchen to grab

a glass of juice. Chase found apple juice in his office-building mall and brought it home. Since when does he have time to shop?

The sun is low and sinking into the horizon. I stand for a moment, drinking my juice, watching the sky turn orange, then red, then dark as the day surrenders. It occurs to me that my day, even this year, is like the sunset. Turning from bright and cheery to dark and scary until I surrender.

I turn and enter the bathroom. I must have dislodged the plug, because I'm just in time to watch as the last of my perfect water swirls down the drain.

"Maybe you're too tired to go." Chase is leaning against the door frame, his arms folded, wearing a white T-shirt, a pair of jeans, and leather sandals. I hate him for his cuteness and the fact that I can't even pry myself off the bed to go over there and kiss him. Which I wouldn't anyway, on account of his accusations.

"I'm not tired." Just because I nod off at all hours, including yesterday during church, does not mean that I'm tired.

"Well, you're certainly crabby."

That's it. I'm going to the Victory Day party even if it kills me. And if it does, I'll haunt him until he realizes that my death was all his fault. I sit up, groaning as I push myself off the bed. Chase comes over to help and I slap at his outstretched hand. "I'm not an invalid!"

He raises his cute eyebrows and dares to look surprised. "I'm just—"

"Don't–" But I'm falling back, so I grab at his arm,

balancing myself as I find my footing. He smirks. "Not a word," I snap.

He wisely keeps his mouth shut as we head toward the door. While I slip into my Birkenstocks, he retrieves the orange salad from the fridge. So far, it looks okay. I dissolved the sugar extra long. And translated the directions, just to make sure.

Chase holds the door open for me. I feel as wide as a Zamboni as I get in the elevator and ride down. Gorky Park is only a half block away but I'm already sweating as we exit the building. The air smells of summer, and I hear loud music pulse from open windows. In Red Square the military will have rolled out their Katusha rocket launchers, a tank or two, and representatives of every military branch. The square has been barricaded for days, and it would take about five hundred dollars and an edict from Putin to get us foreigners past the gates. After a few speeches (including one by Putin), they'll sing the Russian national anthem. It's a tremendously patriotic event and always makes me homesick for America.

The WorldMar group is gathered in a grove of aspen trees. Someone has spread out blankets, and even found a table. Chase sets the Jello salad down on the table then greets his adoring audience of Underfeds, who are wearing shorts so short they just might be illegal. And someone needs to tell them that see-through blouses require *some* sort of undergarment. I avert my gaze and look for Janet. Then remember that she and Jim shipped home.

My ally is gone. Even a sloppy drunk ally is better than none.

I sigh, go and sit by a tree. Lean my head back. Close my eyes. I'm counting the days now. Forty-three. And two hours.

"Josey, are you okay?"

Chase. He's kneeling in front of me, concern on his face. I'm so surprised to see him that I'm blinking. "Uh, I'm just feeling tired."

Little does he know it is an adjective that describes my life. My pregnancy. Our marriage. I smile at him, but it doesn't touch my eyes. I've done everything I can think of to hear the words Noble Wife. I've been Supportive. Long-suffering. And Hopeful.

Now I just feel defeated.

"Do you want to do something?"

Again, I just stare at him, those words not registering. As if he senses my discomfort, he looks away, and I see a pained expression. Oh, Chase. Have we drifted this far apart that we can't even find anything to do together on this beautiful sunny day?

I glance past him and spot the giant Ferris wheel. "I want a ride," I say quietly.

Chase follows my gaze, then smiles, reaching out his hand.

Helping me up, he leads me out of the picnic area and along the sidewalk. "Can we slow down?" I ask.

He flushes. "Sorry. Of course."

We're holding hands. Old feelings rush at me, the ones I've been trying to deny these past few months. This is how I imagined Moscow. Walking with Chase on a beautiful day.

A line jags out from the Ferris wheel, curling around the metal barriers and out onto the sidewalk.

"It's a pretty long line," I say, eyeing it. And thinking about my feet. My back. My bladder.

"It'll be okay," Chase says, and pulls me into the line. Maybe he didn't get that subtle hint. He smiles, but it's an odd, non-Chase-like grin.

We stand there in silence, watching passengers embark, go round, disembark. I let go of Chase's hand, lean on the metal barriers. Stretch. Shift from foot to foot.

Check my watch.

The Ferris wheel has a periodic screech that sends my teeth to clenching. Around me, I smell hotdogs, cotton candy, popcorn. My stomach has awakened, or maybe that's Junior, but something is calling for food. And then Junior sits on my bladder.

We're only halfway in. Chase is sweating, but he's still wearing the funny smile.

"Are you sure?" I ask again. "You look hot." Again, a hint.

Chase glances at me. "I'm okay."

Shoot! Just say it, Josey. But between us I feel a gulf that is not unlike Siberia. Cold. Impenetrable.

Ten minutes later we are at the loading gate. The attendant—a guy who could double for my uncle Bert except in a sweaty button-down shirt and pair of polyester pants—is about to unlatch the gate when he spies me. And my stomach. "*Nyet.*"

Nyet? My eyes are round, but Chase fills in for my silence.

"*Nyet? Potcheemoo?*"

The fact that he's learned enough Russian to understand the attendant's explanation stuns me. What else don't I know about Chase?

Don't answer that.

"What do you mean 'she's too pregnant?'"

Oops, I guess that's the extent of Chase's fluency. I glance at him, and I've never seen this Chase before. Red-faced, anger in his eyes. "Listen, pal, we're getting on that Ferris wheel!"

"Chase, I––"

He glares at the man, who is glaring back at him. I'm seeing international incident and I tug on Chase's arm.

He yanks it away from me. "Josey, you want a ride on that Ferris wheel. You're getting a ride."

He's announced that at a volume they can probably hear in Red Square. Over the reverberation of the rocket launchers. Then, as I watch, trying to figure out what happened to my quiet, sweet Chase, he digs into his pocket and pulls out a wad of rubles. "Here!"

The stunned operator, being savvy as well as underpaid, takes the money. Opens the gate.

"After you," Chase says, his voice suddenly morphing into knight in shining armor. I gulp, offer the attendant an apologetic smile, and climb on the Ferris wheel.

To be fair, there might have been a reason I wasn't allowed the ride. Because the bar barely clears my immensity. "Chase—"

He puts his arm around me. "'Bout time we spent some time alone."

Oh. The Ferris wheel lurches forward. And in a moment, we're rising above Gorky Park.

The view steals my breath and everything horrible about the last thirty minutes. In a way, it even resets the past six months. The canvas of Russia is beautiful. Lush trees, apartment buildings, a sparkling Volga River with paddle boats, Red Square filled with people.

"Looks a lot better from this perspective," Chase says, echoing my thoughts.

I nod. "Wish I'd seen this in winter. I'll bet it was gorgeous."

Chase looks at me, and again I see that pained expression. "GI, I need to talk to you about something."

Something in his tone turns my hands slick on the bar crunching Junior and me. "Sure."

He sighs, and looks away from me.

"I'm a terrible husband."

I watch small people paddle boats on the Volga.

"I didn't think it would be like this, GI. I thought . . . well, I thought somehow I'd be better at being married."

I see a family buying cotton candy. The husband, dressed in a black short-sleeved shirt and black pants, delivers the pink fluff to his daughter. She grins at him, and the wife gives him a kiss. Nice.

"I guess maybe it's the pregnancy thing. It threw me." He

glances at me. I don't meet his eyes. "I always wanted kids, but . . . I keep thinking . . . what if I turn out like my dad?"

I knew it. Did I say this? I did. And now that we know I was right, we can deal with the problem. I look at him, and I'm not sure whether to hit him or feel sorry for him.

"You're not your father, Chase."

He clenches his jaw, turning away. "I just . . . I'm failing at my job, and I can't seem to make you happy. You'd think a guy who studies people could figure out how to make you happy."

Happy would be you coming home each night. A guy doesn't need a textbook to figure that out. As if he reads my mind, he sighs. "I'm sorry I haven't been around much this year."

I'm waiting for him to say he'll do better, but it doesn't come. And I can't absolve him. Because I wouldn't mean a word of it. And, probably with me way up here in the air, God can see me.

"I just wish I could fix this."

Fix what? Him not loving me anymore? Or the fact that we're going to be parents? Or this entire abysmal year? Is Chase apologizing? Or setting me up for the "I'm leaving" punch line? Oh please, God, don't let me end up like Sveta!

"I just miss home," I say softly, probably so softly he doesn't hear me.

We ride in silence until the Ferris wheel finally brings us around the final time, then lurches to a stop at the bottom. The attendant lets us out.

"*Fso Normalna?*" he asks me. I see real concern in his eyes.

Yeah, everything's fine.

Chase reaches for my hand as we meander back to the picnic. I don't take it. Instead, I latch my arms around my stomach.

I can smell hotdogs as we get closer. We're not allowed to cook in Gorky Park, but someone has hired out a hotdog vendor. He's loading in the dogs while others are edging up to the tables, filing their plates with potato salad, chips, pickles, and orange Jello. An all-American meal.

"Want some food?" Chase asks.

I nod, then search the crowd for empty blanket space. I find a corner next to a woman who looks a lot like Halle Berry. Short dark hair, with a skin tone I've only dreamed about. She's sitting with her hand perched on her stomach.

I recognize the gesture. "Hi," I say. "Josey Anderson." I don't add that I'm Chase's wife, because, well, I'm not sure how we feel about that at the moment.

"Maggie Calhoun," she says. Her beautiful brown eyes twinkle. "I see you're a few months further than I am."

"Oh, I hope so. I have two months left, though."

She doesn't say anything, but I see surprise on her face.

"Yeah, I know. My doctor isn't too thrilled with my size either. Says I should eat only pickles and potatoes."

Maggie laughs. "I just got in town a week ago. Can you recommend a doctor?"

Let's see. Can I recommend Luka? He's patient, and is used to my quirky ways, like insisting he use the *real* stethoscope to listen to my baby's heartbeat. (Although, he keeps trying the stethoscope Socrates used. I don't think I'm getting through.) "I go to a Russian doctor near my house. But I've heard there's an international clinic on the south side of town. I'm not going to deliver here, so I figured it would be okay to go to a Russian doctor."

She gives me a grin. "You're brave."

That's one word choice. I pat my belly. "So far so good. Women have babies all the time in Russia, right?"

"That's what I keep telling Dalton, but he's still worried." She glances behind her, at a tall, good-looking, dark-skinned man who's talking to Chase. "It's our first. I keep telling him I'll be fine."

"Does Dalton work for WorldMar?" I'm trying to catch Chase's eye, because I see he's holding a plate, and I'm suddenly desperately ravenous. Please let that food be for me.

"He's taking over Jim Wilke's place as director."

"Have you ever been to Moscow before?" I wave at Chase. Not even a blink in my direction.

"I've lived in Moscow for three years—Dalton and I met here. He was working with a WorldMar sister organization. We went stateside for our first year of marriage."

What a novel idea. I think, perhaps, Chase and I might have this thing backwards.

"What did you do here?" I'm picturing her as some sort of cosmetic representative. Or a buyer for some fashion line. I raise my voice. "Chase?" Nothing.

"I was with the state department." She follows my glance, then looks at Dalton. Of course, he sees her. Starts walking this direction. At least Chase is following. "I helped humanitarian organizations qualify for grants."

My appetite vanishes. "Would that include orphanages?"

"Especially orphanages," she says, getting to her feet. I'm insanely jealous at the ease with which she does this. "They are some of our main clients."

"Is the program still going on?"

Dalton reaches her, hands her a plate of potato salad. "Of course."

And just like that, as if the clouds have parted and I heard a voice of out heaven, I know the answer.

Chase hands me my plate of food. And I smile up at him. Because things are going to be okay.

the perfect day

. . .

I FEEL LIKE A COVERT OPERATOR. LARA CROFT. WELL, A VERY large and cumbersome Lara Croft, but still, the sentiment is there. And, it must be spring, because I've found a new burst of energy, probably in storage from March and April. I've spent the last three weeks alongside my partner in humanitarian aid, Maggie Calhoun, and our sidekick Daphne, putting together the event of the year.

I intend to surpass.

I started by baking peanut butter cookies for the mayor. (Okay, Maggie, Daphne, and even Sveta assisted. Okay, fine! I supervised. And taste tested. But it was my contact with the mayor that gave us the inside connections.) The Mayors loved the cookies, and I convinced them (along with Thug, who ironically used to drive for them, before they were the Mayors) to write a letter of recommendation. Then, taking the letter, I approached Luka with another plate of cookies. He was so taken with the cookies, he forgot to use the wooden mallet thingie on me, and let me go with only a sigh to register my weight gain. (I didn't mention the increasing back pain. I'm attributing it to the fact I can't sleep without a congregation of pillows. Even if Chase wanted to touch me, he'd have to scale the Everest of fluff around me. But he's either not interested or he's afraid to touch me. I wonder if he thinks I might explode. I certainly feel like it.)

After talking Luka into also writing a letter of recommendation, Maggie and Daphne and I made yet a third batch of peanut butter cookies, as well as sandwiches, and pitched the idea to Nurse Stalin and her Director. The icing on the proverbial peanut butter cake was my offering to write the grant needed to secure funding from the state department's program. Which sailed through committee in record time. (Methinks I have my partner to blame for that one. See, Pregnant Women, even with their loss of brain cells, still know how to solve the world's problems.)

Meanwhile, Daphne invited all the orphanage directors who work with her organization to a Peanut Butter Party. At our orphanage. Where we'll serve milk and cookies and peanut butter and jelly sandwiches. (I need to interject here that there is a reason vegemite isn't popular in America. Because grown-ups want grown-up food . . . and kids don't like vegetables. The key is to focus on the target market.)

Caleb helped us design and produce a media packet complete with nutritional information and the two letters of recommendations. Which was a challenge since Caleb is still pining for Daphne, and, short of falling apart and proving that I'm a total mess, I can't convince her that she doesn't have to be perfect to handle marriage. I guess I'm a hard act to follow.

Sveta, now a seasoned peanut butter cookie chef, has made twenty-four dozen cookies.

All this I did in secret, not wanting Chase to think I was, well, taking over his job. But, well, I'm taking over his job. Because I'm a mother. (Even if I haven't actually *seen* Junior yet.) And we mothers know that peanut butter is a mom's best friend. But it hasn't been easy keeping all this from Chase because he's suddenly decided to come home at night. Even if he doesn't massage my feet or sleep with his arm around me, I know he's trying. And that makes my idea that much more delightful.

I finally asked Chase to give Thug the okay to retrieve the jars of prepared peanut butter still in storage in Gorkovich. I told him I wanted to use them for a good-bye party at the orphanage.

I've been seeing our perfect day for weeks now, ever since Maggie sat down beside me on the blanket. I plan to ask Thug to collect Chase (I'm going to pretend to be in labor—he'll be completely fooled!) and bring him to the event, where he'll see not only fifty kids eating (and loving) his peanut butter, but the mayor of Moscow (whom he met in his underwear) will personally congratulate him on his swell idea. And then the director will sign a contract for a monthly supply, which will prompt every other orphanage director in the region to follow suit.

The peanut butter factory will be in the black, and Chase will be a hero. And amidst the applause and laughter, he'll see.

I am a Noble Wife. A wife he needs, who can follow him to the ends of the earth and still be his perfect helpmate. A wife with whom he can face the perils of parenting.

All I have left to do is paint my toenails.

I'm sitting on the bed, trying to figure out where my feet are. I know I've seen them in the last couple months. Somewhere. I try about three different positions, all to no avail.

And my back is killing me. Sharp pains are shooting out from my tailbone, down my legs. And Junior is doing somersaults—complete half-gainers inside my stomach.

But summer scents buoy my spirit. Outside, Russia is lush and green, lilac trees heavy with purple flowers, jasmine in full bloom, releasing its delicate fragrance into the air. Overhead, the sky is a perfect blue, and as I pull on my sleeveless tent-shirt I found at the maternity shop, and a size XXXXXXL skirt with an elastic waist, I refuse to listen to the voices of doubt.

This is going to be a perfect day.

The doorbell rings. I roll over and back off the bed, pushing myself to a standing position, then work my way to the door, grimacing with each step. Daphne stands at the door, all grins. She's looking cute in a pink shirt-dress and pigtails.

"Come in," I say, holding the door open. "Can you do me a favor?"

Daphne nods, putting her bag down on the kitchen table.

"Do I have feet down there? Because I'm not sure."

She laughs. "Yes. Although they're probably a little more pudgy than you remember. Would you like me to paint your toenails?"

I knew it, she's an angel. All this pedestal talk this year was to keep me from throwing myself off the balcony. "Really?"

She glances at the clock. "We have time. Sit down." Going to the bedroom, she grabs the polish. "You want this passion-red stuff?"

It seems like the closest I'm going to get to passion anytime soon. "Yeah."

She returns and kneels in front of me.

"You're an incredible friend," I say to her. "I wish you were going stateside with me."

She grins up at me. "How many days left?"

"Ten. But I'm ready to leave tomorrow."

"No, you're ready to have this baby tomorrow. You'll miss Russia."

I lean back, pondering that. My Russia experience this time hasn't been at all the victory of my last experience. Or maybe it has, in a different way. I will miss subway surfing, *Chiboriki* on the street, Ryslan and my other babies. Lilacs for sale from corner vendors, and Luka's rolling eyes every week as I get on the scale.

"Yeah, maybe I will. But I'd do just about anything to see a friendly face from home."

Daphne nods as she finishes. "Okay, don't move for ten minutes."

"We don't have ten minutes." I push up from the sofa, grab at Daphne, who pulls me the rest of the way. "Just help me slip on my sandals."

Daphne works on my Birkenstocks while I massage my back. Then, grabbing my keys and our bags, she opens the door and locks it behind us.

Thug is waiting downstairs. He's got the windows open and is reading the paper. "Allo," he says, smiling. I love the way his eyes seem to have warmed over the year, and especially this past month. Methinks Spring Fever has bit Thug.

"After you drive us to the village, you'll return for Chase, right?" I settle in the seat, careful not to smudge my toes. Only, for all I know, I've got polish all over my legs, my sandals, and the interior of his car.

"*Da.*" He puts down the paper and soon we're on the highway, the wind in my hair, looking at the houses of the Russian suburbs. The new construction is so rife with old-time Russian values of stately columns, ornate cornices, sprawling buildings. Every house looks like it should belong to Alexander Pushkin.

As we pull up to the orphanage, I see Maggie setting up for the party, putting the pre-made sandwiches cut into festive shapes and the dozens of cookies on tables in the front yard. A gentle breeze plays with the tablecloths. Maggie is adorably elegant in her green pullover sleeveless top and green capris. She carries her baby like a little basketball. Why, oh, why do I have to have a manatee's body?

She greets me with a hug. "How are you feeling today?"

I wrinkle my nose in answer.

She laughs. "I have some news that might make you feel

better," she says. She lowers her voice and brings Daphne into the circle. "Dalton let Bertha go today."

"Go? Go where?" Daphne asks.

I love the fact that sometimes Daphne is more ditzy than I am.

"What happened?" I ask.

Maggie's eyes sparkle. "He found her in a "compromising" position with one of the employees yesterday. And it was apparent that she was the aggressor, if you know what I mean."

My eyes widen, and for some reason my throat turns raw. "Who was it?"

She lifts a shoulder. "One of the other consultants. He wouldn't say who."

I feel lightheaded, and immediately chastise myself. "Was he one of the married men?"

Maggie's smile dims. She nods. Then shakes her head. "Marriages are so difficult to keep together, especially overseas."

Beside me, I see Daphne go white. "I have to go inside," she mumbles.

I watch her go. "Did Dalton let the man go also?"

Maggie turns back to the cookies and sandwiches. "Of course. In fact, I think they're both leaving on today's flight." She looks up at me. "I thought you'd be happy that she's no longer Chase's partner."

I am. I *so* am.

Unless, of course . . .

I smile at her. "Great job on these cookies. Do we have enough napkins and cups?"

Maggie nods, and Daphne and I go inside to check in with Director Stalin.

But my mind isn't on the events of the day. Chase wouldn't leave me for Bertha, would he? He's been so nice this month, but maybe it's an act, something to assuage his guilt.

Suddenly I just want to see Chase, to throw myself in his arms. To remind myself that at the end of the day, I have a husband and everything's going to be okay.

I'm bringing tea outside (because even if it is three thousand bazillion degrees outside, we in Russia still drink our hot tea) when I see the mayor arrive. I greet him and Mayorette, thanking them in my broken Russian for their time. Luka arrives on their tail. He's wearing a pair of dark pants and a white dress shirt. He grins at me and I introduce him to the mayor. That certainly can't hurt his future.

See, someday people will be glad they know me.

Orphanage directors begin to arrive, and with them, some media that Maggie has invited. *Oh, please, Lord, don't let anyone choke.*

I'm keeping an eye out for Chase, but Thug hasn't returned. I do see Sveta, however—helping Maggie hand out cookies. Every time I've asked about Ryslan in the past month, she's dodged my question.

I decide to ask Nurse Stalin. As I'm heading back to the baby room, I see the teachers lining up the toddlers. They look clean and obedient in their blue tights under shorts, long-sleeved shirts (I should be glad they're not still dressed in snowmobile suits), and play shoes. They're so adorable, my heart turns to oatmeal.

Stalin looks up at me and gives me the barest of smiles. "*Zdrastvootya*," I say in formal greeting, but I don't stop.

Until I get to the room. And see that Ryslan's crib is empty.

Empty.

I'm staring at it when Stalin comes up behind me. "*On oshol s'rodeetalmee.*"

He left with his . . . parents?

My mouth opens and for a long time I simply stare at his bed, realizing the ache that centers right on my sternum.

Outside I hear laughter, and even applause as the children file outside. Soon they'll eat the cookies Sveta prepared.

She prepared them knowing her child would never benefit.

My eyes burn. Nurse Stalin is smiling now, and all at once I know exactly how people felt during the communist years, when people they loved vanished without a trace. I knew the woman was trouble, and suddenly I have this absurd urge to wallop her.

To wallop anyone.

I turn and brush past her, outside, trying to get a check on the sudden rush of emotions. I've moved too quickly, however, and my back spasms. I have to brace my arms against the wall and breathe deeply.

"Josey?"

Daphne looks worried as she comes up to me. "Are you okay?"

I take a step back, stretch. "Just a back spasm. I'm okay. Is everyone here?"

She nods. "Maggie introduced the mayor, and he's congratulating Director Ivanka on her innovative approach to nutrition. The kids are eating sandwiches. And the orphanage directors are all enjoying cookies and milk. I think you have a hit on your hands."

I swallow, and can't keep myself from asking. "Is Thu—Igor back?"

Her smile dims. She nods.

I can't wait to see Chase's face. I'm about to go find him, when her hand on my arm stops me. "What?"

She shakes her head. "Chase isn't here."

I stare at her a long moment, uncomprehending.

"Chase wasn't at his office."

I frown. "Where is he? Did someone try to call him? Maybe he's here in the––"

"Igor asked. Chase went to the airport."

The noises around me feel sharp, and too loud. I swallow, running her words through my head. I swallow again.

"The airport?" My voice sounds tinny. High.

"Josey . . . " Daphne's voice is soft, but it feels like a razor on my nerves.

"I see," I say.

Taking a deep breath, I go back out to the yard. Lean against the house as I watch the festivities. The children have prepared a song. They line up, and sing. Their sweet cherub faces make everyone cry. I push my fingers into my lower eyelids, pushing back tears.

Why, God? I thought You loved me. The thought stings my heart, biting down, refusing to let go.

Especially when the mayor announces my name and says some nice things about me. (Although I can't understand them, I can see affirmation of his words on Maggie's face. Even Thug is smiling.) Apparently, someone is rising up to call me blessed. But, of course, Chase isn't here to see it. I smile and wave and say, "*Spaceeba*." But really all I want to do is go home and take a bath. I don't care if the water is the temperature of the polar icecap.

The kids disperse to play and the directors clump in conversation. Maggie is busy talking with the mayor (of course), so I wander around the back of the orphanage, near the gardens, the budding potato and cabbage plants, to be alone with my pain.

I think I hate Chase. I can't believe, after all this patience, all my hard work, he'd leave me. For curves.

I have curves. Just in the wrong places. What was all this be-nice-to-Josey stuff this past month—a decoy? Pity?

Merciless to my agony, my back again spasms. I beeline for a bench and lower myself, holding my back.

And from this position, I can see Thug and Sveta in a torrid embrace under the budding apple tree. Wow. Apparently Thug isn't nearly as stoic as I pegged him. Or maybe Sveta just brings it out in him.

I am caught like a deer in headlights and before I can shake myself free, Thug spots me. He whispers in Sveta's ear and she turns to look.

I wave. Hi. It's me. The peeping Josey.

Then, to my surprise, Thug reaches for Sveta's hand. They walk toward me, smiling, swinging their hands.

The sun is sharp and bright and I wince as it glints off something . . . on their fingers? I stare dumbly at the gold band on Thug's right hand. Now, why didn't I notice that earlier?

Methinks someone's been a little too self-absorbed.

"*Vwe Zheneelas?*" I ask them. I can't believe they got married. And didn't tell me! When did this happen?

Sveta smiles and answers my unspoken question. "*Mesitz nazad.*"

A month ago? My mind travels back to the Day of the Watermelon. Thug's strange absence.

And then it occurs to me. Ryslan's *parents*, Nurse Stalin said. My throat feels like wool and I barely make out his name.

Sveta nods, then turns and kisses Thug. He grins at me, flushing slightly. "*He's vif my mozer during the day.*"

Ryslan has a grandma!

Getting up, I fling myself at both of them. And I'm so utterly thankful that *someone* is happy, I start blubbering.

Sveta has someone with whom to share the joys, the struggles, the parenting.

We stand there a long moment, but my blubbering doesn't cease. In fact, it sounds, even to me, like I might be losing it. Thug notices and leaves me in Sveta's embrace.

Sveta says nothing as I sink to the ground, feeling the cold soil seep into my legs. I put my hands over my face, but I can't stop crying.

"Josey, are you okay?"

Sveta eases me back (and the fact I've soaked her shirt is not lost on me). I look at Daphne, who has been fetched by Thug. "No. I'm not okay!" My words come out in stages, between huffs of breath. "Chase left me!"

Daphne's jaw goes tight and I can see her struggle with denying it. "Why would he do that?" she asks quietly. Oh, good counseling response, Daph. But she knows the truth, and I glare at her.

"Because I'm a mess. I'm fat––"

"You're pregnant."

"I'm fat! Even Luka thinks so. And I can't cook. And Chase doesn't want to clean pools all his life, and people shouldn't be forced to be parents!"

Sveta takes my hand, but Daphne is staring at me, horrified.

"Yeah, that's right!" I snap. "I'm not the perfect wife. I don't get up early, or cook for my family, or even make footies for Junior. I eat caviar and shop online and sit at home blaming Chase for my misery!" My words end in a sort of shriek that scares even me. Daphne is still staring.

Oh, go away. "I don't surpass, Daphne. I don't even measure up."

I climb to my feet, shrugging off Sveta, ignoring Daphne. Turning to Thug, I raise my chin. "Can you take me home?"

Thug nods, but behind me I hear, "Are you sure—?"

I round on Daphne. "You had the perfect guy and you let him go because of your own stupid fears. Don't you know that marriage isn't perfect? It's hard work. And patience. And messing it up. And forgiving." Or, it used to be about forgiving. At the moment, it's about surviving. "Caleb loves you. He wants to marry you, and not a week goes by that he doesn't ask me about you."

Daphne's eyes are darkening, but I don't care.

"Don't give up on Caleb just because Chase gave up on me." The last words emerge in a whisper. I don't wait for her reaction. Just tighten my jaw and, reaching out for Thug, let him help me hobble to the car.

Sveta and Daphne stay behind to help Maggie, who watches me leave with pain on her face.

I turn away and lay down on the backseat. All I want is a cool bath. And someone in my life who cares, who won't leave me.

Anyone.

my perfect life

• • •

I HEAR THE PHONE RINGING AS I UNLOCK THE DOOR. BUT BY THE time I work my way over to it (leaning against the wall, then bracing my hand on the table, then chair, then diving for the other wall and finally collapsing onto the sofa), the caller has hung up.

That's right. Hang up on me. Seems about right.

Sliding to the floor, I crawl to the bathroom and turn on the water. It's glacial. And refreshing.

I crawl back to my bedroom for clean clothes. I dig out my Taz T-shirt, which has never forsaken me.

My back spasms again, and it's so bad I have to take long breaths through it. In the book I swiped from Jasmine, it had introductory breathing techniques. I remember thinking, does a woman really need to be reminded to breathe?

Clearly, yes.

I must have put too much tension on my body today. I crawl back to the bathroom, disrobe (which isn't easy when you're my size), and climb in. The water is freezing. But it only covers half my thighs, so it's bearable. And by the time it reaches my chin, I'll be numb.

Right now, I'd give anything to be numb. Instead of the burning pain in the middle of my chest.

I lean back, close my eyes. Listen to the water fill. The phone rings again, and for a fleeting moment I debate the pros and cons of prying my body out of the tub and crawling wet and naked (and that's a pretty picture, I know) to the phone.

Uh, no.

Maybe it's Chase. Maybe he's worried about me.

But he hasn't spent much time worrying these past nine months, has he?

I close my eyes again, my body starting to relax. My back spasms two more times before I decide to turn off the water. Don't want to freeze out Junior.

I laugh at this. Freeze *out* Junior. At this point, I'd do just about anything to coax Junior out. If it weren't a month or so too early.

But once I get home, with Jasmine to feed me and my mother to give me advice, well, I might just live through this.

Without Chase? My throat constricts. Along with my back. I breathe through the spasm, which seems worse than ever, and decide that probably I'm clean enough.

So I climb out and grab a towel.

And that's when it happens. Something . . . strange. A pop inside, and then to my horror . . . water.

Not bath water.

Oh no.

I stand there, breathing hard, the silence in the flat ringing my ears. Realization is swift and hard and confirming as another contraction hits and sends me to my knees.

I'm in labor.

How can I be in labor? I'm not due for weeks! I drop to my knees and somehow wrestle on my clothing—Chase's Scary Pants (he's never getting them back after what he's done to me) and my Taz T-shirt. Then I crawl to the family room. A contraction takes me down and it occurs to me that I should time them. Or do I time in between? I don't know! When Jasmine went into labor, we called 911 and she got a ride with the sirens on. I am hearing sirens right now. In my head.

I don't want to have a baby in Russia!

I grab the phone and sit up, cradling it in my lap. Dial Daphne. No answer. (Of course, because she's at the orphanage.) Caleb. It rings twelve times before I hang up. Screwing up my courage, I call Chase. It rolls over to voice mail.

I even call WorldMar. No, Chase isn't there, an Underfed says. I'm about to ask her to send paramedics when another spasm hits. She hangs up on me as I gasp for breath.

Everyone I know is still at the orphanage. Or on a plane to America.

I lean my head back, breathing through another contraction. My options are gone, and something inside me snaps.

"Listen here. I did this right. I sacrificed my own needs for my husband's. I was patient, and except for that one time, I tried valiantly not to tear down my house with my own hands. I volunteered at the orphanage, and did everything I could to be noble. So, what's the deal?" I look out the window at the way the sky is turning a dark blue. As if a storm might be brewing.

I'd say it already hit.

"Why can't You be on my side? What do I have to do to make You love me?"

My words catch me. Take my breath away (along with a contraction). Make who love me? God? Chase? Both. Tears burn my eyes and I breathe deeply.

I think back to the beginning, to my fear that Chase would someday stop loving me, and I have to wonder . . . have I been trying to be the perfect wife so that Chase would love me . . . or so that God would love me? Am I hoping that if I do everything right, God will give me the perfect life?

If so, it backfired. I close my eyes, defeated. My ears buzz as another contraction hits. I fold into it, letting the pain take me, tuning out everything else.

"I just wanted you to love me," I mumble as the contraction eases.

"I do love you, GI."

I open my eyes to the soft voice. And stare at Chase. His hair is mussed, his eyes red. I frown at him. "Where have you been?"

He shakes his head, and I see his face twitch. "I know I haven't done a very good job at being here this year, but I do love you GI . . . so much that sometimes it hurts."

He doesn't have a clue what real pain is. "No, I mean, where have you been?"

"I don't know . . . I guess I was so afraid that with this baby all your feelings for me would change. You're so . . . capable. It's like you don't need me. You came here and immediately got a new job and you succeed at everything, and"—his voice catches—"and I'm just a lousy husband who can't keep a job. So, I guess you're right. My heart hasn't really been here, either."

I blink at him. Still hasn't answered my question . . . and apparently he hasn't noticed that I'm sitting on the floor. Grimacing. "But what about Bertha?"

It's so painfully clear we are not tracking with each other, because he looks like I've slapped him. "Bertha?"

I cut to the chase. "Do you love me?"

"Of course I love you," he says, his hand cupping my face. "I'm your Chase-Me, aren't I? I need you, Jose, more than I ever realized. I'm never letting you go."

"I need you too, Chase." I cover his hand with mine. "But seriously, *where were you*?"

He looks stricken. "Picking up your sister." He glances toward the door. I follow his gaze and to my utter disbelief I see . . . Jasmine?

Do hallucinations accompany labor? Jasmine is standing in the doorway, eyes wide, mouth open. Thin and beautiful and just what I need. "Jas?"

She nods, drops her carry-on, and rushes toward me. "Chase wanted me to surprise you."

I close my eyes and wince. Which is not the greeting she expects, I'm sure. "I'm definitely surprised."

"Are you okay?" she says as she kneels beside me. I open my eyes, shake my head. She rounds on Chase. "You told me she was fine!"

"I thought she was fine! She was planning a party today, for Pete's sake. How was I to know she was home, in pain?"

In labor, folks. "It wasn't a party. It was a launch. For your peanut butter business."

"Didn't you take her to the doctor? Didn't you ask her how she was? You're her husband, for crying out loud." Jasmine the Undaunted.

Chase looks bereft. Yeah! What she said! I want to say, and wish I had the strength to pump my fist in the air.

"A launch?" he asks, tracking on me, finally.

I nod. "The orphanage is going to buy your leftover peanut butter. And probably more." I take a deep breath. "But I thought you left with Bertha."

"Where does it hurt, Jose?" Jasmine feels my forehead. I don't think that is where the pain is, honey.

Chase's blue eyes find mine and I see disbelief in them. "I know I spent way too much time at the office." He takes my hands from their place on my stomach. Uh, I need those to ward off the pain, pal. "But, I would never *ever* leave you for another woman. Ever." The tightness in his voice suggests the truth. And I feel sick.

In fact, I lean over and just about lose my peanut butter cookies on his shoes.

He jumps back. As does Jasmine. Yeah, that's probably a good idea.

"Are you okay?" His voice is stricken.

Catching on, are we?

"I think I'm in labor." I whisper.

"Oh, Dear Lord, help us," Jasmine says, and I know it's a prayer. Because I've been saying the same thing for nearly nine months.

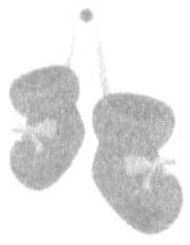

University of Hamburg
Germany

Dear H,

I'm A MOTHER!

But before I get to the details, I have to tell you. I *will* fit into a bridesmaid dress. Even if it's camouflage. (Actually, camouflage might be a very good idea.)

So, remember when I told you (not even a year ago!) that birthing isn't so bad (if you don't look at the person doing the birthing)? Yeah, well, I lied.

It feels much like having your body ripped in half and turned inside out. I suppose you didn't need that visual, but thankfully you're in the land of the EPIDURAL.

I, however, am not. Or, was not. Right now, I'm overlooking the lush and groomed grounds of Hamburg University. It's beautiful here, with flowerboxes overflowing with impatiens, clean cobblestone streets, and delicious chocolate pastries. Jasmine is in heaven—she's already trying to pry the hospital staff's favorite recipes out of them. And every day she brings me a chocolate tart.

But really, it's just for my postpartum recovery. My diet starts next week when we fly home to Gull Lake.

But I started too far ahead. Let me back up to the moment when I discovered I was in labor. (Actually I discovered a number of other things as well, the most important being that Chase didn't leave me for another woman.) Chase had been to the airport to pick up Jasmine (he'd been plotting to get her to Russia all year, and she finally arrived the day of a stellar peanut butter party that I planned, only to have her luggage delayed in customs, causing Chase to miss the party). They arrived slightly after I realized we were in dire straits.

But Chase, my hero, swung into action. He picked me up (although I weighed two thousand pounds), and after Jasmine wrapped me in a blanket (not sure why because it was about eighty million degrees outside, but maybe she thought I might give birth in the car), we went down to the parking lot.

Normally there are about thirty-five cars lined up along the sidewalk. That night . . . none. Chase stood there, and I could feel his heart pounding in his chest. I couldn't manage a suggestion, because my voice was abducted by pain, but then suddenly, my favorite mayor drove up. From the very party I was just at!

The mayor of Moscow and Chase wedged me into the car and Chase and Jas and I took off to the International Hospital. But I made them stop at my clinic, because no one was delivering my baby but Luka.

He wasn't there, but the powers that be promised to track him down (he, too, was at the orphanage . . . and believe me, by this time, I was thinking this was some sort of divine joke, but I'll get to that later), and we sped off to the hospital.

Now, over the past six months, when people have asked me about the International Hospital, I pictured some sort of glitzy American palace, with elevator music and mauve carpets and English-speaking doctors.

Uh, no. First off, we had to put on footies. Like those little booties they wear on Discovery Channel Health shows? Then, as Chase slipped down the hallway on polished linoleum (carrying me), the mayor's chauffeur hauled a doctor out of a room (I'm thinking the guy had a previous life in the KGB), and told him to take care of me. To Mayor Boy's credit, the doctor listened (or maybe it was the sounds I was making by this time) to the urgency of the moment and galvanized the staff.

They brought me to a room with a single bed. Chase plopped me down, and I saw in the adjoining room a contraption that looked a lot like something out of an Alfred Hitchcock movie. Think, stirrups. And hard metal.

"I'm not having a baby in Russia!" I wailed. To deaf ears, because both Chase and Jasmine were talking to Mayor Boy and Hostage Doctor. While I lay there and suffered.

I think Chase paid off Mayor Boy to find Luka because off he went, and no less than an hour later, Luka arrived, flushed, worried, and my hero. (Along with Chase, of course. Funny how I had these feelings of intense emotion when I saw Luka. Very weird.) In the meantime, Jasmine got me some cold cloths and taught me some rudimentary breathing techniques. (Remember when I said I'd never do natural childbirth? Someone, and I'm not mentioning any names, is laughing up there in heaven.)

Chase paced, in between holding my hand. He looked rough around the edges, and in many ways, worse than me. Which was a difficult accomplishment.

The next four hours were a blur. I do know that Sveta and Thug (oh, my driver, Igor) arrived, as did Caleb and Daphne (who did some serious making up while I was bringing life into the world), and Maggie Calhoun and her husband Dalton. It's important to tell you that Dalton used to work in Germany, and thus was on the phone with the neonatal hospital in Hamburg in between his calls with the SOS flight company WorldMar hires for emergencies.

Which, because they thought I was such an early delivery, I was.

But I'll get back to that.

Luka did an outstanding job. Even with his crazy wooden stethoscope. I finally got to ten centimeters (someday, when you're ready, I'll go into more detail. Or maybe not.), and Chase and Luka carried me to the birthing table. I kept thinking about Jasmine's cool birthing bed and how I didn't have that, until I started to push. Then I just thought about pushing.

I'm telling you, babies are miracles. They are born with a scream that you feel all the way through your body. And the rush of relief wrings you out. And all you can do is marvel.

Luka put little Junior in my arms. Incredible. Junior squirmed and screamed, red and wiggly and perfect. Chase kissed the little guy on the head and beamed at me, his eyes moist.

And then I heard Luka say, "*Oy*."

Oy in Russian means something like, Oh No. Or Oops.

Yeah, not a good word.

Luka scooped Junior out of my arms and handed him to a nurse. Then he looked at me with a sort of strange expression and said, "*Ne fso*."

Which translates to, "Not all."

Yeah, me too. I was thinking, what's he talking about?

Until the next contraction hit. And again, I had the urge to push. I panicked, Chase was beside himself, Jasmine had her mouth open, and Luka growled, "*Davai!*"

Push?

So, well, I did.

Little Josey Junior was born three minutes after her big

brother. And she cried, healthy and hard, just as we cried. I think Luka even teared up.

Luka rushed them both down to the neonatal unit, where they weighed in at an okay 2.3 and 2.4 kilograms, which translates to 5.0 and 5.2 pounds. That's over ten pounds of baby in there. No wonder I was the size of a barge. Which gets me back to the due date. They're thinking maybe I got pregnant on our wedding night, or thereabouts.

Which makes sense, because, well, I was pretty distracted that week, what with Jas having her baby, and the wedding. There are times I wonder if I took my birth control pills at all.

I'm also thinking that Luka owes me an apology for all that eye-rolling every time I stepped on the scale. And hello, shouldn't SOMEONE have noticed there was more than one bumpity-bump going on inside my belly? Here's a good case for throwing out Socrates's favorite stethoscope.

Anyway, two hours later, an ambulance shipped Jasmine, Chase, me, Chloe, and Justin (yes, those are their names) to the airport, and we flew out to Hamburg, where there's a neonatal hospital.

Have no fear, the babies are fine. As am I.

Daphne and Caleb arrived yesterday with our suitcases. They're out ring shopping today.

And just because I know you care, yes, after the pain meds wore off, I told Chase exactly what I thought about his late hours, and the fact he missed my entire pregnancy. I made it easy for him to understand, using Discovery Channel metaphors like Sherpa, and the loneliness of the Serengeti Desert, the resourcefulness of Survivorman and even the rather brutal mating habits of the Siberian tiger. He got it. And took it like a man. He's now in full war reparation mode, filling my room with flowers and chocolate and giving me hour-long foot rubs. And although WorldMar offered him a position at the office in Minneapolis starting in September, he's promised me he'll be home by dinner (and to bring it with him).

Here's the part that I want most to tell you. Remember when you told me that Chase and I would figure it out? And asked me the rhetorical question if that was what marriage was all about?

I have some answers for you.

I think marriage, and pregnancy and life for that matter, are more than that. I do think it's about working it out together, but I also have a hypothesis: marriage is one of the ways that God reveals His love, through the good times and bad.

My friend Caleb said something to me when I first arrived. About experiencing God's love in a new way. An unexpected way.

I didn't believe him.

But I've discovered that God's love is in the sun setting in a fiery haze behind tall apartment buildings. It's the scent of lilac in the air in spring. It's caviar instead of pickles, and meeting new friends in your drawers. It's someone believing in you despite your faults, and liking Chase's Scary Pants, and cooking a turkey, and Thug kissing Sveta. It's Jasmine making pastries on both sides of the ocean, and being mistaken for a Bus Lady so I can feed a bunch of babushki bread.

It's babies cooing as I feed them. And Chase holding them, his eyes shining, as he says, "You're incredible, GI." I can't believe that I ever thought he would leave me. I blame it on the four billion lost brain cells.

The short of it is this:

I thought I had to do it all right—be June Cleaver or near it, and create the perfect life, to make sure that Chase, and even God, loved me. Turns out, Chase loves me just because I'm his girl. As does God.

And I know this, because after I got clear of Russia, and

roaches and even the panic over the twins' birth, I realized (over a strong cup of real coffee) that God's love has surrounded me this year, on all sides—in the depths of despair and the heights of my insanity, when I ran away from Him, and when I longed just for a hint of His touch in my life. He's loved me in ways I didn't even realize. Having Chloe and Justin, I got the smallest taste of that incredible love God feels about me. Perhaps that is what it means to know God's love, not just understand it. And to be filled with the measure of God, Himself.

Knowing all this changes me, how? Well, first off, I don't have to work so hard to make things right. I can overflow the bathtub, look like a manatee, or even fall on my face with a watermelon and God will still love me. He'll even turn it into something okay. Secondly, being in over my head is a good place to be.

So, H, here's the best marriage advice I can give you: put your dreams for you and Rex into God's hands. Because He loves you.

Chase just arrived. He's brought me a decaf mocha from the coffee shop across the street (and let me tell you, the Belgian waffles . . .!). He's smiling, and I can see a twinkle in his eye from here. And right behind him, Daphne and Caleb are wheeling in the babies' bassinets. I can't believe I got so lucky.

I know I said it before. But I mean it.

I have the perfect life.

See you soon!

Josey

Thank you for reading *Chill Out, Josey*! Don't miss the sweet and romantic final story as Josey and Chase juggle love, life, and parenthood in *Get Cozy, Josey*, book 3 in the Josey Series!

A Siberian village is a far cry from small-town Minnesota bliss...

When Josey's husband gets relocated to this icy tundra, her dreams of a cozy and idyllic life quickly melt away. Say goodbye to indoor plumbing and junk food—hello to a whole new world of survival. But fear not, because Josey is not one to back down from a challenge. With the spirit of a feisty former missionary, she dives headfirst into multitasking like a pro. From juggling toddler twins to empowering local housewives and spreading God's word, Josey knows how to handle it all with a smile on her face.

But amidst the chaos and the frozen landscapes, there's one thing that proves to be the real challenge: finding precious alone time with the man of her dreams. Will Josey Anderson's determination and quick thinking be enough to overcome the uproarious hurdles that threaten to sabotage her and her marriage?

Grab your coziest blanket, curl up by the fireplace (or the nearest heat source), and prepare join Josey on this unforgettable, heartwarming and hilarious journey as she discovers that true happiness can be found in the most unexpected places.

"With Susan May Warren's trademark wit and flair, you'll find yourself laughing out loud as Josey's quick thinking and resourcefulness shine through." – online reviewer

Get your copy now!

thank you for reading

Thank you again for reading *Chill Out, Josey*. I hope you enjoyed the story.

If you did enjoy it, would you be willing to do me a favor? Head over to the **product page** and leave a review. It doesn't have to be long—just a few words to help other readers know what they're getting. (But no spoilers! We don't want to wreck the fun!)

I'd love to hear from you—not only about this story, but about any characters or stories you'd like to read in the future. Write to me at: susan@susanmaywarren.com. And if you'd like to see what's ahead, stop by www.susanmaywarren.com .

And don't forget to sign up to my newsletter at www.susanmaywarren.com.

Susie May

about susan may warren

With nearly 2 million books sold, critically acclaimed novelist Susan May Warren is the Christy, RITA, and Carol award-winning author of over ninety novels with Tyndale, Barbour, Steeple Hill, and Summerside Press. Known for her compelling plots and unforgettable characters, Susan has written contemporary and historical romances, romantic-suspense, thrillers, rom-com, and Christmas novellas.

With books translated into eight languages, many of her novels have been ECPA and CBA bestsellers, were chosen as Top Picks by *Romantic Times*, and have won the RWA's Inspirational Reader's Choice contest and the American Christian Fiction Writers Book of the Year award. She's a three-time RITA finalist and an eight-time Christy finalist.

Publishers Weekly has written of her books, “Warren lays bare her characters’ human frailties, including fear, grief, and resentment, as openly as she details their virtues of love, devotion, and resiliency. She has crafted an engaging tale of romance, rivalry, and the power of forgiveness.” *Library Journal* adds, "Warren's characters are well-developed and she knows how to create a first rate contemporary romance..."

Susan is also a nationally acclaimed writing coach, teaching at conferences around the nation, and winner of the 2009 American Christian Fiction Writers Mentor of the Year award. She loves to help people launch their writing careers. She is the founder of www.MyBookTherapy.com and www.learnhowtowriteanovel.com, a writing website that helps authors get published and stay published. She is also the author of the popular writing method *The Story Equation.*

Find excerpts, reviews, and a printable list of her novels at www.susanmaywarren.com and connect with her on social media.

facebook.com/susanmaywarrenfiction
instagram.com/susanmaywarren
x.com/susanmaywarren
bookbub.com/authors/susan-may-warren
goodreads.com/susanmaywarren
amazon.com/Susan-May-Warren

also by susan may warren

THE JOSEY SERIES

Everything's Coming Up Josey

Chill Out, Josey

Get Cozy, Josey

THE CHRISTIANSEN FAMILY

I Really Do Miss your Smile (novella prequel)

Take a Chance on Me

It Had to Be You

When I Fall in Love

Evergreen (Christmas novella)

Always on My Mind

The Wonder of Your

You're the One that I Want

DEEP HAVEN COLLECTION

Still the One with Rachel D. Russell

Can't Buy Me Love with Andrea Christenson

Crazy for You with Michelle Sass Aleckson

Then Came You with Rachel D. Russell

Hanging' by a Moment with Andrea Christenson

Right Here Waiting with Michelle Sass Aleckson

Once Upon a Winter Wonderland

DEEP HAVEN SERIES

Happily Ever After

Tying the Knot

The Perfect Match

My Foolish Heart

The Shadow of your Smile

You Don't Know Me

NOBLE LEGACY (Montana Ranch Trilogy)

Reclaiming Nick

Taming Rafe

Finding Stefanie

A complete list of Susan's novels can be found at susanmaywarren.com/novels/bibliography/.

www.ingramcontent.com/pod-product-compliance
Lightning Source LLC
Chambersburg PA
CBHW030607310726
48979CB00003B/605

* 9 7 8 1 9 6 2 0 3 6 1 2 2 *